JOSEPH DARLINGTON is a writer from England. He was nominated for the Dinesh Allirajah Prize for Short Fiction in 2018, and has co-edited the *Manchester Review of Books* since 2016.

The Disruptors is book one of a two part series. Find him on X/Twitter at @Joe_Darlo.

JOSEPH DARLINGTON

THE DISRUPTORS

PART ONE

Northodox Press Ltd
Maiden Greve, Malton,
North Yorkshire, YO17 7BE

This edition 2024

1
First published in Great Britain by
Northodox Press Ltd 2024

ISBN: 978-1-917005-11-1

This book is set in Caslon Pro Std

For Soph, who was promised this story in 2017,

and Kinia; always and forever.

Book One

1

'That's a small?'

'Tell me about it. There's people wheeling bathtubs full of coffee around in there... and those are the mediums.'

'Large is a swimming pool, yeah?'

'Olympic sized, Jonny. Olympic sized.'

Samra Habib, Sammy to her friends, passed Jonny his pint of Americano. It was too hot. He set it down. She drained her espresso in a gulp.

They were sat in Great Northern Square, Manchester. It was evening and cyclists were everywhere, leaning on every lamppost. Most wore the cyan branding of Deliveroo, with fat black carrying cubes hanging off their saddles. There were a couple of Amazon carriers and some from companies Sammy had never heard of. She presumed they had an app. Most put-upon were the rickshaw cyclists. They were on day rates, cycling drunks to Spinningfields as a piece of cheap, hopeless promotion. Everyone was wearing their company's garish colours. They rode in, hitched up, waited for the next call and were off again. If you squinted, the square could almost be the stables at a medieval court.

Sammy and Jonny were in formal attire. Instead of a bicycle they'd a sputtering moped. Jonny was slung with camera gear. Sammy was swiping her phone. Switching between apps, refreshing the feeds, all on the hunt for a party. It was a specific party. A legendary one. She'd not been invited, but she was damned if she'd miss it. This one, surely, would be the story that made her.

Jonny blew on his coffee and waited. He'd mastered the art

of waiting. A rider sidled up.

'Who d'you ride for?'

'I write for the Bantz Testament,' Sammy replied, not looking up. Jonny nodded.

'What, like the Facebook page?'

The rider's eyebrows furrowed. He wore the red and yellow stripe of a Chinese competitor to Just-Eat.

Jonny sighed, sipped, sighed again;

'She's a journalist, mate. I'm her cameraman. We're waiting on a story. Some rich kids having a party or something...'

'I thought Banz Testament was just cat videos and stuff.'

He shrugged his shoulders, half-turning to leave.

'Didn't know they had reporters. Thought it was just, y'know, a bunch of teens copy-pasting links and that.'

'You wouldn't be far wrong, mate,' Jonny replied, blowing and sipping. 'We're freelance. No story, no pay. I ride with Deliveroo three nights a week to pay for all this.'

He waved his hand vaguely at the equipment bags, and tried to ignore Sammy prickling up next to him. She didn't like admitting to the freelance thing.

'Everyone's freelance nowadays!' she'd soon be shouting, 'It's not worth commenting on!'

The rider nodded at Jonny's kit. He recognised a fellow traveller. Nice one, mate. He gave a last bit of advice before he went, 'You should join Sineasy, mate. Pay's better than 'Roo. Not as many jobs, like, but on a good day you're up.'

'Cheers for the tip. I'll check them out.'

As the rider ambled away Sammy tutted. She was flicking between four fake Insta accounts and a soap actresses' Facebook that someone in the office had hacked. The party was clearly in progress. The messaging had stopped and pictures were being posted. Where the hell was it? She was furiously cross-referencing the decor with Google image searches of exclusive Manchester clubs. Why do all these places look the fucking same!?

Jonny went back to staring. He sipped at his megacoffee. He'd barely made an impression on it.

'You know, I hear that if you ask for a large tea at Neros they give you a teabag and throw you in the river...'

'Pretty funny that, Jonny.'

Sammy's swiping was getting erratic. Was she sweating?

'Why the FUCK is no one saying where this is? Why the FUCK aren't they posting locations with their pictures? Don't tell me these posh bitches all learned about privacy settings on the same fucking night!'

A tinny fanfare buzzed onto the screen. She instinctively swiped it away. Then, panicking, tried to drag it back. She opened her breaking news app and read.

'Oh, what the hell?!'

'Something up, Sammy?'

'Helmet on, Jonny, we're riding. And chuck that piss away.'

The moped shot off into traffic. A caffeinated puddle waited for the neon-clad cleaners.

*

Sammy was right about her hunch; something strange really was going down. The story started when she found a decent cashcow in the celeb beat. She could make ten times as much with footage of drunk C-listers and shocking drug revelations than she could with the political stuff. Celebs made for fewer clicks, but better clicks. Better ad revenue. Politicos don't buy like gossipers buy. It was the network of fake accounts, hacks and 'inside sources' (dealers) she'd made in covering this beat that had given her the tip off about tonight's party. The most exclusive in town. Party of the year. A D-list Hollywood actor might even be there. As it turned out, it was at a private suite in the Beetham Tower Hilton, but the story doesn't stop there.

Back when she had been at a real newspaper, Sammy had

worked in the crime section. They waited for the police to send press releases then wrote them up, adding a quote from whichever grieving relative they could get on the phone. She'd not lost that habit and over the past few months her bloodhound senses were tingling again. Disappearances. Celebrity disappearances. At first she thought the obvious – secret rehabs and superinjunctions – but then the cases started coming up in police memos. Not public, yet, but something was up. Celebrities were disappearing and nobody was saying a damn thing about it.

A month before the party, Mel Ditty, minor London R&B star, was found wandering the countryside naked. She'd been missing for a month, though no one had noticed it. Then she reappeared and wasn't saying a word about what happened. Bantz Testament sourced footage of the incident from a local stoner's Facebook page and made a killing off it. They gave it a drugged up sex party spin but Sammy wasn't sure. These celebs were going somewhere. God knows where, but there was money in finding out. It's practically a public service, Sammy reasoned. The world needs to know and all that.

Which brings us back to tonight's shindig. In the hacked DMs, the tastemakers had been calling it a "going away party". Who for? Where were they going? Sammy and Jonny revved past buses and BMWs, their evening gown and tux blowing in the wind.

Only one problem. A rather major one. The story had already hit the nationals; shootout in exclusive Manchester party.

Police had cordoned off the building only ten minutes ago, and shut down the lifts. Two Tactical Aid Units were en route, loaded up with MP5s and combat shotguns. A total clusterfuck, Sammy figured, watching it all play out on the feeds. But the party was still going on. Something was happening up there. All the Evening News hacks were content to sit in their vans outside and point their cameras at the police cordon. No thanks, Sammy thought. She was going to get the proper story. Any means necessary. That's freelance, baby.

Sammy knew Jonny would hate the plan. She would smuggle him in before he realised what was going on. Once he was in there, he wouldn't back out.

She knocked on his helmet like a front door.

'Hey! Jonny! Use the Affordable Homes Initiative entrance, round back. You can get to it through the freight depot.'

They'd made a big deal of including rent-controlled flats in the luxury tower. During construction they'd changed the plans, halved the floor-space and built a separate entrance so the commoners wouldn't track mud across the foyer. The plebs also didn't have a lift, but they did have access to the fire escape stairs.

Sammy had used this fire escape to sneak into many a footballer's coke orgy. Now it would get her past the police line. Being for commoners, the entrance didn't have security. Jonny'd be up on the thirteenth floor before he had any idea what they'd gotten into. And by then, Sammy hoped, his instincts would have kicked in and he'd be all camera and no cares anyway. Solid gold footage.

They pulled up at the poor door. Abandoned as predicted. Grim too.

'Alright Sammy, where are we headed?'

'Eight storeys up, Jonny, and stairs all the way. Hope you didn't bring your heavy camera.'

Jonny dusted oil off his suit. He had in fact brought the heavier camera. It had the big lenses for shooting in nightclub lighting conditions. He stared up at the mighty tower, counting out thirteen sad storeys.

'Couldn't give me a hand with this, could you?'

She was already at the door.

'Have you seen this dress, mate? Carry it yourself.'

'Fair enough, Sammy. Fair enough. I just point the cameras, you're the one that's in front of them.'

*

They were eleven storeys up when they heard the screaming. It was quiet, but unmistakable. Shrouded behind thumping bass and shout-talking. The party was still going on. Glasses smashing, maybe windows. But something was also wrong.

'What kind of party is this, Sammy?'

Jonny was wheezing. His suit jacket was slung over his shoulder and sweat was dark on his shirt. Jonny never looked frightened, but Sammy saw more than curiosity in his eyes now.

'The kind of party where people disappear,' she said, rushing upwards. 'The kind of party the world needs to see.'

As they approached they saw the party had already spilled out onto the stairwell. A blonde teen was hacking his guts up all over his expensive suit and even-more-expensive trainers. A group of girls were shout-talking at each other. Shocked about something. Sammy rushed over to them.

'What's going on in there? Has something happened?'

'It's crazy!' said one. 'Oh my God!' another.

'Someone's been shot, maybe!?' a third girl said, her eyes stretched wide in bewilderment.

Sammy turned back to see Jonny approaching. He hadn't heard them, good.

'Come on!' she urged.

She'd get him into the party and work from there.

Inside the music was pounding. The suite was rammed and it was hard to tell if people were panicking or dancing. Jonny, catching his breath, started snapping. A leather sofa, torn. Rolled fivers and coke residue. Some groups of partygoers did genuinely seem in a state of panic, but there were others who were dancing and yelling and bragging.

No one seemed to be leaving.

Sammy walked over to a smashed window. The wind tore in and out. She looked down over the flashing police lines. Maybe a chair had been thrown out? Perhaps it was gunshots? She couldn't tell. Jonny was clicking away.

Just then a tall young man, blonde like the last, with the same floppy hair, stumbled out of the bathroom with blood down his shirt. Sammy leapt at him.

'What's going on? Where's the blood come from?'

His eyes wouldn't focus. He was squeezing at his shirtfront like he'd only just noticed the mess. He didn't know if it was real or not. Totally mashed.

'Where have you been?! Who did this?!' she shouted.

He gestured toward the bathroom. Sammy turned to go but the boy grabbed her. His hand was firm on her wrist.

'Men. Black suits. Black suits and sunglasses! Illuminati!'

'Thanks, yeah'

She brushed his hand off and ran to the bathroom.

It was the kind of scene that would have made her day back on the crime desk. A giant of a man, strapped in a too-tight suit, lay in a wrecked mess on the floor. He was cradled in the arms of a young medical student, shirtsleeves rolled, medical supplies scattered across the linoleum. He was leaning with all his weight on the man's neck. He was trying to staunch a thick stream of blood. He had three or four bullet-wounds.

The blood poured out of him like water from a rusted bucket. He had about a pint of living left in him.

'Stop gawping! Pics! Now!'

Jonny clicked. Sammy screamed at the Doc over the music.

'What happened? What's going on?'

'Who are you? You need to ring for help! I just found him like this and...'

'What?!'

She turned her attention to the dying man, waved her hand before his eyes.

'You! What's going on? Who did this? Where are they?'

His eyes wouldn't focus. He was slipping away. He wasn't

seeing this world, only the twinkling of the next.

'Oy!' Sammy yelled, snapping her fingers.

Getting no response she slapped him. The Doctor, horrified, made a grab at her hand.

'Keep your hands off me, Doc!' she yelled, and she slapped the fallen hulk again. This time his eyes came back a bit. He saw the bath he lay against. He saw his blood. He ran his eyes along the red-slicked tiles and looked up into Sammy's face.

'What happened? Can you tell me? Who did this?' she yelled.

He flinched, screwed up his eyes, and tried to answer. He opened his lips and from his mouth came a huge, expanding bubble of blood. It swelled to the size of a grapefruit, then popped. The mist splattered all down Sammy's front. The dying giant's eyes went back to searching the air.

'Fucksake!' she spat, straightening up.

The Doc, shaking, hyperventilating, jumped back to staunching the hopeless flow.

'Stay here and keep shooting!' Sammy yelled at Jonny. 'I'm going to find out what's going on.'

She waded through the blood and out of the door, her dress trailing red. The young medic looked up at Jonny, pleading. Jonny sighed and shook his head. He lifted the viewfinder. He better make extra for this.

The next room was empty.

Trashed, smashed and overturned tables were evidence of a struggle. Maybe a full-blown gang fight? Or maybe just a mad rush for the door. Bags were strewn across the floor, a couple of phones and, spinning around on a stained sofa, a yapping chihuahua.

Sammy crept forward carefully. She noticed a series of bulletholes in the wall. She noticed a blast of crimson, perhaps where the big man next door had first been hit. The bass dropped and a strobe light kicked into life, sending Sammy tumbling, screaming to the floor.

She checked herself. Alright. It wasn't a machine gun. She

looked up. From this angle she could see shadows moving in.

This is it, she realised, either I go now and get the story, or I stay here and probably don't get shot.

She was already on her feet and running. Don't think. News doesn't think.

She skidded round the corner, found herself in the kitchen. The lights were blinding white. She raised her hand, shielding her eyes. Through her fingers she saw it. Time seemed to slow. She knew she'd made a mistake. Time shuddered to a halt. She was turbo-charged. She was there.

Between her fingers, dazzled by the lights, she saw a tiny Indian baby. It wore an impeccable suit and tie. It wore sunglasses. In its tiny hands it held a shotgun. It fired at her once, and missed. It pulled back the pump-action. She had lost her footing and started to fall. The baby fired again. She felt percussion in her belly; a punch in the left of her guts. She hit the floor. Bashed her head. Blinked. Blinked. And the baby was gone.

'JONNY!' she remembered screaming, 'I'VE BEEN FUCKING SHOT!'

And then darkness.

2

Sammy heard beeping and the sound of raised voices, so she assumed she was in the newsroom. Her arm was caught in some kind of wiring. She grabbed at it. Pulled. There was a push of bodies around her, a spiking pain in her arm and she fell back to sleep.

*

Sammy came to in a hospital bed. Fuzzy all over. The lights were too bright. She needed to get out of there.

She ran her hands along her body, taking inventory of her appendages. All there. A pain came from her middle region. Lifting her bedclothes, she saw the beige bandages wrapped around her like a National Health mummy.

She remembered being shot. She ran her finger over the rough fabric of the bandage and caught her breath a moment. She turned and rooted around the nightstand until she found her phone. Still 26% battery. That'll do.

She tried to drag the unlock pattern across the screen but her finger was still fluffy with morphine. Come on! She shook it around in the air, trying to drive the blood back down to the tips. She tried again. That's cracked it! Now, where to start...

'She's awake. Sister, she's awake!'

Uh oh. Busted.

'Thank you, Mitzi. I'll take care of this one.'

A matronly figure approached her bedside.

'Mrs Habib, you shouldn't be awake now. You've gone through major surgery. The road to recovery is going to be a long one. You need your rest.'

'Thnks m'm,' Sammy's lips were sleepy – she smacked them together a few times to wake them up. 'Sorry, but I need to get out of here. If I don't get this story then someone else will; and if I don't get this story then I don't get paid.'

'That's very admirable, Mrs Habib, I shall make sure that your employers are told of your commitment to your work. However, there will be no leaving the hospital. Not for a good long while.'

Sammy noted the patronising tone.

'-and I'm afraid that, while you're in here, there are no mobile phones allowed. It can be very dangerous. So if you'll please put that away, Mrs-'

'It's Miss! Miss Habib. Or... what am I talking about – it's Sammy. Call me Sammy. Do you see a wedding ring?'

She wriggled the fingers of one hand around, quietly sliding the phone beneath the bedsheets with the other.

'I'm sorry, Miss Habib. Sorry... I mean Sammy. It's just that being a Muslim woman of your age we presumed that-'

'What?'

'It was our in-patient care team. They're Muslim too, you see. They said that a woman your age-'

'I'm not a Muslim.'

'Oh, I'm sorry, Sammy. Very sorry. Are you a Hindu? We must change your dietary requirements checklist if so-'

'No. No I'm not.'

'Oh, I'm very sorry, Sammy. I didn't want to presume. Our in-patient care team you see... Well, I'll just go and update your preferred name on our system.'

The matron had gone bright red. As she walked away, Sammy was left unattended. It was time to escape. I'm Sammy-fucking-Habib, she reminded herself, and I serve no God but News.

She threw the covers over her head and lifted her knees to

make a tent. Her gut twinged a bit. It's going to start hurting soon, she supposed. First thing was to open up messages;

CONTACTS > JONNY (CAMERA) >
Need a lift asap. Stuck in hoipitl.

Fingers still not quite working.

Next she opened her news app. Start with the BBC and work down from there. She didn't see anything in the nationals. They must have run it as *Drugs-Related Shooting in Manchester*, she guessed, making it about as clickworthy as *Bear Shits in Woods*. The good news is; that means they'd missed the celebrity angle entirely. Sammy still had the exclusive.

She found the piece in the M.E.N. She read voraciously, her eyes picking out the valuable passages and automatically filtering the padding. *Beetham Tower - exclusive party – celebrities as yet unnamed – one fatality, reported as a professional bodyguard – woman remains in critical condition.*

Critical condition? Those sods had given her the death sentence! And what happened to "*a journalist remains in critical condition*"? The private school mafia were closing her out of the circle yet again…

Get a grip, Sammy. The drugs are getting to you. A buzz:

JONNY (CAMERA) >
Jesus S! They letting you out already?
I'm bidding on a lens. Be 1 hour.

Fucksake. She didn't enjoy lying to Jonny, but sometimes he made it necessary.

REPLY > Need go NOW or they charge $$$ for bed!!!

She switched to her dummy accounts. She would check out the aftermath in the socialite circles.

A hot mess all around, she noted. Crying emojis for days

and pity-likes through the roof. They'd already started posting inspirational memes and the targeted ad software was having a bonanza selling trauma counselling services. Sammy posted a couple of 'so sad for everyone, where is the love?' messages to keep herself in the discourse. She had a brainwave and sent an @ reply to Lil Shooshy – a grime artist she knew would have been there – 'so worried. U alright Shoosh?' That's when she saw it. No word from Shoosh since last night. No, nor KayKay either, and the one from Hollyoaks (whatshername?), gone too... *Buzz*

JONNY (CAMERA) >
Bloody Tories. B soon.

Buzz.

JONNY (CAMERA) >
there*

Sammy got onto the celeb pages, checking for any leads and – lo and behold – the Bantz Testament had a message from the Home Secretary on the incident.

That was bad. If they'd posted this to the feed then they must have someone else on the story. She really needed to get out of this bed. She'd watch the vid first.

The Home Secretary was a caricature of a man with a caricature of a name: Sir Tallow-Wandsworth Mosley. An old aristocrat who was, out of what Sammy could only guess was some strange kink, attempting to single-handedly bring back the Hitler moustache. As a result, the news would often roll the audio of his statements without showing footage of him speaking. It was bizarre. It was England.

Bantz showed him in the flesh. The 'stache was always good for the lol-clicks:

'The security services are aware of the situation and I can

confirm that currently we do not consider it to be a situation. Gun crime is a reprehensible scourge, and the incidents last night in Manchester are being fully addressed by the security services. We do not comment on ongoing investigations. As to the so-called disappearances of youth-cultural figures, Her Majesty's Government are not inclined to cast aspersions at this time.'

Sammy paused and filtered. Her head rushed with the morphine. Okay, so the disappearances are on the Home Sec's radar, but not the national papers'. Can't be. It means they know but won't say. Perhaps a superinjunction? Or maybe worse? Sammy had the horrible feeling she wasn't the only one who knew about this story.

'Sammy?' it was a nurse. 'Sammy, what are you doing under the bedclothes?'

'Sorry,' she poked her head out. 'It's the lights. They're so bright.'

It was a different nurse. Might be harder to get rid of. Sammy mimicked blinking in the lights.

'Oh, Sammy. I'm very sorry but the doctors need to see what they're doing.'

She rubbed a towel across Sammy's head. Sammy must have been sweating. She hadn't noticed.

'How does your tummy feel, eh?'

'My... my guts?' Sammy had to admit, the towel was nice. 'They're hurting, I suppose. Not too bad though. They're fixed up, right?'

'What do you mean?'

'Like, I've had all the surgeries and things, right? I'm just waiting for it to heal now.'

The nurse passed her a glass of water.

'Has no one told you? Oh, I shouldn't be the one to tell you...'

The nurse was looking around. Sammy guessed from her uniform that she was a junior.

'Please tell me,' Sammy made with the big eyes. 'I'm so worried.'

'Well,' the nurse ummed, walking gingerly to the set of clipboards at the bottom of the bed.

'You were really lucky, Sammy. The gun they shot you with was a miniature. The surgeons were able t-'

'It was a shotgun,' Sammy cut in, 'I saw it.'

'What?'

'It wasn't miniature. It had a pump action and everything. It was like something from *Call of Duty*. It wasn't miniature-'

'Do you remember it happening?'

'Yes. Clear as day. There was a... a baby. It was a baby in a suit... with the combat shotg... an Indian baby.'

The nurse was smiling. She rubbed Sammy's head with the towel again.

'Now Sammy, that was just a bad dream. The medicine you're on gives you very vivid dreams, and that was one of them. There weren't any babies. It was criminals, or gangsters or something. It was on the news. You were on the news! And, in terms of the injury, you were very lucky. They used a miniature gun, it says here, and so the surgeons were able to retain a large amount of intestinal integrity.'

'Intestinal integrity?'

'It means that you'll still be able to consume liquids and partial solids. It's far more than we could have expected with an injury of this type. You're very lucky.'

'What the hell's a partial solid?'

'Well, think of it this way, they had to cut out – sorry, I mean remove - about twelve inches of short intestine. Then they sewed the rest back together. Now, you have a little hole inside you – like this.'

She made an 'O' ring with her fingers and put it up to her eye. Looking through it she continued.

'So everything has to be teeny tiny in order to pass through. So only liquid and partial solids. Think of it like... nothing thicker than a milkshake.'

'Fuck.'

The nurse jumped at Sammy's sudden expletive.

'You mean like a McDonald's milkshake?'

'If you like.'

'What about the Shakers ones with bits in?'

'Sorry, no bits.'

'Damn. Well, at least I can do the McDonalds ones. Those are pretty thick. And, how long is this for?'

'Oh, I'm sorry Sammy,' the nurse did a little pout. 'It's forever. The other nurses might say "for the foreseeable future", but it's pretty much forever – that's what they mean when they say that. You're still very lucky though. The surgeons had never seen a miniature shotgun wound before. You're a medical miracle!'

'Ah. I see.'

'You get some rest now, Sammy. Lots of healing to do. In fact, by tomorrow morning your whole injury will have healed up. They've put a special gel on there. You might not even be able to tell what caused it! From the outside at least. Oh, I've said enough. I've got to go. You rest up, Sammy.'

'Sure.'

She wasn't shot by a miniature shotgun. Sammy was certain of it. Miniature shotguns don't exist. They wouldn't make any physical sense. She saw it! In that bastard baby's little hands! Like something out of *Call of Duty*. No. She had to prove this. It was essential.

She lifted her legs up and disappeared beneath the blanket-tent again. She searched the internet but there was no sign of miniature shotguns. Not even custom ones. She checked the news again and again, chasing all the links and helplessly refreshing social media. No word of the shooters. Nothing about evidence being taken from the crime scene. Seemingly no pictures either.

She knew what she had to do, but she didn't want to do it. She was looking down at her mummified middle. Only a day and it'd be unrecognisable, the nurse said. It was her only evidence. The only evidence she had that the shooting took place at all, nevermind the weapon. But, maybe... Maybe a decent Doc would be able to tell from the scar as it was now, what kind of weapon had done the damage? Someone with experience. An American maybe. She didn't want to do it. But she did.

It took ten minutes of scratching and stretching the bandage. It came away in fibres. She had to keep stopping as pain spiked through her. She was sweating now. Furious. Working by the light of her mobile. Some sick-looking blood seeped out and she panicked, but she hadn't popped open. The pain was getting more intense as she got closer. The spikes were shooting up into her chest. Nasty, like internal punches. Like – well – like spikes. Her metaphor was correct from the start.

She tore the outer layers away and held on to the dressing around the wound. She was starting to feel it now. She was getting to know it through the different pains. She threw up a little bit. Acid pangs like a bad hangover. She cleared away the bandages and had only a cotton pad over her middle.

Now was the time, she thought. She took a deep breath. Burped. Deep breath again. She looked.

It wasn't that bad. A tangled mess of flesh and wiring but not big, not unsightly. There was no bruising. She ran her finger along it and realised it wasn't the end of the world.

'You better like soup, my friend,' she whispered to the wound. 'Cos there's going to be a lot more of it from here on in.'

She whimpered a little bit. Oh God, why did she do that?! Why was that the thing that made her want to cry? Oh, Jesus...

It's the morphine, babe, it's the morphine. Calm down. Now, let's get a photo. Come on, you can do it. Just a couple of photos... shit.

NOTIFICATIONS >
Warning! Battery below 10%.
Some user functionalities now unavailable.

'What?' she swore aloud; 'the fucking battery?! The flashlight function – oh God, it's eaten the fucking battery.'

'Are you alright under there?' it was nurse one.

Sammy panicked. She didn't know what to do. The phone wouldn't take pictures on low battery mode. Suddenly, she was in the harsh light of the ward.

The nurse had torn the sheet right off her.

She was gaping at Sammy's open wound. Her face was half-shock, half-fury. Like she'd caught Sammy masturbating.

'WHAT is this?! WHAT have you done?!' and just as quickly she turned, ran for the corridor. 'Orderlies! I need orderlies in here!'

Sammy snapped her head around. The figures in the beds around her were leaning up, gawping. There were no nurses left. Suddenly, Sammy was up on her feet, holding the medical padding to her wound with one hand and her phone in the other. Spikes of pain shot out of every part of her body. But she was on her feet. She stumbled to the end of the ward. The nurse was shouting something out in the corridor. Sammy launched herself out of the room - and into a wheelchair. Thank God! She let the padding and her phone fall into her lap as she heaved at the wheels with both arms. She was roaring with the agony, but she was moving.

Down the corridor, handbrake turn, down another, and screeeeech into the lift! Floor 7. They won't be expecting her to go up. She'd find a base. Camp out there. Work out her next move.

It was only then that she realised she was naked under the medical gown. What had happened to her clothes? Probably destroyed, she guessed. And expensive, too. Tragic.

Up on Floor 7 she wheeled herself down a corridor, natural as anything, hoping no one would look at her bum. She only passed a couple of patients. If they did see anything they kept it to themselves. Through a set of double doors she found a disabled toilet. She wheeled herself inside.

This'll do as a hiding place. She lifted herself off the chair and onto the floor. It was cold, soothing.

The pains subsided, slightly. She pulled the padding from

the chair and pushed it against her belly. She pulled down the phone and saw it had a message.

JONNY (CAMERA) >
Here now. Where you?

REPLY >
Come to Floor 7 disabled bogs. NOW!!!

She wasn't going to try and explain.

JONNY (CAMERA) >
What?

Let him work it out when he gets here.

JONNY (CAMERA) >
What?????

He'll come. He'll come. She turned off her phone. Save the last 3%.

She closed her eyes as she lay on the toilet floor. She thought about the baby. He was real. And then she thought about the celebrity disappearances and what the Home Secretary had said about them. They were real. And then she thought about the documentary they'd make about her – *Sammy Habib – The One Who Broke the Story of the Century*. The scandal of the century. Then there was a sheepish knocking on the door.

She lifted her foot and opened the lock with it. In sidled Jonny. He looked panicked, in his eyes at least, but still together and – this is why she loved him – he'd brought along his DSLR. It hung on his shoulder like hope.

'Jonny, you're here. There's no time to explain.'

'What the hell happened to you? I was told it would be months before you were back on your feet. Why are we in a toilet?'

'There's no time, Jonny. Here...'

She pulled back her robe. He grimaced, turning his head away. She snapped her fingers at him.

'Come on! Take a photo. Quick!'

'What the hell, Sammy? Are you on medication or something?'

'Yes, but that's not the point. I need photos! Come on, look at it! No Jonny – not that! This! Yeah, the massive fucking hole in my belly? The place I got shot by a fucking baby? Yeah, that's what I need photos of.'

Jonny shrugged. He took out his camera, screwed on the lens.

'This is a bit weird, Sammy, you've got to admit. Taking photos of your... injury in a toilet.'

But he started clicking. He got a few angles. He negotiated the small space to try get as much light as possible. He didn't ask. That was why she always asked for Jonny.

'Now turn over.'

'What?!'

Now it was her turn to be shocked.

'Why should I turn over? What are you taking photos of, Jonny?'

'Look Sammy, I've shot enough dead guys in my time to know that there's always an exit wound. I don't know what you want this for, but if you're after a proper record of it then you're going to have to flip yourself over.'

It made sense. She'd not even considered the exit wound. That might have been one of the spikes of pain, perhaps? Had her guts been leaking out of her back the whole time?

'Nice arse, Sammy.'

Jonny was snapping away.

'Fuck off, Jonny.' She said, spitting out excess saliva.

It was then that the orderlies rushed the room. Jonny's instincts kicked in and he pocketed his memory card.

They stole his camera but found nothing on it. He nevertheless earned a lifetime ban from visiting the hospital.

Sammy, for her sins, was carried unceremoniously back to bed and placed on a heavy dose for the night. By the time she woke up the wound was closed. It could have been any wound at that point. In Sammy's mind, she'd made the right decision.

3

She had a vague memory of grabbing at someone, of begging. It was the nurse, Mitzi. Sammy was out of bed. She remembered the feeling of bare feet on lino. She was struggling with wires, begging, bartering. It was her phone! Mitzi promised to charge it. Mitzi promised and so she got back into bed. All was dark then. Nothing but the thought of charging. You dreamed you were a phone. You dreamed you were plugged in. You were charging. Filling up. Turning green and healthy.

*

'Sheryl! It looks like Sammy's waking up.'

The fuzz. Jesus, the fuzz was all over her. They'd hit her with another dose when she was sleeping. Now she couldn't feel her lips.

'Trrl!'

Work on your jaw, Sammy. Come on, stop clenching.

'Taaaaaal!'

'What's that Sammy? You want the towel?'

She could hear the nerves in the nurse's voice.

'Ysh plsh. Hot. Hot!'

Sammy felt the careful hand lifting a towel to her forehead, wiping off the sweat. It brushed down her cheeks. They felt sore, like she'd been gnawing in her sleep. The towel soothed them. Next, she heard something clicking open on the bedside table. Sammy waited. She controlled her breathing. She felt a baby wipe brushing against her left eyelid, cleaning out the sleep. It came over to the right, repeating the process. She blinked her eyes open. White light. It took a while to adjust.

Out of all the nurses, only Mitzi was here. She was the student one. The one who-

'Thank you, Mitzi.'

'Oh! You remember my name?' the nurse beamed. Mustn't get that very often. 'Well you're very welcome. You had us very worried, Sammy. You've not been very restful at all. I promised the sister that you'd behave. They wanted to put you in a secure unit. They say you're a danger to yourself.'

'I'm very tired.'

'You will be, Sammy. You had a big operation and then lots of... medicine, after you tried to-'

'I just need to rest.' Aaaaaaand yawn. Classic.

'Okay, Sammy,' she patted her on the shoulder. 'You sleep tight.'

'I'll just send my family a message to say I'm okay.'

'What?'

'My family. In Iraq. They'll want to know I'm okay.'

The nurse looked dubious. Sammy could see the thoughts swirling around her head. Should she say no? Her eyes were darting to the ward door, checking for other staff. She might say yes. Lean into it, Sammy, lean in.

'They're over in Iraq so I have to send them emails. There are no telephones there after... you know, the war.'

'Okay.'

The nurse slid the bedside cabinet open and pushed the phone into Sammy's hungry hands.

'Okay, but only this once. Let them know you're okay and then you get some rest, okay?'

'Sure, Mitzi. Definitely.'

Big smile. Big smile back. Job done.

Sammy noticed it was turned off. Did she do that? She never did that. Must have been one of the nurses. She held the button for a second and watched the screen come to life. The blue light hit her eyes and scraped back her tiredness like a windscreen wiper. She melted back into her body, her anxiety briefly subsiding. She had her phone and all was right with the world. Now she needed to ring Jonny.

Her phone buzzed. Old messages. Only 12. Wait... only 12? Something was up...

She started working through them. The latest was promising:

JONNY (CAMERA) >
Got it. Ring us.

Got what?

Then came one from her editor. That wasn't good. Oh, and it was long too. Shit. Sammy knew that long emails from the editor were always templates. His actual emails never exceeded three sentences. This one had four paragraphs.

Sammy's eyes moved across the lines searching for keywords. She kept seeing "rest" and "rest up" alongside words like "opportunity" and "development".

She was getting fired.

'They can't fire me!' She whispered furiously. 'I'm not even on staff!'

Someone had got to them. She knew it. They wouldn't just drop her like this, would they? Bantz Testament had done some pretty stone cold firings in the past but it was always when people crossed the line, went too far, got pregnant, or else tweeted something culturally insensitive back in 2005. She'd taken a bullet for this story! No, it must be the private school wankers. The mainstream media getting to them. Or the lawyers... the superinjunctions! Sammy knew she was onto something big and this was just more proof of it.

She needed to get out. That was all there was to it. But first, she needed to check in with Jonny.

'Mitzi.'

Sammy tightened her gown beneath the sheets, clamping her phone to her side.

'Mitzi! I need to go to the bathroom.'

'Wait a minute.'

The nurse was feeding an old woman a series of brightly coloured pills. She asked the woman's date of birth and checked her wristband before each one and then, after each one was swallowed, she checked it off her chart.

'Do you need some help with the bedpan?' She asked, walking over to Sammy.

'What? No. No, it's the other thing. It's okay. I can walk.'

As Sammy lowered herself out of bed the nurse instinctively went to help her. Once Sammy was vertical, it was clear Mitzi regretted giving this help. Something in Sammy's movements just screamed escape attempt. Sammy slipped on the pants she forgot last time and made for the door.

'Thanks. Back in a minute.'

'Sammy, it says here that you shouldn't need... the other thing. You can't eat solids anymore, remember?'

'Oh, well...' and Sammy leaned over, resting her arm on the nurse's. The nurse helped her to limp along, unable to refuse her. At the door to the ward Sammy turned to her.

'I suppose it's just what's left. It'll be my last ever... movement, I guess'

'Don't say that, Sammy.'

The nurse was sad for her bowels.

'You never know what might happen in the future.'

'Thanks, Mitzi.'

*

As the ward door swung shut behind her, Sammy was on borrowed time. She bolted straight for the lifts again. The grumbling in her belly was already starting to turn spikey. She hadn't long until she was incapacitated again. She would get in the lifts and then-

'Wait! What's this?'

Sammy was talking to herself. The adrenaline was getting her giddy.

Down the corridor, she saw the scrub room. Where there was a scrub room, there were scrubs. If Sammy liked one thing and one thing only, it was dressing up for a story. She'd almost forgotten her pain as she limped down the corridor and through the scrub room door. As she suspected, she saw lockers, she saw shoes, she saw… yes! Doctor's coat! She pulled it on. It went all the way down to the floor. She wasn't the tallest reporter in the world. Never mind, she rolled up the sleeves and made her way back to the lift, grabbing a stethoscope on her way out.

'Dr Habib.' If my dad could see me now!

She got into the lift and wondered where to go. Somewhere counter-intuitive. Somewhere they wouldn't suspect. X-Ray? No, might mess with her signal. Paediatrics? She hated kids. Loathed them. The thought of them made her physically spew. It was perfect.

She hit the button for floor three and burped. A big wash of stomach acid shot up her throat, burning and making her spit.

See, what did I tell you?

She strutted along the corridor to paediatrics. She leaned into the limp, trying to stifle her grunts of pain. Look like you're going somewhere important and nobody ever stops you; undercover journalism 101.

As she limped along, Sammy passed a room of sick toddlers. She felt a twinge as she remembered her shooter. Hopefully it was just the morphine. Then she saw it. Storeroom. Perfect.

She creaked open the storeroom door. The light was low. Her eyes could rest.

She reached for her phone. Dialled Jonny. Ringing. Ringing. Come on…

She noticed the room was filled with toys. Rows and rows of toys. Squeezy ones and fluffy ones. Ones with funny faces and ones from TV shows that didn't look very fun at all.

Ring-ring. Ring-ring. What is he doing? Oh, he's picked up-

'-idn't think I'd ever-'

'Sorry Jonny, you were cut off. Start again.'

'Never mind. You okay? Not dead?'

She thought back to his enigmatic message.

'Not yet. You said you'd got... it?'

'Yeah, Sammy, the stuff you asked for. I found a guy. Were you drunk or something when you sent those messages? Have they got you on drugs?'

'Yeah, it's pretty bad in here. I've got to get out and quick.'

'Well, I spoke to that American doctor you were talking about. I don't know if it's the same one, but I found an American doctor anyway.'

Oh yeah, the wound! That's what he was supposed to be finding out. It came back to her.

'And..?'

'...and I showed him the pictures and he confirmed what your surgeons said. It's like a normal shotgun wound but tiny. Like, at least half the size... and he says it's not something to do with gauge either, whatever that means.'

'I know what that means,' she said.

She didn't know.

'So you're saying the gun itself was smaller. Like a tiny shotgun? For babies?'

'Yeah, a small shotgun. The thing is though, and this is the weird bit-'

' It's all pretty weird.'

'Well the weird bit is, this guy's seen like a billion shootings. He's a consultant specialising in gunshot wounds and he's from Miami. He's seen it all, right? Well, he'd never seen this.'

'Never?'

'Never. He said he didn't know why anyone would make a smaller gun. But I guess he's an American, so...'

'Yeah, they always want everything bigger.'

Sammy was playing with a toy tank now. She'd lined up two weird plastic baby dolls and was driving over them, turning the cannon to shoot them in their weird eyes. Jonny was rambling.

'Who was it that said Americans are like midgets or something? Was it you, Sammy? It's the sort of thing you'd say. Like they're six-foot-tall but feel like they're midgets or something? So they make everything big? That was funny that. Think you were onto someth-'

'Shut up, Jonny. I'm trying to think.'

She placed her free fist in front of a baby doll's face and slowly spread out her fingers, mimicking an explosion from the tank.

'So I was shot with a tiny gun that no-one believes exists. They certainly don't believe me when I say it was a proper shotgun.'

'There's another thing, Sammy.'

He audibly swallowed, as if he shouldn't say.

'What? The dead bodyguard? Did they say what shot him?'

'Oh no, that was a sidearm. Their words, not mine. I guess they meant a pistol?'

'So what?'

'So I managed to get some photos of the scene before the ambulance came for you. I was going through them and I noticed the hole in the wall. The first shot where the guy missed you. You know?'

'Okay'

She'd forgotten that bit. It came back instantly.

'Well I took that to a ballistics expert that I know.'

'You know a ballistics expert?'

'He used to drive Uber when I was driving Uber. Still does, I think. There's not much money in ballistics. Not in the UK. So I showed him the pictures and made sure they were in scale and everything and, what he said was that the first shot which hit the wall was from a full-size shotgun.'

'Yeah, but...'

She stopped playing with the toys now. Something was up. Correction, another thing was up.

'But if he's driving for Uber then he can't be a proper expert, right? He's just your mate.'

'No, he's legit. He works for the police when there's a major shooting incident, and then he lectures at Manchester Met on the forensic science degree. Name's Dr Sandro Bannetyne.'

Sammy flicked open Google, searched the name. Sure enough, there was his profile – two of them. First result, lecturer at MMU, the second was a private page for his business. He was officially affiliated with the Greater Manchester Police. Sammy put the phone back to her ear.

'So, if he's this big expert then why's he driving Uber?'

'He's freelance.'

'Gotcha.'

Sammy had seen the finest minds of her generation, starving, hysterical, freelance, dragging themselves through endless finance departments looking for some progress on their unpaid invoices.

She believed this expert and, more than that, she knew he was on her side. Something was up. One shotgun and two sizes of shot made absolutely zero sense. Someone was covering something up and she'd be the one to track them down. She needed answers.

'Alright Jonny, nice work. We'll go fifty-fifty when I run the story, yeah?'

'I'd rather just invoice you for my hours.'

'Well that invoice isn't getting paid, Jonny, so I'll go fifty-fifty with you on a byline. Anyway, I need picking up. Come down to the hospital and get me.'

'I can't.'

He sounded put out, Sammy couldn't work out why.

'You got me banned for life, remember?'

'Oh yeah.'

She couldn't remember, but never mind. Her legs were starting to wobble and the spikes jabbed at her middle again. She Googled the nearest pub.

'I'll meet you at the Thatched House asap.'

'The Thatched House? Is that a pub?'

'Well it's not a thatched house.'

'Alright, calm down. I was trying to do my taxes before you rang. I'm halfway through a stack of bus tickets. No, no I can already hear you down the phone. I'm going to do these and then come. I'm not your bloody slave, Sammy, much as you treat me like one. I'll be there in an hour.'

BEEEEEEP-

He hung up. Ingrate!

She looked around the store room. She could either leave now and risk being sent back – they'd definitely drug her then, which would mean game over, bye-bye job, bye-bye flat – or else she could hold out in here for the next forty-five minutes. Tough choices. She couldn't risk being caught.

Grimacing through the pain, she lay down. There, surrounded by stuffed animals, in the cool dark, she tried to sleep. What had her boss' template email said? 'Rest up?' She lay on her back and rested.

But it wouldn't stop niggling. She had to keep on the search. She opened up Google:

CUSTOM SHOTGUNS

CUSTOM SHOTGUNS UK

MINIATURE SHOTGUNS UK

MINIATURE CUSTOM SHOTGUNS UK

MINIATURE CUSTOM SHOTGUNS UK SELLERS

MINIATURE CUSTOM SHOTGUNS UK SELLERS NAME

SHOTGUN SELLERS NAME

SELLERS SYNONYM

MINIATURE CUSTOM SHOTGUNS UK DEALERS

She eventually found the list she was looking for on an obscure board on Mumznet. Some discussion was taking place about when to start taking your children shooting. The argument was passionate. Sure enough, within a couple of pages the board started discussing the best shotguns for children.

'Not that the government want us doing it, but then my Toby is very mature for his age and-'

...it was the list she needed.

There were only twenty-eight licensed gun dealers in the UK who dealt in customised shotguns. Twenty-three were in London. Typical! Suppliers of Team GB and the like. How many in the North? Six. It's not as if it needed to be bought in the North, Sammy supposed, but as a starting point it made sense. Things go missing a bit easier out in the country.

She scrolled down the list, checking the location of each. Suddenly she saw it:

REGINALD GUNSMITH'S – AVON MURRAY

Avon Murray. That's where Mel Ditty turned up. Drugged up sex party but-not-really-it-was-a-disappearance Mel Ditty. Avon Murray! That couldn't be a coincidence. This was where Sammy had to go next. To Reginald Gunsmith's – wait... is his name Gunsmith, or is that the name of the shop? What is that apostrophe for? Never mind. She was tired. It was Avon Murray. By the sounds of it, the middle of nowhere. They probably don't have grammar there yet. She lay back in her hideout, surrounded by toys. She reached a hand out and stroked a rabbit with her fingertips. She'd wait here, hidden. And then she'd go to the pub. And then she'd go to Avon Murray.

4

There was a buzzing in her head. It started in her right eye socket and buzzed right round her skull. It was a pulse. As it brought her back to consciousness she felt her stomach start to moan. She lifted her legs up - BANG! Knees hit something above her. She opened an eye. It was coming back to her. A line of teddies surrounded her, looming over her.

She pulled the phone from her face. She'd slept on it. She wiped off the dribble and silenced the alarm. Only 15 minutes late. Cat nap.

She sent a quick text:

JONNY (CAMERA) >
On way now. S.x

She hit send. Instantly regretted the kiss. Nevermind. Onwards.

She looked around the room and spotted a pile of crutches. They were in kids sizes. She picked out the largest pair. Too small, but they'd do. There were occasional benefits to being a midget.

She pulled her doctor's coat straight, retied her bobble and headed out the door.

She hit the G in the lift and headed for ground.

JONNY (CAMERA) >
At Thatched. What you havin?

REPLY >
Usual. X

Stop with the kisses, Sammy, gees.

The lift stopped a bit too quickly. The wobble sent her belly into spasm. The crutches wouldn't hold her. She crashed against the wall.

As she slid down it she bashed helplessly at the Doors Close button. The doors slid shut. She hoped no one had seen her.

She was getting used to the pain now, but it still paralysed her. There was no powering through. Even staying upright and hitting the button she felt like she might shit herself. Come on. Let it roll over you. Let it do its thing. It's healing. It's healing like yoga or sit-ups. Just tell yourself it's healing.

JONNY (CAMERA) >
Don't think they do massive bags of cocaine here, Sam ;p

REPLY >
Fcu yuself Jonnny. Rum ncoke

It was passing. Nice and slowly it was easing off. The pain faded. She lifted herself up to a dignified position. She picked up a fallen crutch. She let the lift door open.

Thank God. Praise Allah. Jumpin Jehosafat. The lobby was empty. Just the receptionists locked in their bulletproof admin cube. They wouldn't try to stop her, would they? No, not with the doctor's coat. There was even a wheelchair on the steps outside. Whose was it?

Can't be that important if someone's just left it there.

She started crutching herself out of the lift. She'd forgotten to put shoes on. Never mind, she could make it barefoot. She was halfway across the lobby when she saw the neon yellow. She froze. Span. Practically launched herself behind a big plastic fern. No, they hadn't forgotten her.

Outside the door two female police officers were patrolling. One was in the standard patrol kit, which was intimidating enough, but the other was even scarier. She stood half a foot taller than her partner, and was dressed all in black. She had the stabvest. She had the MP5 carbine. Sammy had written articles about those things. Hollow point bullets, they had in them. Vicious. She'd seen the bodies.

'No thanks,' Sammy whispered. 'Not today.'

For all she knew they'd still got her religion listed as Muslim. Or they'd have noted that she'd changed it from Muslim, which probably looked even worse. Oh, come on, Sammy. How many times have you met the police? They're alright. They sent women too, so as not to offend your delicate sensibilities! It's just the chemicals that are making you paranoid. This might just be a routine patrol.

No, fuck it. She wouldn't take chances. She crawled back down the corridor. Kept crawling until she saw the sign for the courtyard.

Sick people were milling in the courtyard, looking like a diagram of states of human mobility. They walked, limped, rolled and stumbled. All of them smoked. Sammy crawled through the crowd, trying not to catch anyone's eye. They, for their part, were studiously ignoring her too. In her doctor's coat, they probably thought she'd come out to tell them off.

Sure enough, as Sammy had predicted, or at least hoped, the courtyard led to a side exit. It was a gate with a padlock. One with spinning numbers. Four of them: 1 – 9 – 4 – 8. CLICK. And she was out.

Date the NHS was established. Predictable.

By the time she was out in the car park she realised she'd missed her chance to steal a wheelchair. Never mind. She had her freedom, and that's what mattered. That, and not getting riddled with Her Majesty's bullets.

She checked Google Maps. The pub was only five minutes' walk away – or ten minutes' limp. The app even started loading up reviews. It did pretty nice food, apparently.

'Jesus, Sammy! Don't go in there!'

'What?'

She was limping through the beer garden. Her wound was hitting her with a steady pulse of pain now, and her feet weren't doing great either. Her soles were black.

She turned to see Jonny sitting at a table. He was halfway through a mild. The ice looked to have melted in her rum and coke. She began to limp over.

'A bit cold for a picnic, isn't it Jonny? Can't we go inside?'

'No.'

He had his hoody pulled up over his head. He would never normally wear it like that.

'Why not? It's raining.'

'Sit down and have your drink, Sammy.'

He was serious, or as close as he got to being serious, which was mildly peeved.

'You're going to get us in trouble.'

'Strict beer garden?'

She clattered down onto the bench. Jonny took out his phone. He placed it on a miniature stand and selected a video.

'That's a cool stand, Jonny.'

'It is, isn't it? I was shooting a corporate and some company was giving them away. Says it on the side: *Lund Corp.*'

'Never heard of them.'

'Me neither, but that's not the point.'

He pressed play. The BBC News started rolling.

'...and we're going to return now to the crime desk. The police have released photos of people wanted for questioning. This is in relation to a shooting in a Manchester penthouse three nights ago.'

'Three nights?' Sammy looked up. 'How long was I in hospital?'

Jonny shushed her and pointed to the phone.

'...three men and a woman. The woman has been identified as a Ms Samra Ruwayda al-Baghdadi Habib, a journalist with links to Al Jazeera.'

'I did one story with them!' Sammy sputtered, 'and they

picked it up through AP!'

'Shhh!'

'...was her accomplice; a cameraman with the Bantz Testament-'

'I see they get your job right, Jonny!'

'I'm freelance. I do more work for Deliveroo than Bantz!'

'...unknown Asian man and a suspect with a history of violence. Witnesses have identified him as Baz Clemford. If you or anyone you know has information regarding these individuals, the police have requested that you contact them immediately on the number at the bottom of the screen.'

Jonny picked up the phone and its stand, placing them neatly back in his pocket. The mood was sombre.

'Okay, Jonny, so... I'm a terrorist apparently?'

'No, we're just wanted for questioning. It was the other two who are considered suspects. If you read the article alongside the video...'

'Oh, I bet everyone's going to read the article! Jesus, Jonny, how long have you been in news? Have you not been paying a single bit of attention this whole time? People – do – not – read – Jonny! We have the stats! I can take you to Bantz and literally show you the point where people click off our articles. No prizes for guessing where – it's exactly where the written words begin, Jonny, because people are dumb and illiterate. We are now truly screwed. You might as well wear a turban because you're now the associate of an Arab with two middle names. Jesus, I knew they'd come for me, but I didn't think it would be this banal.'

'Coming for you?' Jonny snorted. 'Is that all you care about? Yourself? Sammy, I like you, but you don't make me anything in terms of money. I need to work or I'm going to be homeless and then they'll never let me see my kid again, will they? The amount of crazy stuff I've done for you... you got me banned from a hospital! God forbid any of my family ever end up sick in there... what am I going to tell them? You've, you've... you've got me fired from Bantz!'

'You're resting up too?'

'It's not fucking funny, Sammy. My name is mud now! I'm freelance. My name's all I have! I'm tempted to just go to the police right now. Go and tell them the whole story. All my mistakes, crimes… whatever they were. They were all done to help you! I don't care about your missing celebrities. I didn't even want to know about it. I want out. Now. This is the end of us, Sammy. I just can't be seen with you. Sorry, sorry, but that's the case. That's the way it is.'

'Really?'

Sammy had been searching on her phone while Jonny was getting emotional. She knew he'd never go to the police. He'd probably ditch her, though. That's what she would do after all. Can't blame him. But, yet, she did still sort of blame him, the cowardly little shit. If he wanted to play the victim then let him play the victim.

She leaned back. Put her phone down. Looked him dead in the eye, and spoke:

'Boo-hoo, Jonny, boo-hoo. My heart weeps for you. Do you feel better now? Have you got everything off your chest? Are you all done?'

'No! No, I'm not all-'

'You're all done, Jonny, and I'm going to tell you why you're all done. You're all done because while you were out delivering cheese pizzas, I was out there perfecting my trade. A trade in ruining people's lives. You see, I can see through that news story because I wrote those things every day. If a teenage girl posted a cute video of her hamster in the morning, and that shit was viral by lunch, then by mid-afternoon I'll have found at least three transphobic things she posted six years ago and turn her into the biggest hate figure since Myra Hindley by dinnertime. Hell, she could be a saint, and we'd just quote her out of context, making her say the exact opposite of what she really intended. None of it matters, Jonny, because people – don't – read. They would rather pull each other apart in a ditch than read more than three sentences. That's who our customers are. That's who we specialise in enraging. We make them feel righteous and Holy and Right... and you're worried about the BBC? You're worried about the police? My poor little Jonny, those noble institutions are there to protect society from people like us. People like me. Do you get me? Do you know what I mean?'

'Jesus, Sammy.'

'I didn't come out here to hear you being a victim. You be a victim if that's what you want to be. I hear it's really fucking satisfying. I can see why you want to do it. It sounds great. I support your life choices. It's a free country, after all. But if you try and fuck me on this one, you hoody-wearing fuck, then–'

'Alright, alright!'

He pulled the hood back off his head.

'You're so dramatic.'

Sammy had not always been like this, of course. Her furious cynicism was something life had done to her. Fifty years ago, her curiosity, her bravery, and her unswerving commitment to the truth might have made of her a legendary journalist. The top of her field even, with medals and everything.

Instead, living in the Twenty-First Century, she was just another sucker inputting information into the information machine. It was her daily battle to squeeze an income out of this service – a service the majority of the population provided to the corporations for free – that had made her cruel and bitter and in need of redemption.

The question of her redemption, as I'm sure you've intuited by now, is the primary concern of this novel...

Sammy sipped her rum and coke and looked down at her phone. She had the story open. They'd used her byline photo which was flattering. Jonny, by contrast, looked like a serial killer. Must be a passport photo or something. The "unknown

Asian man" looked familiar. Too familiar, in fact. She saved his photo and the photo of the other guy. Who was it? Baz Clemford. 'Baz': nice! On second thoughts she dropped his photo into messages and sent it over to Jonny.

Still moping, he felt the buzz in his pocket. He lifted out his phone and looked at her.

'Alright, Jonny, if you're going to abandon me then at least make yourself useful before you go. See if our mate Baz has any known addresses. I'm looking up the other one.'

Jonny perked up, glad to be useful. He lifted a finger to his lips for a moment, thinking.

'Hrmm... okay, I'll start on the GMP database, then do the phonebook, then look up any associated IP addresses...'

'TMI, Jonny, TMI,' she smiled. 'You'd make a terrible criminal.'

The photo was too blurry for Google Image recognition. She dragged it in and it just spat back a parade of low-def Asian faces. There were a couple of identikit faces in there but they didn't seem relevant. Top search was a celebrity from... Bollywood. Well, not him. Closest looking match was... she clicked on the link to find it was dead. An advert for online slot machines popped up instead. Even with AdBlock she got these things. This didn't seem to be going anywhere.

She sat back and thought about the party. It was forming into a generic image in her mind already. She, a trained journalist, and her memory was a blur. She remembered the bodyguard dying on the bathroom floor. She remembered the medic. Why wasn't he wanted by the police too? They probably already had him. The rest were just overexcited rich kids... and then the baby.

Was it the baby that reminded her of this guy? Were they family? ...and then the baby disappeared.

Maybe it was the drugs, or the shock. Maybe she had remembered wrong? But she wouldn't remember this man as a baby, would she? With a tiny shotgun... for which she had evidence. Some evidence... with other evidence contradicting it: the hole in the wall, her own memory of the full size gun, like something out of *Call of Duty*. No, this guy couldn't be the baby. She wasn't crazy. Maybe he was the baby's dad? Some kind of relation? There was a similarity in her mind. Something uncanny going on in their faces. And now she couldn't remember the baby at all.

'Okay,' Jonny grinned, 'that was actually really easy.'

He was sitting back, pausing for effect. He wanted her to ask for help again.

'Alright Jonny, pretty please. What have you found?'

'So, the Police database had a few leads but nothing useful. Instead I went back a bit and ran Barry – not Baz – through a few old phonebooks. There's a site where they've put them all through OCR, you see, so they're searchable.'

He was clearly very proud of himself, showing his workings to the teacher.

'So, through this I compiled a list and found addresses. I put these addresses into the BT installation service database – that private log-in information has paid for itself, by the way – and from that I've got about ten, no, twelve places where Barry Clemford has, at one time, been living.'

'Barry Clemford, or a Barry Clemford?'

'Get this. There's only one!'

'Really?'

She grabbed Jonny's phone from him. She began reading down the list.

'Bad luck Barry! You're not going to last long as a criminal these days with a unique name. This is a lot of addresses! I guess he was trying to move house to keep anonymous? Sorry, Baz, but there's a thing called Google and it loves us all very much, and watches over us always, no matter where we go. WAIT!'

'What?'

'Are you sure this one is right?'

She pushed the phone over to him. He focused his eyes.

'Avon Murray?'

'Avon Murray!'

'Yeah, yeah, it's right.'

He took the phone off her and expanded the information.

'And he was there only a few weeks ago. The last place of accommodation was listed as Manchester city centre. He was in Spinningfields apparently. Very fancy!'

'Well Avon Murray is one of the only places in the North that does custom shotguns, and – get this – it's where Mel Ditty turned up after she disappeared for months. How's that eh, Jonny? And here you were, thinking I've been living a fantasy this whole time.'

'I still don't really get what you're on about, Sammy…'

At least he was smiling. He had a tactical unknowing, Sammy remembered. It was part of what made him a great cameraman. A capacity to instantly forget any information that might lead to trouble down the line.

'No bother, Jonny. You're off the story anyway, right? Well, do us a last favour and drive me to the station. I can't be messing around here. I need the first train out to Avon Murray and then some kind of B&B or whatever they have out in the countryside. I dunno, a manger or something. Is that what Jesus slept in?'

'He did when he was a baby, yeah. I don't think he always slept in one though, did he? Not when he was grown up like.'

They walked out to Jonny's moped. As Sammy swung her leg over she thought of the nurse… what was her name? Mitzi? Perhaps she'd lose her job over this.

Oh well, nothing to be done. Sammy pulled a helmet on.

'Just got to stop for some petrol, Sammy. If that's alright?'

'Sure!' she laughed, pulling a thickly-packed wallet from the doctor's coat. 'This one's on the National Health!'

'Have you nicked that? Bloody hell, Sammy, I'll be glad to be rid of you.'

He kicked the moped into life. The seat between Sammy's legs started to vibrate intensely. Oh God, she realised, this is going to hurt.

5

The train pulled into the station. Sammy presumed it was Avon Murray. The station had no sign. She jumped off and the doors slammed shut behind her.

The train pulled away. She was left alone. This was definitely the countryside.

The station was two platforms and nothing else. Two platforms on a mound. Around them was forest. There were no signs. No clue as to where to go.

It was easier to walk downhill, so she walked downhill.

A hundred yards later, she passed the station sign. Someone had thrown it in a bush. Judging from the moss it had lain there a very long time.

Despairing, Sammy took out her phone. She clicked it on and entered her unlock pattern. She'd look on Google Maps. She stood still for a while and waited for it to load. It didn't.

She checked the internet. Nothing. She checked signal. Emergency Calls Only. What the hell does that mean?

Nothing for it. She needed to suck it up and move. Think of the B&B, Sammy. Think of a bubble bath. Her hand moved automatically to her wound.

Whatever, Sammy, you can wrap it in a bin bag or something... think of the bubbles.

So she walked on into the woods. She pushed through brambles and nettle patches. It was supposed to be summer but the light through the dappled leaves was grey. It sucked the life out of everything. The forest looked like a film set. Sammy began to suspect that if she walked off the trail and pushed at one of the clumps of foliage she'd find it was two dimensional.

After half an hour of forest, which felt like a lifetime, she emerged onto a paved road. Not paved well, mind, but at this point she'd take anything.

On the other side of the road was a field. It was bare. Dry stone walls carried curls of barbed wire. She decided to stay on the forest side of the road. Couldn't risk some farmer with a shotgun. Twice in two days would look careless... three days? She couldn't remember how long it had been... her slippers were hopelessly mangled, kept on only by brambles.

She felt sure her wound was seeping. The bandages were turning yellow and, in one worrying patch, brown. She still didn't know whether to go right or left.

No cars in sight. Not even the sound of cars in the distance. She could see the road ahead curl downwards, up, down, and ahead of that, yet another forested hill...

The damn countryside! It went on forever!

She lifted up her arms and swung them in tiny aerial circles. She closed her eyes and tried to feel gravity pulling at her. She could feel the ache in her guts. It had shifted over to one side now. Counterbalance, counteract. Come on Sammy. Then could it be? Yes! She felt it, she was sure. Some seagull part of her brain had assured her that turning right would lead her down the hill. Down the hill, she had decided, was where she needed to go.

And so Sammy limped on and on. Two or three cars passed but gave no sign of stopping. She gave up the idea of thumbing a lift. The sun moved along behind the clouds and Sammy realised she'd never get there. She'd bleed out on this godforsaken road. She should just roll herself up in the barbed wire and die. She passed another empty field, and another. All fortified: stone and wire. Then a field with cows. She avoided them. They waddled over and tried to meet her eye. She refused to meet theirs. She became interested in the forest instead.

Then the forest died back and there were only fields.

She had to keep going. She got into a rhythm with her crutches, rocking forward and back. In her head she started humming a tune. What was it? She couldn't remember. The field beside her was full of wheat. She saw vapour trails crossing it, psychedelic ocean effects. She could hear the music now in her ears as well as in her head.

Head down, girl. Just to the top of this hill. Just to the top. You can make it.

She crested the hill. Another forest.

'Fuck it, Sammy, you've earned this' she said, before collapsing into a pile and crying.

She stayed down there ten minutes, which also felt like forever.

The descent into hell, via the forest. Abandon all hope, and all that.

Sammy lay there, feeling sorry for herself. Trying to convince herself that, down here at her lowest point, the only way was up.

Back on your feet, Sammy, come on.

She spat out the wash of saliva that had filled her mouth. The reflux was bad.

She trudged on into the forest. She was moving downhill again. She saw a signpost. The sign had been snapped off but even finding a bare post was, at this point, a good sign. Enough to keep her hopes up.

Then, between the trees, she saw it. A different tree. A taller one. In red brick. A mill chimney. Goddamnit, two! And a third! That was enough! Somewhere down in the base of the valley was a town.

*

She passed through the outlying houses, the churches and newsagents. All closed. She took out her phone. Still no internet, no signal. Eventually she reached the main street. The shops were different here. No supermarket – just oldie worldie things like butchers, ironmongers, opticians... three opticians? And everything closed. No cash machines. No phone boxes, though Sammy couldn't remember if cities even had those anymore.

She checked her phone. It said 16:36. It couldn't be that early! She wandered on. But sure enough, there was a clock tower in the village square: 4:36pm.

Why is everything closed? What day is it? A Tuesday. It can't be a bank holiday. Did no one live in this town? The streets were empty. She was alone. In the centre of town in the middle of the afternoon on a weekday, she was alone.

'Zombie apocalypse...' Sammy said to the breeze.

She limped along until she found a crossroads.

It was here, at both a literal and metaphorical crossroads, that Sammy Habib made her first contact with the people of Avon Murray. Across the road, sheltered beneath a weeping willow with an old and unreadable sign – are there no readable signs in this town? – she noticed a pub. The Hatters. Outside, two men in flat caps smoked in silence, their hands were clutched tight around their bitters. Through the frosted glass she saw lights and movement. Lifting her crutches, checking she still had the Doc's wallet in her pocket, she swung herself over to the big black door.

The wrought iron doormat read 'WIPE THY RUDDY FEET!'

She entered. Stumbled to the bar. A hush fell. Not a total hush, but enough to tell her she'd been noticed. Behind the bar was a dark haired whippet of a girl.

'Glass of water,' Sammy coughed, 'please.'

'Water's for customers, love.'

For a girl who looked about fourteen she had the voice of a lifelong smoker.

'Well, I'll have a pint of... have you only got one lager?'

'Yeah. And a bitter, and a mild, and a stout. Or a cider, if you're that way inclined.'

'Yes, that's all of them. All of the drinks. Luxury! In that case I'll have a bitter, I guess.'

Sammy was not in the mood for this.

'Alright. Pint of bitter,' the girl said.

'And a glass of water.'

'Alright. Pint of water.'

The girl spoke like she was reporting it to a supervisor. She was the only one on the bar.

'Tap water?'

'Sure,' she was giving up now. 'I mean, I'm guessing you don't have anything else?'

'Well, my love, I could get me hiking boots on and go scoop it from a clear running spring for you? Or Gerry here could fly his 'ellycopter up to the Scottish highlands and bring you back the purest mineral water, if that'd suit you? Might take a while though, mind.'

'Wahey! You want to see my 'ellycopter, Tina?'

Gerry dribbled as he grabbed at his crotch.

'Keep it in your pants, Gerry. It's only early.'

She pushed the glass of tap water onto the bar and started pouring the bitter.

'Maybe at home time though, eh love? You always get it out about then, don't you? You could fly us all home on it.'

She pushed the bitter over to Sammy.

'That's Gerry. He's got an 'ellycopter. That'll be £2.20, love.'

'£2.20?' Bargain.

Sammy collapsed behind a table in the corner. Other than the clump of people around the bar, the pub was dead. There were a few groups of older men. Some with their wives. All sat silently sipping at their drinks, occasionally passing a comment. Some of the comments seemed to be about her. Is this all people do in Avon Murray, she wondered? Close up shop at 4pm and drink in silence?

She felt like she could see a thin string of time. It was hooked around the necks of the blokes by the bar, the teens giggling in the front room, and the silent old men in here with her. They were all tied up in this invisible fishing line. Doomed to repeat. Doomed to the process. The cycle. The horror of it made her sick. She burped.

A few eyes darted at her. She chugged the water down to stop the acid coming up. Urgh! It just made it worse! Try the bitter. That's better! She glugged it down. About a third of the pint in one go. It soothed the oesophagus. She knew it'd only make her worse later. Less capable of asking for help. Less capable of finding, what was it? A gunsmiths? No, a B&B first.

She grabbed a paper from a nearby table. Might as well check if she was in there.

Nope.

The front page was a nightmare of local pointlessness: Duck Race Goes Bad: Local Dog Blamed, Government Targets Farmers, Bread Wins Prize. She turned the pages anyway, looking for something, anything to do with the case, or with local accommodation. She saw an advert for a shooting competition; one using shotguns. And then an article about the competition. And an interview on the same thing, with Stanley Reginald, of Reginald Gunsmith's. So Reginald was a surname. Then what is the apostrophe doing there? Nevermind. They were pushing this shooting competition anyway.

First prize was a gun. A little redundant. It was something to look into anyway.

She turned to the ads. No hotels. No B&Bs. An ad for Reginald Gunsmith's. The bastard's everywhere.

As she was looking down at the paper she felt dizzy. Was it the bitter? Poisoned! No, no Sammy you idiot you've just not eaten in... three days? How is it three days? And she looked down at her middle and... oh, Jesus. No! No, that's not right. The brown bit was going red. This wasn't good.

She tensed herself and reached down, pushing her fingers under the bandaging. Ooof! It felt moist in there. She pulled them out. Yes. Blood. Not good. Not good at all. Emergency in fact, Sammy. That's an emergency, that is.

She stood up. Pulled out her phone. No signal. She rolled up the newspaper and pushed it into her doctor's coat. She gazed at herself in the mirror. She was covered in mud. How had that happened? She turned around. Mud on the seat. Mud on the floor.

Just ignore it, Sammy. Move on. You're just hitting the wall is all.

All eyes turned on her as she staggered toward the bar. She'd left her crutches behind. She couldn't have lifted them anyway. God, this came on quick. She hit the bar and leaned on it, heavy. The barmaid came over. Her eyebrow raised.

'Alright, love? What do you want?'

Sammy parted her lips. She couldn't speak. Nothing would come out. She couldn't think what words to say even if she could speak. The panic set in. She was shutting down. She lifted up her fingers, dipped in blood. The bar went quiet.

'Oh, you sick cunt!'

It was Gerry. He seemed furious. Thankfully, this sent his mates into hysterics. It sounded like barking.

'Bloody hell.'

The girl behind the bar shook her head. She'd clearly decided Sammy was disabled or foreign or something. Sammy felt incompetent, helpless, humiliated. They don't know! They couldn't know what she'd been though.

'Here love,' it was the girl, 'women's room's round that corner there.'

Sammy looked down at her hand. There was a tampon in it.

Okay. Okay, if that's what's happening then let's go. She stumbled back, her head whirling, vomit on its way. She rushed to the toilets. Bang. Through the door. Bang. Into the cubicle. Bit of vomit. Just a little. Not much there.

Aaaaaand... sit back on the seat. Lock yourself in, that's a girl. Go on, Sammy. You can do this. Just chill a second.

She looked down at the bandage. The red was there still. Something was bleeding, but wasn't bleeding too much. She might be okay. She reviewed her situation.

What she probably should do is redress the wound, but the toilet of the Hatters didn't seem the best place for that. What happened to the B&B? Her head span.

Okay, so if you can't redress it then you have to do something to stop the bleeding. Will it go tighter? She tried vaguely pulling at the bandages. No, nothing doing. What's that in my hand? She still had the tampon. She'd forgotten about it. The tampon, it occurred to Sammy, might just work. Maybe that was why the girl gave it to her? No Sammy. Don't attribute magical powers to the yokels. It's just a thing for blood. Coincidence. Sort of. Come on, let's fix it up.

She opened the tampon. Felt its softness. Tore at it a little to make it look more medical. With one hand she heaved back the bandage, with the other she pushed the tampon onto her wound. She moved it where she felt the blood leaking. She cried out. A new pain. A different one. Stingie. Very stingie.

But the stinging stopped quick. The blood seemed to stop too. Holy crap, Sammy, you could be a doctor after all! You've earned your stethoscope.

Now what? You're stuck in Avon Murray with nowhere to go. You've no signal, no internet. Everyone thinks you're a weirdo and hates you. You're a total mess. There's no pursuing the story like this. You've got to rest. Just for a moment. Just till morning. Just get out of here and find a hotel. She held her breath. She stood up and hobbled out of the door. Just get out there and ask for-

'Hey. I like your coat.'

It was a young man with brown eyes. He was smiling. It was a cocky smile, but it didn't seem cruel. He was stood outside the toilet door. She'd almost run into him.

'Were you... were you waiting for me to come out of the toilet?'

'Maybe. Look, you made quite an impression in there. I wanted to see if you were okay.'

'I'm fine,' she said.

He didn't believe it. She was staring at him. Why? She should probably walk to the bar. What was she supposed to be doing again?

'You look fine. You look great in fact.'

He was being ironic... or was he? Do they have irony in the countryside?

'I really like the muddy doctor's coat... and the bandages. They look great.'

'I'm... I'm an NHS mummy.'

What are you doing Sammy? You're an idiot. He was laughing though. He had a nice laugh.

'Right. Right. I was thinking like, zombie surgeon or something but NHS mummy is pretty good too.'

He said it with that cocky smile again. He's probably a dickhead. Probably.

'Zombie brain surgeon!'

Sammy added through giggles. Sammy, you're drunk. He was laughing though. He was laughing. It felt nice to hear. She'd missed laughing – laughing at funny things instead of cruel things. He brushed her arm.

'Well look, Doctor Frankenstein, I don't want to be the bearer of bad news but you've made a pretty weird impression on the guys in there.'

He thumbed the air behind him.

'And I don't want them to get out the torches and pitchforks. They're a nice bunch, really, but there's just nothing to do around here. That's why Gerry's always getting his knob out. Then Baz gets his arse out-'

'Baz?'

'Then before you know it, cows are getting tipped over and everyone's criminal records are getting just that little bit longer. They get excited easily. That's all I'm saying. You're new here aren't you?'

Don't trust him, Sammy. You wouldn't fall for this schtick in town.

'How did you guess?'

'Well the closest thing we get to a brown face in this town is when the Polish stay outside too long and get sunburned. Oh, and Mr Lund. But Mr Lund doesn't count...'

'Right.'

'Where are you staying anyway? Are you visiting someone?'

She burped. Froze. Waited. There was no acid. It was just a normal burp. Maybe everything was going to be okay. She looked up at him. He was chuckling. He was nice. She liked talking to him.

'What's your name?'

'Mine? Oh, I'm John. John Barton.' He put his hand out and she shook it. 'And you?'

Should she make up an alias? No. Too much extra thinking.

'I'm Sammy. Sammy Habib. Like the BBC. I don't know why I said that. I'm a journalist. I... I was hoping to find a hotel or a... B&B maybe?'

She realised when she said it that maybe those weren't real. Maybe B&Bs were an invention of the cosmopolitan elite?

'Are there any in Avon Murray?'

He arched his eyebrows. 'I don't think I've ever seen any. I can't see why anyone would want to come here in the first place. Why are you here? You're a journalist?'

'There must be something? A Travelodge? An... inn?'

'An inn?'

'Yeah.'

'Like Jesus?'

She giggled. 'Yeah. Like Jesus.'

'Well, I've got a spare room if you want it.'

He smiled at her. It seemed friendly, not creepy. But damn it, Sammy, it is creepy and you know it! Maybe that's how things work out here.

'Or I have a manger. You can stay in the manger if you like?'

'What even is a manger?'

'I don't know. I think it's like a trough. Like, what you feed cattle from. I live on a farm so I should probably know these things.'

'You have a farm?'

That made sense. He looked country but like... smart country?

'I don't have a farm. I just live on one. I'm the odd jobs guy. I do a bit of this, a bit of that. It's fun. It's a big house, anyway. It's got a spare room. In the harvest it gets filled out with the seasonal labourers from Poland. Good guys but God, there's a lot of them! At the moment it's pretty empty.'

He turned back to the bar a moment. Sammy could hear the punters were starting to shout. It was getting rowdy, she could sense it. The bad type of rowdy.

'Look, come back to the farm. Stay in the spare room tonight. In the morning we'll see about finding a proper place for you to stay. I have the internet up there and everything. My Jeep's outside. Ten minute drive.'

'Internet...'

Oh Sammy, you're an idiot. You're not really contemplating this are you? But, what choice do you have? Plus, he's sort of like a puppy dog. Just pocket a steak knife from the side of the bar on your way out and you'll be alright.

'Sure. That sounds good. I'll stay in your spare room.'

He picked up her crutches on the way out. She would have forgotten them otherwise.

6

The jeep bounced in through the farmhouse gates. It shook Sammy awake again. She was surprised it wasn't dark. It felt like 2am in her head, but the evening was only just starting to roll in. As they pulled around the farmhouse she saw it was part of a large complex. There were two large sheds, maybe for cattle but she couldn't tell, a free-standing roof covering farm machinery, and a series of cottages built at strange angles. It was at the front of one of these that the young man – what was his name again? – pulled-up the jeep.

'There we are,' he grinned, 'home!'

'Urgh...'

A wave of nausea hit her through all the tiredness and ache. Plus, somewhere under there, she now realised she was starving.

'You don't sound great, Sammy. I didn't make you sick with my driving, did I?'

'Maybe.'

Suddenly she heard two loud bangs against her door. If she were more awake she'd have flinched. The air was filled with mad barking. Turning her head, she saw two Rottweilers flecking her window with angry drool. The guy had jumped out of his door, slammed it, and was stamping around to the beasts.

'Oy! Lay off! On wi'yet! Outerit! Bugger off!'

He waved his arms above his head. One dog immediately retreated. The other, still baring its teeth, received a series of vicious slaps around the face and, as it span around in panic, a swift boot up its arse sent it on its way. The guy walked over to

Sammy's window.

'Sorry about that. They're the farmer's dogs. Right shitheads.'

'Okay.'

She pulled on the door handle only to find herself rolling out. He caught her. She looked up into his daft eyes.

'What's your name? I've forgotten your name?'

'My name? I'm John Barton.'

'I'm... Sammy.'

'I know,' he said.

He heaved her to her feet. He'd started to look very concerned.

'See here, Sammy. Are you alright? You're wobbling everywhere. Could I get you something to eat? I've got a steak and kidney pie in the fridge.'

'No. No, I'll die.'

'What? Are you one of these vegans or something?'

'I can't eat anything that's not a McDonald's milkshake... or like a McDonald's milkshake. It's my guts. My guts are all messed up and I'm messed up... are you Jonny?'

'If you like.'

She leaned her full weight on him. She couldn't work out which way was up. He walked her towards the nearest cottage door.

'I mean, it's John but you can call me Jonny, I suppose.'

'Not your Jonny, my Jonny...'

'You're Jonny?'

'NO! Nobody's Jonny. He's gone. He went away.'

She crossed the threshold. Inside, the place was clean. Lots of wood panelling and a few hulking old sofas. She let her slippers slip off her feet. One still dragged behind her, attached by brambles. She couldn't remember where the brambles had come from.

'Nobody's Jonny, anyway. It's not important. I need... I need to eat a milkshake.'

John Barton set her down on one of the big sofas. She felt her body sink into the too-soft cushions. She sank in, deeper and deeper. She needed to be horizontal. She rolled over. She was lost in the soft cushions now. She fell asleep.

*

She woke up and couldn't remember much. Least of all where she was. She felt in her pocket for her phone. 5am, sure enough. That was her wake-up hour. She felt like a wreck but, somehow... better? The memories of the past few days returned to her. She'd been shot, what, three? No, four days ago now. Well, she was feeling better than could be expected. She looked around the room. Let it come back to her. The farm. The man... or boy? He was sort of halfway between the two, she guessed. Vicious dogs outside. What was his name? She couldn't remember.

She looked to the table. There were two glasses there. One held water which she drank down without thinking. She was parched. The second had some bizarre mess in it. She couldn't work it out – like a kind of yellow-brown gloop.

She went to the tap and poured another glass of water. Downed it. Poured another. Same. She stopped to taste the fourth glass. It tasted strange. Like moss.

The counter was a mess. It didn't seem in keeping with the rest of the cottage, which was otherwise spotless. She investigated.

Start with the small mysteries, Sammy, and work your way up.

The mess had come from a beaker-type device. Picking it up she realised it was a blender. A blender from the 90s. But what was the mess? Wait a minute... she picked up a discarded pie tin and noticed the single washed dish beside the sink. She looked back over to the congealed mess in the glass beside the sofa.

The boy must have eaten half the pie and blended the rest for her. She had told him about her injury then.

She opened his fridge. Nothing in there she could eat. Same with the cupboards. There was a brown banana in the fruit basket. She peeled it, placed it on the plate by the sink and bashed at it with the base of her hand until it resembled babyfood. There were still brown bits in it, but she was past the point of caring. She hoovered up the pulp, her face to the plate, and felt the sustenance moving down into her belly. Her mind was clearing. She clicked on the kettle. Instant coffee? It would have to do.

Coffee in hand, she started flicking through his bookshelf. Mostly manuals and annuals, but there were a few books of local history in there. A half-read copy of Nietzsche. Very ominous. The books she thought might be useful, she threw on the coffee table. Time to start orienting herself.

'Morning.' It was the boy, rubbing sleep from his eyes. 'You're up early. Sleep well?'

'I did, yeah.' She looked down at her pile, realised she'd probably woken him up. 'Aren't you farmers supposed to be early risers?'

'Farmers, maybe. I'm not a farmer though, am I?'

He walked over to her. Looked into her empty mug.

'Another coffee?'

'Sure, thanks.'

She turned back to the shelf. If he was set on staying up then she'd continue the hunt.

'You not want this?' he said, lifting the blended pie glass up at her. She gestured "no". He shook his head.

'Wasteful. Sheer wastefulness. It's a sin, you know.'

He dumped the mess in the bin.

She got to the end of the shelf and then, doing one last scan to check she hadn't missed anything, returned to the sofa to look through her haul. There were two Olde Tyme Avon Murray collections, one history of the Greater Strines area, a couple of Ordinance Survey maps, a history of the region during the Civil War, a collection of short stories about the town, and a pamphlet called *Avon Murray Makes the News* made up of photocopied news clippings.

On closer inspection, it included all the Mel Ditty stories

that mentioned the town by name. God, nothing must happen here, she thought. Making national news was worthy of its own commemorative pamphlet. Jesus, and from the inside cover it looked like he'd paid £4 for it.

'What are you looking at?' he asked, the kettle rising to a boil. 'Judging me by my books? That's a special kind of snobbery that is.'

'Look!' she smiled, 'it's me!'

She held the pamphlet open on a page filled with Bantz Testament coverage. The photos hadn't photocopied into black and white very well, but you could just about make her out.

'Oh, yeah?' he laughed, walking over like she was making a joke. He took the leaflet off her. His eyes focused. He looked puzzled. He took it over to the widow to get a better look. The dawn light flooded into the living room, onto Sammy's face.

'Oh my God,' he looked genuinely taken aback, 'but... this is you!'

'Yeah,' she'd never seen anyone quite this starstruck before. 'Yeah, I told you I was a journalist, didn't I?'

'Well, I guess you did...' he was looking back and forth from the admittedly touched-up picture to the crumpled mess on his couch. 'But I thought you meant like a local paper or something. Bantz Testament are massive! Everyone round here reads it. I thought you'd all be from London?'

'Our Facebook page gets more traffic than all the other news sites put together. So yeah, we are pretty big.'

About time you got the kudos you deserve, Sammy.

'And I am from London. Bantz isn't though. We're in Manc.'

'Manc?'

'Manchester'

'Oh... Manchester.'

He gave up staring at the leaflet and passed it back to her.

'I was supposed to go to uni in Manchester but it didn't sit right with me. I didn't get on with the place. I thought they were all a bunch of wankers. No offence.'

'Students are wankers, yeah.'

*

He realised what he'd said and went to pour the coffees.

'You don't seem like a wanker though. It's just... all that other lot.'

'It's alright. Until you came along, I thought everyone in the countryside was a wanker.'

She reached out and took the mug from him. He made a good instant coffee. Scratch that, nobody made a good instant coffee. He made a passable one.

'I think most people are wankers in general,' he said, reflectively. 'It's just that out in the countryside we're more honest about it.'

He stretched out and yawned, raising his hands above his head – Sammy noticed how high the ceilings were – and then brought them back down, his mug still full in his hand and somehow unspilled.

'So, what brings you out to Avon Murray, then? Is it that Mel Ditty thing? Cos you're a bit late on that one.'

'Sit down.'

She lifted out her phone. Still plenty of battery left. Good. She opened the voice recorder, hit record and set it down on the table between them.

'I'm here because celebrities have been disappearing and nobody's talking about it. In fact, so few people are talking about it that I'm beginning to think there's something funny going on. The only one of these celebrities to have come back is Mel Ditty, and she turned up here. What do you know about that?'

She could see he was a little intimidated. He wanted to ask about the phone but didn't dare.

'What do you mean? I just read about it in the papers. The stuff in the leaflet...'

'Yes, but was there anything said around here? Did the locals know anything? Were there any rumours?'

'The locals? What? No. No, I don't think so. I never heard any.'

She was staring at him intently. She was silent, waiting. 5-4-3-2-1 Sammy, count down. No? He's still not saying anything. Okay, move on...

'What do you know about the gunsmiths around here. The one that's holding a shooting competition?'

'Reginald's? I don't know. I mean, the farmer bought his shotgun from there. Reg isn't the most cheery guy in the world. I wouldn't say I know him at all, really.'

'Does anyone strange use his shop? Do people come from out of town? Dodgy people?'

'Yeah, all the time... Sorry, no, not dodgy people. I meant people from out of town. It's a gunsmiths. Not every town has one – they're pretty rare. It's one of the only reasons people come in to Avon Murray from outside. I don't think he has anything to do with gangs or anything, if that's what you're getting at? Shotguns all have license numbers. If any of his were used in a crime or anything then they'd know who made it straight away. It's not that kind of thing... I mean, we're in the country... everyone's got guns around here.'

'Everyone?'

'Well, no. Not everyone. There's not that many of us. There are a lot though. Lots of guns about. We need them – for work. Look, why are you so concerned with the gun shop? What's it got to do with you? Reginald might be a bit of a sour-faced prick but he never hurt anyone that I know of.'

'Celebrities disappeared from a party I was at...'

She leaned forward. Maybe not a good idea to get this on tape but hell, no one believed her anyway. Might as well get this guy on side.

'It was at that party that this happened to me.'

She pulled apart the doctor's coat, pointed to the bandage around her middle.

'A custom shotgun. Miniature, apparently. Or at least equipped to fire miniature bullets-'

'Shot'

'What?'

'Shotguns fire shot. Or cartridges, though that's not really how you'd say it... you can just say "round". Everything shoots rounds.'

He sipped from his mug.

'Thanks, Tom Clancy.'

Where was she?

'So, celebrities disappear. I get shot by a custom shotgun. Where have disappeared celebrities turned up before? Avon Murray. I Google custom shotguns, where do you think they turn up? That's right, Avon Murray. One of the heavies involved in the shooting; he's only got a former address in Avon Murray.'

'So you think it's all connected?'

'That's what I'm trying to find out.'

She realised she'd been recording the conversation as it if were an interview, but then she had proceeded to do a monologue. She picked her phone up and deleted the sound file.

'Well,' he stood up, drained the last of his coffee and put his mug in the sink. 'I don't think you'll have much luck with Mr Reginald. He's pretty tight-lipped, even with the locals. If you come at him the way you came at me with that phone then he'll probably report you as a terrorist.'

'A terrorist?' she smiled.

He didn't smile. Now it was time for her to feel out of her depth.

'You can't wander around small Northern towns asking questions, Sammy. Firstly, they won't get answered. Second, the word will immediately go around that you're a threat and, eventually, something will happen to you. Not like... murder or anything. There'll just be something. You'll get arrested and not be told the charge, then dumped back in Manchester. Your car will keep getting flat tires. My car, in this case. You might end up having a run in with a farm animal that's got loose.'

'That's mental. You're just trying to scare me.'

He shook his head in a knowing way. He seemed genuine.

'But what are they even trying to protect? What secrets are out here that they don't want people knowing?'

'There's no secrets. Not as you'd understand them, anyway. I mean, most people around here believe in faeries, but then the faeries are strong enough to protect themselves. They don't need our help. No, it's something deeper. It's in the mud. It's the North.'

'But, Manchester's in the North!'

'Is it now?' he was pulling on his farmer coat. It looked a bit ridiculous on a younger man. 'Good luck convincing folk round here of that. To us, Manchester's just London with an accent.'

'Bollocks!'

She was up on her feet. Say what you want about London, but you don't diss Manc.

'Manchester's the fucking future! Manchester is the North! All this out here? This is just a... a desert. It's just a wasteland.'

'We'll agree to disagree.' He screwed on a flatcap. 'You want breakfast?'

'Yeah.' She was angry, but also hungry. Perhaps she was just hungry.

'What do you want? I'm going shops.'

'Granola.' Then she corrected herself. 'I mean, a fine granola. Not the cluster stuff.'

She needed something with a lot of fibre. Something to clear the pipes.

He was shaking his head.

'...and what exactly is granola?'

'What? It's like, grains and cereal and stuff. It has nuts in sometimes, and raisins. Look, it's in every shop. I'm telling you.'

'Well, alright. I'll ask...' he sounded sceptical. 'I don't think they'll have it though.'

'They will. Trust me.'

And he left, clattering the door shut behind him. Maybe it was just an old door, she thought. Or maybe she'd offended him. Ah, damn it. He started it. Bloody yokels. She picked up a booklet from the top of the pile and flicked through the pages. Country stuff. Nostalgia and nostalgia. She couldn't bare to look at it. She threw the book back down. She wasn't in the mood. She went to make herself another instant coffee and started searching for hotels on her phone.

First problem: the internet moved like treacle. She could watch the loading bar moving, slowly. She hadn't seen that bar for years! Oh, and second problem: Avon Murray didn't seem to register in the front page rankings. Try 'Avon Murray'; with quote marks. Okay, better. But no hotels. No B&Bs. Should she try Air B&B? Couchsurfer? No, she couldn't wait for external websites to load if it took this bloody long just to navigate Google.

Sammy returned to the books. She flicked through, scanning the pages for relevant details. It was soothing to receive information at scanning speed again. The slow internet had distressed her. The coffee was working as well. She was coming back to life. She found that Avon Murray was an Anglo-Saxon village which had been expanded during the industrial revolution – thus the chimneys – and it had then shrunk again as Manchester and Liverpool outstripped it technologically. All the local milliners sold up. She saw photos of the station she'd arrived at. In 1889 it had a loading bay on one side with a whole collection of heavy machinery to lift goods from the cars. Over the wrought iron footbridge – scrapped in the war – there was a cafe, signal house and public lavatories. They were doing an offer on Eccles cakes, it looked like... and there was a sign; "Avon Murray". It could have been the same one she found in the bush coated in slime. This place was once important, she realised. Nobody could watch those long trains pull in and out and think otherwise.

The one she'd come in on was just a bad bus on diesel-powered wheels. Wasn't quite the same, somehow.

She wondered what it did to these people, to live here and to know all of this. To know that there wasn't anything ancient here. Even that forest had been grown in the last forty years. It wasn't an ancient landscape, like some countryside down South was. It was just a mill town without any more mills, that wouldn't even classify as a town anymore. It looked like the countryside but... everything here was man-made, she realised, and it was all relatively new. Nobody living had chosen to be here. They just were here.

Depressing.

Soon the boy was back with breakfast. She needed it, she was starved. She sat herself at the small breakfast table in anticipation. He pulled off his flatcap and coat, looking almost his own age again, before dropping the bag of shopping onto the table in front of her. He lifted out a bag.

'That's porridge,' she said.

'I told you they wouldn't have granola,' he said. 'This is the closest they had. I asked the guy and everything. No granola. No cause to stock it when no one's ever asked for it before. Anyway, this is better for your... stomach thing. Or, gunshot wound, I guess I should call it.'

'I'd rather you didn't.'

She had been looking forward to the granola.

'I guess porridge will do. Are you having some too?'

'Hell no,' he laughed. 'I'm having bacon and eggs. I'll make you the porridge though. Don't get up – I said, don't get up! It's fine, Jesus. I'll make it. You just sit there and play with your phone or whatever.'

He started clanging about. Saucepans, a frying pan, cups and saucers, a bowl. In spite of the racket he was moving quickly and efficiently. She sighed. She liked that he was neat. He turned on Radio 4. It was the Archers. Bloody hell.

'Hey,' she shouted through the din, 'there aren't any hotels in Avon Murray, are there?'

'You work that out on your phone?' He sliced open a pack of

bacon. 'I could have told you that. In fact, I think I did tell you that.'

'Yeah, well. It's confirmed now.' She checked her phone again. 'You were right.'

'I like being right.'

'Look, can I...'

'Can you what?'

'You know what I'm asking.'

'Yeah, but I want to hear you say it.'

He cracked two eggs into the frying pan and started stirring the porridge with his other hand. He was a good cook.

'Can I stay here? Just until the story's done?'

He was humming the Archers' theme tune to himself, pouring two glasses of orange juice. She was beginning to resent his grin.

'Please. Is that what you're waiting for? Pretty please can I crash on your couch for a couple of days?'

'That's all I wanted to hear!'

He swung around with two breakfasts. He set hers down in front of her and sat down opposite.

'Courtesy will get you places that poking a phone at people won't. Especially out here in the country, Miss Habib.'

He pointed at her with a fork.

'It's an important lesson to learn.'

'Thanks, I guess...'

She realised how starving she was. She dug in. They ate in silence. She tried not to concentrate on the smell of eggs and bacon as he stuffed it all into his face, barely chewing. The porridge was pretty good, she supposed, but watching him eat was ruining the experience. It was still only early, she realised. All that crap about him not being a farmer... he was definitely a farmer.

Then, as suddenly as his food had appeared, it was gone. She'd only eaten about a third of her breakfast. He was already cleaning off his plate in the sink. He was throwing on his coat and flatcap. What was he doing?

'I'm off to work. You going to rest up here today? You'll need a bloody wash at least, before you walk into town again. Rest up though. You're injured.'

He walked over to the bookshelf, lifted down a ceramic hedgehog and pulled off its head. He lifted something out, put the hedgehog back on the shelf and walked over to her. Next to her orange juice he put a joint.

'This will help you chill out, you psycho.'

'Cheers,' she mouthed through porridge. She wouldn't have thought they had weed out here. Makes sense though. Something to get through the days.

He dipped his cap and was about to slam out of the door again. She swallowed her porridge and shouted,

'Oh, just one more question!'

He leaned his head back in, expectant.

'What's your name again?'

'Jesus, Sammy. It's John! John Barton!'

He slammed the door and jumped into his jeep. She could hear it roar away down the drive. She turned her phone recorder off. Hit playback; "It's John! John Barton!". That would do. She'd remember now. She saved the file as "Boy's Name" and turned back to her porridge.

7

John pulled the jeep up beside the shearing pen. They'd situated it on the furthest end of the farm, away from the housing complex, in the hope it'd keep the shearers from wandering off for a cup of tea. Whatever time this saved was more than made up for by the long drive out there, not to mention the exposure. The wind and rain mucked about with the bearings something rotten. Swinging the jeep's rear door open, John pulled out his toolkit, overalls, gloves, a power drill and, most importantly, his specially designed Mueller-Kueps wrench extender. It was his pride and joy.

Today's job was the gate. Intended to let one sheep through at a time, the recent heat wave had expanded the metal so much that no sheep bigger than a Yorkshire terrier could fit through. It was John's task to expand it back to a serviceable size again. Dilate it, as the shearers were fond of saying.

It was a delicate job. He needed to find the wobbliest bit first and address that before working his way around every last nut and bolt. Finally, once it was all in place, he'd get out the Mueller-Kueps and tighten the ever-living-shit out of the thing. That'd save him coming back there any time soon. He lay his tools on the ground. Donned his gloves and overalls. Set to work.

It was a greyish day out in the fields of Avon Murray. No sign of rain but certainly no sun promised either. It was a close, monochrome sky that seemed to suck the life of out everything. These were the days that could pass without you noticing them. Days that didn't touch the sides on their way through. John tried to concentrate on his work, but he kept thinking back to the journalist. "Sammy Habib", he thought, trying the name out in his head. Roving reporter for the Bantz Testament. He thought about her being shot. Thought about her walking around in a muddy doctor's coat. She must get into some scrapes in that line of work. He'd always thought journalism boring but then, it was Julia's job.

Julia was the girl, sorry, woman that he'd dated for those fleeting few months in Manchester. She was tall and slim. Very tall in fact. He'd never seen a woman like her, or heard one that spoke the way she did. Feminism this, capitalism that. He could never work out whether she was for or against these things, but he was interested. He really was. All the times he'd changed the subject came back to him. The times at the end where he'd told her to shut her face. But those weren't the good times. He remembered being proud, having her on his arm. He remembered cooking her vegan ravioli and they drank wine out of proper glasses, and he felt like a millionaire, even in those grotty student halls.

She had a long nose. He called her Julia Caesar.

She'd said he only liked her because he didn't know his mother. That she was a mother substitute. Some Freudean thing. Then one day he didn't deny it and said "So what?". She said they needed counselling.

The problem with all that psychobabble stuff was that John had had a pretty great life so far, or at least he thought so. Sure, he was raised only by his dad, but his dad was great! They still went to the pub together every Friday. He came round for lunch on Sundays. He'd played every sport, some of them to a high standard. The high school coach said he should go pro. He was no slouch in lessons either. He got a B-average across his GCSEs, A*s in A level. Missed out on the Oxbridge train – the Hogwarts Express, as his dad called it – but he was still one of the smartest in his class. Plenty of friends too. Long college days skimming stones and smoking sput. What was his girlfriend's name again? He couldn't remember, but he was definitely in love with her. That was before Julia, obviously. But no, he'd never had any more than his fair share of hard times. He didn't hate society. He just, for whatever reason, hated Manchester, and London thrice that.

As John rattled the gate, trying to wrench it back to the correct size, two figures approached. One was tall and lank. He slipped over in one cowpat, then another, losing his hat each time. The one beside him was short and squat. He swore under his breath each time the lanky one lost his footing. It was Khaki and Morland, errand boys for the farmer. They stumbled up the field towards John Barton, their smell arriving before them.

'Jesus, boys! You two been sleeping in the pig sty again?'

'John Barton,' the shorter one grumbled. 'You keep thy lip to thyself.'

'Yeah!' the taller one added. The short one swiped at the back of his head. Ducking the blow, his cowpat-muddied flatcap fell to the ground again. The short one, Khaki, continued,

'The farmer's wanting to see you, our John. Something about you bringing strange women back to the cottage wi'yer. Now, Morland and I were thinking, these wouldn't happen to be your friends from university now, would it?' He had a fat grin on his chops.

'Trust me, Kharky. Any time you two get to thinking, rest assured that the opposite of what you reckon is almost always going to be the case.'

John tightened a bolt on one side of the gate, watching a bolt on the other side loosen as he did it. He scratched his head and tried it the other way.

'As you may have noticed, boys, I'm rather busy at the moment. If the farmer wants to see me then I suggest he either wait until I'm finished, come down here himself, or else not set me such tasks in the first place. I'm not averse to doing them, but it's a twenty minute drive coming out here. If I drive back up to the house now and talk to him, say, quarter of an hour, then what? By the time I'm back down here it'd be time for me to pack up.'

He then grabbed both bolts, one in each hand, and tightened them simultaneously. Success! He slapped his oil-slick gloves together and stood up.

'So, in other words, I'm not currently at liberty to see him. Please do send my apologies.'

'Ah well, that's where yer wrong, y'see.' The short man's eyes were glowing and he had a nasty sneering grin on his face. It was a face that revelled in seeing other people get in trouble.

'Y'see the farmer, he's considering this a matter of – what's that phrase again – oh yes, "national security", or so he says. He's taking it very seriously indeed, young John Barton. And, on account o'that, he's specifically stated that we should tell thee that he is not asking, he is very much telling.'

'Yeah!' Morland added, ducking, and then reaching down to pick his hat from the mud. Khaki looked at him, shaking his head. He hadn't even swiped at the taller man that time.

'So,' John questioned, tightening a last bolt before leaving the job half-done, 'the two of you have come all the way down here to drag me back to the farmer, with or without my say so?'

'That is accurate, yes.'

'And I haven't a choice in the matter.'

'Afraid not, young John Barton. The farmer was very specific in his orders. We were to bring you back to the farmhouse whether you liked it or not.'

'Excellent,' John said, fixing his work in gaffer tape in the hope it would hold until tomorrow, 'and I'm guessing you two will be wanting a lift back up to the farmhouse in the jeep, yes?'

'Oh yeah, ta. That'd be great!'

'Shurrup Morland!' and this time the swipe connected, knocking off the taller man's hat. 'Though he is right, young John. We would be most amenable to a lift, if it wouldn't be too much hassle. We'd be very much obliged.'

'No skin off my nose,' John answered, throwing his tools in the back of the jeep. He opened a passenger door, indicating they enter, then climbed in himself. As they set off he straightened the mirror so as to keep Morland in his rear view.

'Listen, you two. Promise me that if you ever go into organised crime that you'll buy your own car first, yeah? You'll never make decent mobsters by trudging about in wellies everywhere.'

The rest of the journey was silent. Morland bashed his head on the roof every time they hit a bump. They hit quite a few on their way back to the farmhouse.

They reached the farmhouse in exactly twenty minutes. It rose from behind the dry stone walls like a postcard or a wartime drama. If you'd grown up here, however, it was just a building. More than that, it was an ugly one. A building of large size, ostentatious perhaps, or at least showy. John found it obnoxious. He pulled the jeep to a stop outside the front door and hopped out. The other two were slower to get out, lowering themselves down from the jeep's high seats. John waited for them to dust themselves off and straighten up their coats and flatcaps. He locked the jeep and walked to the farmhouse door. As he pressed the doorbell he noticed they'd sidled up behind him like jailers.

'So you two are going to pretend you've manhandled me all the way here?'

'It's our jobs, young John Barton,' Khaki mumbled. 'No hard feelings, eh?'

The door opened to reveal the farmer's wife. It was mid-afternoon and she already had a red wine in her hand, her long nails scratching on the glass. She was wearing leopard print. Skin tight leggings and a suit jacket. Nobody had ever been able to work out whether she was a rich girl slumming it or a council estate girl come good. She stared at the ragged threesome, perplexed.

'Shouldn't you be at the tradesman's entrance?'

'Awfully sorry, ma'am. Normally, yes.'

The two automatically doffed their caps. John left his on.

'But we were tasked with bringing young John Barton to see... His Grace.'

'His Grace?'

She raised a pencilled eyebrow.

'The err... the farmer, Ma'am.'

He scrunched his cap in his hand. Morland, following suit, did the same, grinding mud and worse into his palms.

'Well, in that case you best come in, young John Barton,' she smiled. She stepped to one side, leaving just enough room for him to enter, 'come on in.'

John doffed his cap and slid in past her body. Morland then stepped forward.

'Sorry, but you two will have to wait outside. Or, better yet, go and find some other job to do. You've brought him here, after all. Job done. Toddle on now. Ta-ra.'

The door closed firmly in their faces.

'Well, Morland. That's another job well done. This calls for a couple of scrumpies, eh?'

The two rattled on down the drive, out of the gate and away in the direction of the nearest offy.

Up in the house, John was shown into the farmer's office. He sat down in a leather-bound chair, across the table from the farmer's slightly higher leather-bound chair.

'Anything I can get for you boys?'

'No my dear, I think we'll do very well as it is.'

'John Barton?'

She squeezed his shoulder.

'No, I'm quite alright. Thank you very much for the offer though.'

'Get out of here, woman!' the farmer snapped. 'We're talking men's matters in here!'

She slipped out, closing the door behind her. They sat in silence, listening to her heels clicking along the hall and down the stairs. John hated the farmer's office. It was such a cliché. Golf trophies. A picture from his first marriage that he'd never taken off the wall. A globe with a liquor cabinet in it. A wall of books. The only ones he'd read were the almanacs and account books. There was a stack of Top Gear magazines around here, John just knew it, but wherever they were, the old man did a good job of hiding them. There was even a fire in the fireplace. The farmer was sweating from the heat of it.

'Now, John Barton,' the farmer began, his moustache unmoving on his stiff upper lip. 'I've been hearing rumours about you.'

John nodded his head. Registering the comment but not responding.

'What I've heard, young man, is that you've been consorting with the wrong sort.'

He lifted a well-chewed cigar to his lips. Of course, John thought, of course he'd do that. Where was he hiding it before though?

'I've heard that you picked up a very intoxicated young Muslim woman at the local public house last night and have proceeded to stow her away in one of my cottages. Now, look, I can see you getting your hackles up already over this. I'm not judging you. I've played around a lot in my day, don't you worry. I was young too once, oh yes! I'm not having a go at you for that. Not at all. No, it's just that I'm worried about you lad, and I've got to keep an eye on everything that goes on out here. It's my jurisdiction you see. My responsibility if something were to happen.'

'What do you mean if something were to happen?'

'I mean... look, I can see yer making a face, but we've got to be careful here. I know how it goes, trust me. They come on all smiling and nice but, pretty soon my lad -and you mark my words on this one- pretty soon she'll be talking to you about converting. Next thing you know we'll have you walking around here in a headscarf. They ruin men, do these... types. They take advantage.'

I'm going to put this one down to projection, John thought.

'Look, I'm very grateful for your concern, but you don't have to worry. She's not like that. It's not like that... the situation I mean.'

'Oh Johnny, you poor naive lad. They're all like that. There's no helping it. You can't change the world with good intentions.'

He relit his cigar where the flame was meeting the saliva.

'Wait... who are all like that? What are you talking about?'

'The Muslims, lad. They're just different to us, that's all. There's no harm in it. I'm a very liberal man, myself. Live and let live, that's my motto. But a pig can't change its spots.'

'A pig? Look. Sir. I agree with what you're saying and everything... it's just, she's not a Muslim. At least I don't think so. She's a famous journalist–'

'Journalist?!' he spat the cigar out. 'Why, that's worse! We can't have her snooping around the farm. Putting it all out on, on... Al Jazeera!'

'She doesn't work for Al Jazeera! She works for Bantz Testament!'

'So it's a religious newspaper?!' he took out a napkin and wiped the sweat from his face, 'My dear John Barton, this gets worse and worse. You can't be having a religious nutter walking about here, living here. I know your dad's a Quaker like, and no harm to the man, I'm all for religious toleration, but my dear John Barton, this is some't else. You've got to see that?'

'There's nowt to see! She was new in town and lost and... and I offered her a place to crash. We're not going out. We're not getting married. Jesus Christ, I only met her yesterday. How fast does gossip travel around here? I only offered her a place to sleep'

'Jesus Christ is right, Johnny. You should be asking for guidance from above. I'd consider your actions. You must have a screw loose bringing a stranger back to sleep in your bed–'

'She slept on my couch!' He took his cap off and scratched at his head in frustration. 'And, look, she will be sleeping on my couch for a while, alright? We looked for a hotel and there aren't any. Not in the whole of Avon Murray.'

'Then she should consider moving along elsewhere, shouldn't she? It's not our job to take in every waif and stray. Good Lord, John Barton, you'll have us packed to the rafters with every no-hoper with a sob story this side of the bloody Pennines if we had things your way! Well no, I say no! I'm not having valuable space taken up by scroungers and religious maniacs, and I don't care what you say. If I see her, John Barton, she's out!'

He relit the cigar. Composed himself. Wriggled a little in his seat and opened his arms in an expansive manner.

'Look John, I'm just thinking of the farm. You know that's my business, right? To think of the farm? Well, if we put her up then where are the Poles to stay come harvest time, eh? Have you thought of that?'

'She won't be here at harvest time-'

'That's the spirit, Johnny. I'm glad you understand. Tell her we're sorry, but there's just no room.' He smiled, his top row of teeth showing through his moustache, 'and may she go in peace.'

'I'll...'

John stuttered, and scratched under his cap again. Figuring it was fruitless, he changed tack.

'I'll pass that on to her, sir.'

He stood up, bent a little from the waist. The farmer nodded and turned his chair to the fire, his face glowing red and shiny in the light. At the door, John turned back to him with a last request.

'Oh, and sir... I noticed while I was up fixing the shearing gate that there's a bunch of holes dug near the sheep-feeding stacks. I figure that the rats might be making a comeback.'

'Really?' He swallowed. 'But we just got rid of them six months ago.'

'Aye. Well, looks like they might be back. Maybe. If you want I could take the shotgun out to the top field and wait for them at dusk? You know, try and take care of it ourselves before wasting any money on pest control.'

'That would make sense.'

The farmer lowered himself back into his chair, pondering.

'So, do you think I could get the latest combination to the gunsafe then? I mean, I could go out tonight if you're really interested in getting on top of this?'

The farmer fidgeted with his moustache. He leaned forward and stared into the fire. After a moment's contemplation he turned to the young man.

'Look, John Barton. I think it's best we take care of one problem at a time, don't you?'

'What do you mean?'

'I mean that... and I'm sorry to have to say this Johnny, but what I mean is that until your present house guest has vacated the premises, I think it best if the shotgun remain under the supervision of myself and myself alone. Do you understand?'

'I suppose I do.'

'I'm just thinking about the farm, John Barton, and I suggest you do the same. You're a good lad, but sometimes you let your heart get in the way when you should be thinking of yer responsibilities. They might not teach you that at University, young John, but that's what being a man's all about.'

'I understand, sir. Thanks for the advice.'

He closed the door behind him. He needed to get his hands on that shotgun. He didn't know why but he knew he had to teach Sammy how to use it. He'd had it in his head since last night. It was something they could do together. Something he could offer her which she couldn't get in the city. He thought about moving close behind her, adjusting her aim, feeling her hair on his cheek. He thought of ruder things, private things. He was letting his fantasies lead him.

He passed the farmer's wife on his way out.

'Have you been a naughty boy, John Barton?' she raised her wine glass and winked. 'I hear you've been playing with the wrong type of girl? Well, if you ever want to come round here and play with me, John Barton, then I'm sure I could... fit you in somewhere!'

She broke down in hysterics as John closed the door.

Back in the cottage he found Sammy asleep on the couch. Around her was a pile of maps and books and old newspapers. He lifted one up. Property of Avon Murray Public Library. So, she couldn't help herself, eh? Somehow she'd gone all the way down to the library, on the other end of town, and brought half of its bloody contents back with her. She'd washed though, and he noticed she was wearing his clothes. They were far too big for her, but she'd arranged them in such a way that they almost looked intentional. On the floor, beside the unfolded map she was now using for a sheet, was a book; Learning Shotgun Discipline, for Kids. There was something in your fantasy then, John.

He got out the pork pie he'd bought for dinner, sliced it in two. He'd mash some potatoes with it, perhaps a little gravy. The blender was cleaned and ready to prepare Sammy's portion in. He'd wake her up when it was ready.

8

The next morning John came down to find the mess had changed. Sammy must have got up in the night to do more reading, and was out cold again. He mixed her a cereal smoothy and left it on the table as he went to work.

The gate to the shearing pen took the whole day. The tape had done nothing. The metal had sprung back in the night. What should have been a dilatable entry became abstract art. Still, there was nothing that couldn't be put right and, with the sun setting, the gate was finally held firm with a twist of the Mueller-Kueps. Calloused and oil-slick, John Barton headed home.

*

When he got to the door his heart stopped. There, on the white wood, a hand-print in blood. A solitary drip ran down from it, still wet. John swallowed and turned the handle. The door was unlocked.

He hadn't believed the farmer when he'd made his threats. He didn't think his two buffoonish helpers were capable of... Or, he shivered, maybe the person who'd shot Sammy had come back for her? Maybe, he was still here now?

In the hall he noticed drops of blood. They left a trail leading to the stairs. No-one on the sofa. No-one in the kitchen. He saw Sammy's coat, slung from the banister. He touched it. The inside was wet and glistening. He pulled his hand away and found it dripping red. He heard a noise upstairs. A... a... splash?

'Fuckin, Bitch!' it was Sammy's voice, muffled behind a door.

As John mounted the stairs he could hear the splashing clearly now, echoing from the bathroom.

'Sammy?'

'Oh shit!' The splashing stopped. 'Sorry, erm…'

He heard her fiddling with something. From a small, tinny speaker he heard his own voice coming back to him – 'It's John! John Barton!' – before more expletives and the sound of a phone skittering across lino. She shouted out to him.

'I'm really sorry, John. I'll sort it. I didn't think you'd be back so early.'

'Are you decent?' He was at the bathroom door now.

'Erm… yeah?'

She seemed uncertain. He could only imagine the mess she'd got herself in. As she moved he could hear everything from running water to plops and splashes, and the rustling of a mass of paper.

'You don't seem very certain. Are you sure you're decent?'

'Yep. Always decent, me.'

'Well I'm coming in.'

He pushed the door open and immediately shielded his eyes.

'Bloody hell, Sammy!'

'What? It's a bra. Do they not have those out here?'

Sammy was spread-eagled on the floor wearing only bloodstained jeans and a bra. Her – correction: his – bloody shirt was scrunched up in the washbasket, dripping on the rest of his clothes. She was fighting a losing battle with the blood seeping out of her shotgun wound. She had taken off the bandage and, finding John wasn't the type to keep bandages in the bathroom, she had attempted to patch herself up with a mosaic of sticking plasters. Needless to say, it wasn't working.

'What in God's name has gone on in here?'

'Yeah, as I said, I'm sorry.' She brushed her hair back to reveal a face red with warpaint. 'I needed to change the bandage, like'

John looked at the bath full of pink water. 'And what's that for?'

'I'm dripping.'

'I can see you're dripping!' He laughed. He'd never seen so much blood.

'Look here, Sammy. One job at a time. I know you're bleeding and that's distressing and all, but you've got to take this one slowly. Be patient.'

'I'm always fucking patient.' Sammy snapped. 'That's the nickname they gave me in hospital. Everyone called me that there!'

'Right- well, you need to strip off-'

'Oh yeah?'

'-get that bath drained. Have yourself a shower instead, right? Then I'll go get my patching up kit from the stables.'

'You keep your first aid kit in the stables?'

She pushed away John's hand as he tried to help her. Instead, she pulled herself up by grabbing at the toilet seat.

'That's stupid. First aid kits are supposed to be visible. That's why they put massive red crosses on them. X marks the spot! You should put it up here.'

She pointed at the medicine cabinet. It had bloody fingermarks all over it.

'It's for sheep,' John muttered, closing the door behind him.

'You what?'

*

Ten minutes later, Sammy stepped out of the bathroom. She was wrapped in a towel. John Barton waited for her in the corridor. He'd put bin bags on the floor and he had a neon yellow bandage in his hands.

'So, you're still dripping then?'

He nodded towards the patch of crimson darkening at her middle.

She had a towel around her midriff. It hung an inch below the oozing wound. Sighing, John lowered it slightly, sensing her indignance, and slapped on the bandage before she could say anything.

It was freezing, he knew. That was part of it. Something to do with the chemicals. She sucked in air. Wiggled her fingers. Before she knew what was happening he'd stripped off the plaster coatings and slapped one yellow arm around her left side, another around the right. She was embraced by a sticky yellow hug. She smelled of chemicals, but the bleeding had stopped.

'It's doubled up on the back,' John commented, pulling at it, checking for potential seepage and finding none. 'That might make it a bit lumpy under your... blouse, but it can't be helped.' He stood up and looked her in the eye. 'You're not so big as a sheep.'

She was pretty without make-up. That's why she hardly wore it. Benefits of the dark complexion. It's all in the genes.

'I'll take that as a compliment,' she chuckled.

After a moment of gazing into each other's eyes, she noticed his vision turning to the trashed bathroom and the mountain of wrecked clothes.

'Sorry about all your blouses, John. My head's not on right today.'

'Where are you clothes Sammy? Are you naked under that towel?'

'Piss off, perv!'

She strode on down the corridor. She knew where his wardrobe was now. She'd find herself a new blouse in there. As she slammed the bedroom door she could hear the farm boy mooning about in the corridor outside. He yelled through at her.

'So, how did you end up bleeding this time?'

'What do you mean?' She pulled on a t-shirt and tucked it into her newly-donned boxers. 'I was in all day.'

'Yeah, I bet! Look, I saw the handprint on the door outside. You've left a trail of blood all down my hardwood floor. I know you've been out. Something's happened. You've been on your travels again.'

'Oh, pardon me! Didn't realise I was crashing at 221B Baker Street.

She took a moment to prod at the bandage in the mirror. It made her look like a guide dog.

'Where have you been?' He was staring at her now. Being persistent.

'If you must know,' she pulled on a hoody, 'I was at the gunsmiths.'

'Fucksake. Reginald's? What did I say about–'

'I know what you said, but if I listened to what everybody said then I'd be back at home doing exactly what mummy and daddy tell me to. I'd probably be a doctor or a lawyer or something. And married, pshhh.'

'So, how did it go? I'm guessing from my bathroom looking like something out of Hellraiser that the answer's "not well?"'

She swallowed, sighed. Annoying boy. How did they have know-it-alls, even out here in the middle of nowhere?

'They said I was too short to shoot…'

She could hear him laughing. Bastard.

'You might laugh, but the way he looked at me. It's just straight-up racism. I can tell.'

'Not everyone out in the countryside is racist, Sammy. Some hate all outsiders an equal amount, regardless of creed or colour.'

She opened the door. Somehow she'd taken his clothes and managed to assemble them into the outfit of a gangster. Oversized hoody. Jeans hanging down. That scowl, my God, that scowl!

'–but in Reginald's case,' John finished, 'I grant you it's probably racism.'

They went downstairs where John Barton baked up a spinach pie. He forgot to properly drain the spinach so it ended up runny enough for Sammy to drink unblended. She was reading up on Avon Murray again in between checking her phone. The news was on the TV in the background. John couldn't understand her. It was either everything all at once, or passed out. Those were her two states of being.

'Look, Sammy, I can tell you're busy,' he sighed, pushing away his plate. There was a garden of spinach leaves caught in his teeth but Sammy was too absorbed to notice. She replied with an '*mm*'.

'Well, Sammy, I've been thinking. It occurs to me that it's my day off tomorrow. Seeing as how leaving you alone seems to inevitably result in a bloodbath, I was thinking that it's probably for the best if you spent tomorrow hanging out with me. What do you think?'

'Mm,' she replied, not listening. She finished the article on her phone and frowned. Not so useful as she'd thought. His question finally registered and she looked up, 'could you get me in to the gunsmiths?'

'No, Sammy, not like that...'

She went back to her phone.

He frowned. 'I thought maybe we could go horse riding or something?'

'Mm,' she replied.

John was perplexed. He'd never known a woman turn down horse riding before. Even she-who-must-not-be-named, the one from uni, she was as keen as the rest. More keen, in fact. But now here was a woman so caught up in her business that-

'Maybe,' she said.

'Maybe?'

'Maybe.'

'That's all I needed to hear.'

He collected their plates, took them over to give them a quick blast under the tap. He mounted the stairs and gave her a salute.

'Enjoy the news, Sammy Habib, you famous journalist. I'll see you bright and early for a day of riding!'

He could still hear the TV blaring as he shut his bedroom door.

*

The next morning John Barton woke up to find Sammy in his bedroom wearing a riding helmet. She chucked a plate of toast in his lap as he sat up and plonked a tea down on his bedside table.

'Wake up, lazy arse! We're riding'

He bit into the blackened bread. He'd slept terribly. Probably the noise from downstairs, or the nightmares about blood. Still, the horse riding idea had worked. Women, he thought. Doesn't matter who they are – they love those horses…

'…and I know exactly where we're going!'

'What? Where?'

'Here!' She lifted up her phone. John focused his eyes and on the screen he saw a page from the Bantz Testament. It was about the celebrities, the missing ones.

'Jesus, Sammy. Can't you go one day without-'

'One day without what?'

'Never mind.'

'It'll be nice. We'll have a picnic. I have the coordinates locked in to my maps app and I've found a way to boost the signal when we inevitably end up in some tree bullshit. I've turned my phone into a satnav, basically. It says that Mel Ditty was found at this point, in a field by a river. So there you go, that sounds restful, eh? And that she was noticeably drugged, incoherent, and refused to clarify where she'd been or who she'd been with. The police treated it as misadventure but we'll be treating it as a kidnap. They weren't even looking, you see. So there might have been clues everywhere. Might still be. Eat your toast. I'll boil us some eggs.'

*

The horse ride, as it turned out, was a travesty. Sammy was alright on the back of a moped but six feet up on the back of an animal? No thanks. If she lay down with her arms wrapped around its neck she felt a bit more secure but John, for some reason, wanted her sitting upright. She insisted on her way. As the horse started to move, however, it soon became clear that her 'being as close to the ground as possible' method was going to lead to her falling off. An image flashed into her mind of being dragged under the horse's hooves. Jesus, she hadn't even considered the hooves until that point. She just thought of it as huge and terrifying. Now she realised it had offensive capabilities too. Who invented these fucking beasts?

After an hour of messing about she finally got it moving. It sort of ambled. It jigged her up and down in a vaguely circular motion. What was it she used to say about the horse girls in her old school? Sex-substitute. If they weren't actively having sex with their horses, they were definitely using them as some creepy sex-substitute.

Well God help anyone who thought this was like sex. It was closer to being in a mosh-pit. She asked John Barton if he'd ever been in a mosh-pit. Unsuprisingly, he hadn't.

The farm boy's good-guy act hadn't served to impress her. He was nice, she supposed. He didn't reek of dung like some people around the town did. But someone who was content to fix – what was it? A cowgate? – being content fixing things just for them to break again. Jesus! He must have something wrong with his brain, surely?

A couple of hours of riding and she felt like her arse had been used as a speedbag. Finally, finally, her phone announced 'you have reached your destination.'

John dismounted without effort then walked over to her. Was he annoyed at her? She had probably spent the whole ride swearing at the horse, but it was pure reflex. Unwrapping her foot from the stirrup, she fell sideways, out of the saddle and into John's arms. He laughed as he lowered her to the ground. She wasn't amused.

'You're loving this, aren't you?'

'Maybe a little, aye'

'Oh aye?'

'Aye.'

He led the horses over to the river to drink.

She stood and measured out the field. It was the same one as the photo. She was standing roughly where Mel Ditty was stood in the photo. Too bad it wasn't a real photo. They'd photoshopped her in afterwards.

It was this field though. The police report Sammy had dug up wasn't specific as to where in the field, but it was this field. No doubt. In her mind, she broke it up into a kind of grid pattern and set about pacing it. It was time to focus. Time to be meticulous. Time to earn her money.

'You not having a sandwich? I've made it into a smoothie for you.'

'After, John. After!'

John Barton yawned and stretched. She wondered why he didn't offer to help. That's the sort of thing he'd normally do. He'd only get in the way anyway, she told herself. Useless bugger. He seemed content to kick about near the river, skimming the occasional stone, while she went about her work. After a few minutes, she noticed him sit down. Not that she was paying attention to him.

The field was shaded on all four sides by trees. It was set in a natural dip between two slopes. It was open to the sky but there was no looking down into it from any of the surrounding land. A good place, Sammy reckoned, to dump someone. The only routes in were a couple of stiles for walkers, the bridleway they'd rode in on and a gate, locked.

The lock was rusted. She got crud all over her fingers even picking it up to inspect. Seemed like the mechanism on the padlock had wasted away as well. Long story short, no one was driving in here. There was no point looking for tire tracks. She looked anyway. Didn't find any. No, whoever came in here with Mel Ditty must have either walked in or dropped in by helicopter.

Both approaches were weird and made no sense. They also undermined the whole point of using this perfect dropping-off site. Why find a good field to release someone in if you're going to have to risk meeting someone on the way to it? You'd only do it if you were confident of having the whole town on side.

So either the whole town was in on the conspiracy, or Mel Ditty had simply appeared, miraculously, out of thin air.

Sammy searched the rest of the field. It took two hours. She found nothing. Not a single thing. She didn't know what she was looking for but, whatever it was, she didn't find it. She gave up and limped back to John. He was napping by the river.

'You finally done?'

Okay, maybe not napping. Resting with his eyes closed.

'Yeah.'

'I've already eaten my half of the picnic. Your half is there.'

He waved his hand idly at a basket.

'There's sandwiches and eggs and cress and tomatos and even a chicken drumstick. A hand-blender too. You should be alright. Are you limping?'

'I might have overdone it.'

'Not bleeding are you?'

He didn't bother to open his eyes and see for himself.

'No.'

'Did you find anything?'

'No.'

'Wonderful.'

He sat up and yawned. He was a bit annoyed, she could tell, but he was doing well at hiding it. He was giving her the quiet treatment. She was familiar with that one; the silent sizzler!

She wasn't going to apologise for doing her job, or what was left of her job anyway...

'I've been enjoying the sounds of the river. The horses. The trees. You know, nature stuff that you don't care about.'

He was being pathetic now. Then, all of a sudden, he pepped up.

'Oh, speaking of trees. Check these out!'

She leaned over to where he was pointing. On the other side of where he lay there were a patch of tiny, miniature trees. They were growing from a patch of equally minuscule pebbles, like a tiny replica of a Chinese garden.

'They're cool, aren't they?' He was smiling now. More genuine, less pissy.

'What are they?' she asked.

'I think they're little bonsai trees. They're not usually out in the wild like this. I mean, they aren't natural things. They take years of cultivation. But, being here, it might be that someone put them out in the wild. You know, to see what would happen? That's all I can think of. Or maybe someone threw them out and they've managed to survive all on their own? Very cool anyway. Extremely cool.'

'That is cool,' she admitted, 'they are very cool.'

'Have you ever had a bonsai tree?' he asked her.

'Me? No,' she shook her head, 'can you imagine? It wouldn't last the week.'

'I used to keep them,' he brushed one very lightly with his hand. 'I had them in our flat in town…'

'I thought you hated town.' She was speaking softly now. She wasn't sure why. 'Manchester's just London with an accent, you said.'

'Well I lived there for a bit with a girl. A woman, sorry. She was a bit older than me, like, and talked about the stuff you do. You remind me of her, actually.'

He'd been talking to the plants, but now he turned to look her in the eye.

'You're prettier than she was though. And tougher too. I don't think she'd be wandering the countryside with her guts hanging out. No, you're special, Sammy. You're something else.'

She was close to him now. He was gazing into her eyes. She smiled, 'Am I your type, John Barton?'

'No. I mean, yes? I suppose.'

'Shut up, mate. You're waffling.'

She rolled onto her back and started to blend up a sandwich with a hardboiled egg. The sound of the machine and the smell of egg broke the tension. Thank god.

'You're mad, John Barton, if you think you can get a kiss just for a ride on your wobbly horse.'

'They're not my horses. They're the farmers. And I didn't want to kiss you either. That's you imagining, that is. Wishful thinking, like.'

'Oh aye?'

'Aye.'

She stopped the blender for a moment. The field was silent.

'Well, if you don't want to kiss me and there's bugger all in this field, then today's been a total wash out, hasn't it?'

'All you care about is work.'

He lifted the remaining corner of an unblended sandwich and bit into it. The torn remnants of lettuce hung from his mouth.

'That's where you're wrong. You might think that work is work, John, living out here and fixing gates all your life. But out there, in the real world.'

She could see he was chuckling again.

'It's all well and good you being incredulous but the city is the real world now, mate, and there is no such thing as "just work" anymore! You should pay attention. It'll be the same here soon when you lot finally catch up. There is no work. Not any that's distinguishable from life. Everything you do needs to pay. There's money in everything. Everything that there is and everything that you do, there's money in it all. And it's not a case of find it and you're rich, no. No, mate, nowadays it's find it or you're bust!

'Right now, my horse-riding, gate-fixing, hidden-bonsai-fetish-having friend, I have to find who's behind… whatever the hell this is, or else I'm done. They might kill me, sure. But I'm a freelancer. I GET IT DONE! If I don't get a story, I'm as good as dead anyway. The police are after me. My apartment was shared between three of us, so that's long gone. Now I've nothing left but the goodwill of the industry and a shotgun hole in my abdomen, and if I don't find out who made the one, then I won't find anybody to give me the other!'

'You're being very dramatic,' he whispered, taking a pack of Polos from his jacket pocket. 'Can you have mints?'

'I can and I will,' she said.

They sat for a moment, John sucked his mint while Sammy

chewed hers up to dust. The river was calm here. It pooled in tiny, crystal clear bays, looking from above like little sandy beaches.

'So I've been thinking, Sammy,' John passed her another Polo, 'about these shotguns-'

'Will you teach muh?' she asked, mouthful of mint.

Then, before he could speak, she lifted out her phone and started furiously flicking at it. Again he started to speak and she grabbed his lips to stop him. Her flicking slowed down and she started clicking now. She'd brought up an image. She raised the brightness and showed him. She must have taken it in the Hatter's the other night. It was the shooting contest poster. She smiled, shifting crunched Polo around in her mouth.

'I need to win this.'

'You want to win the shooting competition?'

'Yes.'

She nodded and continued, ignoring the his incredulous face.

'Yes, because once I win, they'll have to take me into the shop. Winner gets a custom gun, right? So I'm going to go in, trophy in hand, and say "give me whatever made this!"' she pulled up her top and the neon yellow bandage shone bright in the daylight.

'Good plan. Two problems. First, people here have been shooting since the age of seven, so you'll never win.'

'You watch me!'

'-and second, the only gun I have access to is the farmer's, and he won't let me have it right now.'

'Why not?'

'No reason. The point is, that if we want the gun, we'll need to go in to his house and take it from him. Now, I'm not about to start breaking into my boss's house just like that and-'

'Yes you are.' Sammy smiled. 'We're breaking in there tonight. Now, saddle up cowboy! We've got varmints to... er, smoke! Yeehaw!

...and, while you're there, can you saddle me up first? I hate this goddamn massive horse.'

9

It was 11pm. Sammy and John had fallen asleep on the sofa. The TV news blared over their snores. Somehow, cutting through it all, Sammy's alarm woke them. Sammy, launching herself from the sofa, fell over the coffee table. John got up and decided to make tea. It was time for action. Almost.

They arrived at the farmhouse at 23:35 sharp. By now, John knew, the farmer should be deep in a whisky-drugged sleep. He slept in the spare bedroom, his wife in the main bed, passed out on wine. The only ones awake were the dogs. They prowled around in the front yard, sniffing out trouble.

'Racist bastards,' Sammy whispered, as she unzipped her raiding bag. She had a string of six Cumberland sausages. John Barton had sacrificed his most potent weed for her to sew into them. She flicked open a knife and cut each respective sausage off her string, passing them to John.

John knew the yard well enough that even in the dark he could lob the bangers exactly where they needed to go. There were three dogs, six sausages. Ideally that made two each, but hopefully just one would contain a sufficient dose to put them out of action. You can't be too careful though, John had told a disgusted Sammy, one of Khaki and Morland's favourite games was getting the guard dogs stoned. They might have built up a tolerance.

The night had no clouds. Not optimal for night manoeuvres, but Sammy wasn't going to wait. The stars sent shadows twisting along the ground as the trees blew in the wind, bats twanged the telephone wires and then, yes, there they are! The dogs, two together, one behind, trotted into the yard. Sammy and John were looking down at them from atop the stable building. Now John could see them, he could guess what they were thinking.

He launched the first sausage to the other side of the yard. The rear dog heard it land, jumped and whimpered. The top dog revealed himself with a grumpy harrumph and bounded over to it. He snarfed it in one bite. Looking around, the dog saw no other sign of food, so came back to the other two. In turn, they both sniffed at its muzzle.

'Good,' John whispered. 'I knew they'd do that.'

He flung another sausage to where the first had landed. They waited a second, then flung the remaining four in two other corners of the yard. The underdogs, seeing the top dog caught up with the first sausage, saw their chance. They gave each other a moment's side-eye, before blustering to grab their own.

'Two each,' Sammy whispered.

'Dumb dogs,' John nodded.

They held their watch for ten minutes. They'd predicted anywhere from twenty to forty for the sausages to take effect but within five the dogs were rolling around, licking each other and digging at the ground. First one collapsed, thumpf, and lay on its side, tongue lolling. Then the second, thumpf, and the third, who lowered himself carefully down before taking up the same position as the rest. Their tails were wagging for another couple of minutes after they stopped moving. Eventually, the tails too dropped, and they were in.

The two figures, svelte in black clothing, sprinted up to the ground floor bathroom window. The downstairs toilet, John knew, had terminally dodgy plumbing and spent each night clanging and groaning like Marley's ghost. Sammy, who he planned to push through the small, high-up window, could make as much noise as she wanted in there and it'd be no worse than the plumbing on any other night.

They squatted beneath the window. It was higher than he

remembered. A small window, normally levered open to let out smells, but tonight it was closed tight. Still, it was the plan. They'd get through it.

'It's up to you now,' John told her. 'Smartarse,' he added.

'Get down on your hands and knees,' she grinned. 'Be my dog.'

'How about I just boost you up?'

'And take the chance to grab my arse? Fuck off, I know your game.'

She lifted a set of unusual looking tools out of her bag and zipped it back up. Two looked like gardening implements The third was a mirror the exact size and shape of a credit card. John had assumed the position. Sammy ruffled his hat, 'Good doggy!'

Standing on his back she could just about reach. She inserted one of the gardening tools between the caulk of window and frame. She managed to drag it round the circumference, extracting a long string of caulk with it. The string dropped down onto John's head, sticking for a moment on his face.

'Gross! What was that? Are you chewing gum up there or what?'

'It's the dark arts, John,' she whispered, giving him a quiet kick in the ribs. 'Now shut up!'

Into the space left by the first tool she inserted the second, twisting it into the lock from behind and popping the internal mechanism. She put her whole weight into it. Once it was out, she could use the same tool to push the button, lift the handle, and open the window from the inside. John heard the click.

'I don't know what you did, Sammy, but that was pretty nifty.' He felt her boot against in his ribs.

'There's the alarms yet, dumbass! Be quiet!'

She lifted out her phone and started flicking through apps.

'Don't tell me,' John sighed, 'that there's an app for that now too?'

Sammy ignored him and ran AlarmTrackr, the new app she'd downloaded that afternoon from Journocity.

'It's everyone's worst nightmare,' the embedded video had

said. 'Your alarm's going off and you can't remember where you located the sensors.'

Cut to shot of baffled mother. 'Well that's no longer a problem thanks to AlarmTrackr.' As Sammy opened the app she saw, marked out as red points on a Google Maps overlay, the six sensors in the farmhouse that might pick them up. Two were broken or without batteries. That made it easier. It also showed he location of the wireless port. Turning this off would disable the whole system.

There had been eight different versions of the app, all of them free. Sammy picked this one because of the ad.

'Okay,' she whispered, 'I've got it.'

'Aren't you going to do it with the zapper?'

'Yeah, John,' she mimicked him, putting on a moron voice, 'I gon do dat ting with zap-pah!'

She snapped the back off her phone, mounting the mirrored credit card onto it. The card was good for unlocking car doors but today it was her refractor. Her phone, bought from Taobao, used an infrared beam to focus its camera. God knows why. The dark arts community had found a bunch of extra usages for it, however, including disabling alarms. Sammy bounced the beam off her mirrored card and swirled it in the direction of the wireless alarm hub. She kept it going for about a minute, strafing everywhere possible. The beam was able to pass through walls.

So, even without great accuracy, something was bound to connect. Sending infrared down one of the receptors should overload the system, producing a factory reset. She opened AlarmTrackr and nodded. No lights. Alarms deactivated.

'That's a good phone that, Sammy.'

'Yeah. Rubbish camera on it though.'

He backed himself against the wall and made a cradle with his hands. Sammy, pushing her tools back into the bag and zipping them up, aligned herself with John then, perhaps before he was expecting her, charged at him, leaped up, into his hands and off, up, into the window.

She was half way in before she realised she was stuck.

'Shit,' she mouthed, 'have I put on weight?'

She heard John calling up from behind her.

'Have you put on weight?'

He could see her legs cycling in the air, her middle stuck firm in the window.

'It's all that Northern tripe you've been serving me!' She was whisper-shouting, a speciality of hers on missions like this. 'Every meal I've had here has been brown brown brown! Potatoes and pasties and pastry and meat meat meat! BROWN! You bloody bumpkins; it's amazing you don't all die at fifteen, your bloodstream replaced with gravy!'

'Fair enough, Sammy, fair enough. It's probably that, as you say. Well, that, and the bandage we put on you yesterday.'

'Oh yeah.' She remembered her lumpy middle. 'Do us a favour in that case, John Barton. Pull me out of this window. Much obliged.'

A brief struggle and he eventually unplugged her. She brushed herself off and looked up to find him gesturing to the wall.

'What?'

'What do you mean 'what'?'

He grabbed her by the shoulders and manoeuvred her beneath the window.

'You're giving me a boost. Here, come on. Do this with your fingers.'

He made a crossweave pattern in front of her eyes.

'Then put it down like this.' He made a cradle.

She tried it. She got her fingers tangled up.

'What's wrong with you? Haven't you boosted anyone before?'

'I'm 5'4", John! I don't boost, I'm boosted!'

'Well your boosting me. Grab my foot.'

She held on to his muddy walking boot as he pushed off her, up, and straight through the window.

A minute later he was back at her side, lifting his pack onto his back.

'Come on! I got the front door open. This way!'

There was something strange about sneaking in through someone's unlocked front door. Both Sammy and John stopped at the mat to wipe their feet. John was about to take his boots off before thinking better of it. They walked in, closed the door behind them, and went silent.

The inside of the farmhouse was much darker than outside. John tapped Sammy's shoulder. She let out her hand. He caught it. Together, they moved slowly through the dark, John leading the way by memory and touch. Sammy waited for her night vision to kick in. She felt the plush carpet beneath her feet. Hopefully she hadn't dragged anything too nasty in with her. They got to the end of a deceptively long corridor and she felt John fiddling with a door handle. It squeaked ever so slightly as he turned the knob. It clicked open.

The door creaked too, as he pushed it open. He pulled her in, close to him, and shut the door behind them. For a moment, it was perfect darkness. Then, after a fumble down the cobwebbed wall, John found the switch. The stairs to the basement lit up.

Sammy realised she was very close to him. She looked up and found he was looking down at her, thinking the same thing. She suddenly wished it was colder, then she could see how his breath met hers in the air.

'Come on,' he mouthed, and they silently crept down the stairs.

Down in the basement there was exactly what one might expect to find in the house of an aspiring-to-be-gentleman farmer. A huge wine rack with only a little wine in it but plenty of bottles of spirits, probably given to the family as gifts. A number of golf bags, various clubs and a couple of powered trolleys from the 1990s. Fishing equipment. Unused tools and a workbench with a big stack of Top Gear magazines on it.

So that's where he hides them, John thought.

Sammy had AlarmTrackr open again. It had a function for locating hidden safes.

'Oh no!' the mother on the advert had said, 'Grandpa passed away and left everything to the grandkids, but I don't know where he left it all!'

Sammy found where the farmer left it all. It was behind a propped up sail.

'Of course he'd gone through a yachting phase,' John thought, 'I bet it lasted all of three weeks.'

The gun safe was old. Old enough to be crackable just by listening to the combination roller. Luckily, Sammy had held on to the stethoscope she'd stolen from the hospital.

'You're breathing very loud, John. Can you calm yourself until I've got this done. I can't hear a thing.'

'Sorry,' he whispered.

It was then she realised that half of the heavy breathing noises were coming from herself.

She held her breath. Cycled the roller. Slowly. Slowly. Heard a click. Yes! And then another. Oh Jesus! And, then, carefully, one more! *CLICK.*

The safe popped open and she lifted down the shotgun. It was longer than she'd expected, and thicker too. 12 gauge. She ran her fingers down the black metal and the carved walnut stock. John picked up three boxes of cartridges. He pushed them into his backpack. Sammy lifted the gun to her shoulder. Smiled. Pulled it away and sniffed at its oily barrel. She heard John close behind her.

'You're such a bloody smartarse, Sammy.' He wrapped his arms around her from behind. 'A tiny, deadly bitch…'

'Oh it's so hot!' she admitted, breathing heavy, turning her mouth to meet his, kissing him over her shoulder. His arms wrapped around her, a hand clenching her wounded belly, a hand grasping her breasts. She could feel his body over hers. She could feel his heat. She was holding the shotgun tight to her, caressing its barrel with hungry hands.

'Fuck,' she whispered onto his tongue.

Then she felt it. No, it couldn't be. But it was. It must have been. She felt him, hard, ready, pushing up against her, and he… wasn't huge. She gasped a little. Took a hand off the shotgun and felt back there. John was moving now, rhythmical. She put her hand back and felt him through his trousers. Only about a handful. Goddamn it, John Barton!

'I need you, Sammy,' he was breathing. 'I want you. I'm going to take you right here.'

'Actually, John,' she pulled away. 'I'd rather not go to prison for the sake of a shag-'

CLANG!

They heard a noise from outside. How long had they been in there? Sammy checked her phone. They were nearly twenty minutes on from doggy downtime. The dogs must have been coming to. The noise sounded like it came from the yard.

Then, barks. Yes, she thought, definitely the yard.

And now – "Whatsallat'ownaire?" – the farmer yelling. Sounds of movement above them. Creaking and banging. Shit. They were close to bust. If she'd succumbed to John's small but rather charming charms then she'd definitely have had it. As it was, they'd come prepared.

'Quick, Sammy! Before they find the window! Save us!'

'Save us?' she flicked her phone over to an app she'd made herself that afternoon using EasyAppBuildr3.5.

'That's a bit melodramatic, isn't it?'

She opened the app (she'd called it "RenningBlud" as "Raining Blood" was taken) and after a couple of tense seconds of buffering, she hit the button: 'Fire!'

For the farmers' fiftieth birthday bonanza he'd wanted a bouncy castle. After judging the rental prices to be "a total ruddy scam", he'd bought his own. That afternoon, John Barton had dug the blower out of the barn and installed it in the stables.

He aimed into the farmhouse yard. Sammy stuffed it with all the clothes she'd bled across the previous evening, then the ones she'd bled in when she arrived.

Now, hitting the trigger, Sammy sent the blood-sodden clothing bursting out into the yard.

The yard was suddenly a tornado of red, white and black fabric. The clothing span in the air like a bloody, windswept washing machine. The dogs, surrounded suddenly by a mob of ghosts and the smell of fresh kills, howled and yapped and barked for their lives. As the farmer thrust open the front door – too panicked to realise it was unlocked – he screamed out into the haunted sky, "Blooming Nora!", before being slapped in the face by a wet bra.

Sammy and John Barton were already out of the back door, sprinting away into the long grass of the rear field. They strafed across in zig-zag patterns, leaving only a confused trail behind them. They broke out into the woodland on the far side. There, tied up by a stream, were the two horses. John loaded his bag onto the larger stallion and mounted up. Sammy stood staring at him.

'Is this really the best plan we could think of?'

'Yeah, get on,' John waved, his eyes still full of adrenaline, glinting in the moonlight. 'Horses don't have license plates. Horses don't use roads. Horses, Sammy, are bloody lovely and everyone likes them except you! Now, get on!'

'Fine,' she nodded, fastening her bag onto the horses' saddle and mounting the shotgun on the other side. 'But you still need to get down and help me. I'll ride this knock-kneed donkey but I'll be damned if I'm getting on him without someone holding him. I've seen the rodeo videos. I know what these bastards'll do if they smell weakness.'

'Fine,' John sighed, 'come here.'

*

They rode on through the fields and forests until near dawn. Only forty-five minutes outside of Avon Murray by car, it had nevertheless taken them four and a half hours to ride there. Sammy's riding had not improved. John saw her reach for the shotgun whenever she felt like she was falling off. It was an improvement on strangling the horse, but it wasn't doing much for her balance.

At four a.m. they stopped to pitch their tent. They had a pop-up but John insisted on pegging it down properly, setting up a groundsheet and a top sheet, all of which Sammy considered pointless showing off. Man shit. They were set up soon, though. The horses fed, watered and left to wander in the next field. They took out sleeping bags, used their backpacks as pillows. They would have zipmarks on their faces in the morning.

As they lay in the dark, zipped in, their bags warm around them, Sammy heard John whisper, sleepy. 'Want to zip our bags together Sammy?'

'You're alright, mate,' she whispered back. She had brought the shotgun to bed with her. She felt the weight of its heavy stock resting on her bandaged middle. She held the long metal barrel close to her face. She had the gun. Soon she'd have the rest.

'You wanted to before though. Didn't you, Sammy?'

John was still whispering, almost asleep now.

'Quit chatting shit, John,' she yawned. 'It's time for bed.'

10

'What's this?'

'Whu... JESUS!'

John Barton woke up with a shotgun pointing right at his crotch. He shrieked and batted it away. Sammy pulled a disgusted face.

'Calm down, you big wuss. If I was going to cap you I'd have done it in your sleep.'

'Oh my God.'

He gathered up his bedding, his heart moving quick. He only had a vague notion of where he was. All he could see was the shotgun and some grey light seeping in behind Sammy's silhouetted head.

'Sammy! You DO NOT point guns at people!'

'Whatever...'

'That's, like, lesson number one!'

She pulled back the gun and snorted. He couldn't see but he could tell she was rolling her eyes. She pushed the gun back at him, stock-first this time.

'In my defence, we haven't had lesson one yet, right? So don't be giving me shit. I just want to know what this is...'

She rubbed her finger along a small tin badge, screwed to the base of the shotgun.

'It's a serial number.'

'Okay,' and she left the tent. John Barton was alone in the dark, his head spinning. The raid came back to him, and the fact that he was harbouring a wanted criminal. His brain then began some rudimentary reasoning and told him that he would now also be a wanted criminal. He wondered for a second, sitting in the dark, why he did it. Then he remembered Sammy's kiss. Her hands on him. His hands on her.

'Bloody hell,' he breathed to himself. Then, to the dangerous abductee beyond the tent; 'what time is it?'

No reply.

'Sammy!'

'What?'

'What time is it?'

'Eeerm,' he could hear the impatience in her voice through three layers of canvas. 'Quarter to five.'

He sank back onto his rucksack-pillow.

And a fine bloody morning it is too he thought.

How was he, a lifelong farmhand, one the most infamously early risers in the county, being beaten out of bed by a phone-obsessed millennial? It was a sickness, he decided; she had a sickness. Half five is healthy, half four is sick.

John Barton rubbed at his eyes. It was time for breakfast.

By the looks of Sammy she'd already been up for over an hour. This was more to do with her alert appearance than the state of the campsite. Sammy had prepared nothing.

As John staggered out of the tent she registered him with an '*mm*'. She was deep in her phone. It was plugged into a huge pink battery which was, in turn, connected to some unusual satellite arrangement. She'd plugged in a travel keyboard too, its keys tiny and cluttered together in a ball. It looked vaguely like an ocarina.

'What is that thing?' John asked, lighting up the stove.

'The Mueller-Kueps? It's a writing ball. Nietzsche had one.'

'Nietzsche?'

'He's a philosopher,' she grabbed the ball as if to demonstrate, her hand massaging it like she was wringing out a hedgehog.

'He was a philosopher,' John batted back.

He poured water into the camping kettle and lit the fire.

'I thought Mueller-Kueps only made tools. I have a Mueller-Kueps. It set me back a bit.'

'A keyboard's a tool,' Sammy said, then furrowed her brow. 'Will this conversation wait? I'm knee-deep in a government database here.'

Oh good, John thought, not even had breakfast yet and we're already doing crimes.

As the kettle slowly began to steam, John plodded around. They'd nestled themselves in behind the cover of a bush, just beside a clearing. It was some of the deepest and least interesting woodland in Avon Murray, so they'd have nothing to worry about either from locals or from weekend walkers. The foliage would soak up the sound of shots.

There was room in the clearing for a shooting range. He heaved a stump onto another stump, then a rock on top of that for good luck. He then turned and took twenty-five paces. It would do.

Sammy was deep in the official gun registry database as the kettle boiled over. She could deal with the screeching and the hissing but now with all the bubbling too, she couldn't concentrate. She gave in and made the tea. She did it one-handed, her thumb rubbing at her phone. If she stayed idle for more than ten seconds, the registry's software could detect her. The app she was using had an option to override this but it would meaning signing up for a premium account. Fuck that.

'Okay, so I now know where to get the number so I can track the gun straight to its owner. This one, for example, bought from Watson Brothers in London, customised at Reginald Gunsmith's and is now registered to the place we borrowed it from last night. What do you think, John, shall I update the 'current location' field?'

'What are you talking about?'

The kettle was replaced by the frying pan. John Barton was making sausages.

He was tentative about shooting at six in the morning, but as there was no one around to hear, he hadn't much of an argument against it. Sammy, as always, was persistent. She had wanted a target and insisted that shooting at some piled up logs and rocks was too easy. Thus proceeded the first argument of the day, with John finally giving in and placing a sarcastic acorn on top of the pile. This would be her target. She would miss it all day.

The first ten minutes were taken up by John snatching the gun off her every time she was about to kill herself. He'd never seen a person so eager to point the barrel at their own feet or, on two different occasions, look directly down the barrel while the weapon was loaded. The safety catch seemed to baffle her.

'But guns are meant to be shot! Why would you intentionally put a don't-shoot button on it?'

Then, after having finally managing to fire a shot, the lead flying six feet over the head of the target, she tried loading two cartridges at the same time.

'It's twice the power that way!'

'That's not how you do it.'

'I don't care how people have done it before, John. We've got to think disruptively to get the edge on everyone else. You yourself said they've been shooting since they were little. Well we've not-'

'I have.'

'Okay, I've not. So I can see stuff they can't, get me?'

'You are the worst pupil I have ever taught.'

She fired a few more times. The gun was double-barrelled and she insisted on firing both barrels at once. She kept flipping the gun over looking for… well, John doubted she even knew. After an hour of shooting, which felt like a lifetime, she wouldn't stop grabbing the barrel.

'It's hot, John! Feel it! So nice.'

'Don't-' and she grabbed his hand and rubbed it against the barrel. All the shooting had warmed it. He felt it in his fingers, then his palms. Losing concentration for a moment, or maybe a minute, he felt himself rubbing the barrel, watching her rub the barrel. Did this mean something? He turned to look into her eyes. She looked into his.

'Do you feel… weird, Sammy?'

'I love shooting, John Barton,' she smiled, then giggled, then rolled her head back and guffawed. 'Aha! I fucking love shooting shit! HaHA! Bang BANG!'

He felt a strange tingling in his fingers.

'Do you love shooting too, John?' she asked. She turned to him, looked him deep in the eyes. She was hypnotising. So beautiful, he thought, so strange. So… stoned.

'What was in the sausages?'

'What?' Sammy stopped to think, 'the ones before? Were they from the pink baggy?'

John nodded. He had seen the size of her pupils. He looked down at the swaying grass. He longed to get down on his knees and touch it.

'My bad,' Sammy giggled.

John stopped, frozen in time, thought back.

'So, that's why the dogs woke up so quickly? We only gave them half the stash?'

'Seems that way…'

'And we've just eaten what's left.'

Sammy giggled, went back to rubbing at the gun.

'Never mind, John Barton. We still have the gun. Plus there's, what? Two days until the shooting competition? We'll smash it!'

'Two days?!'

'Come on, y'big baby,' she laughed. 'Shooting's fun!'

So they went back to firing. After another twenty minutes or so, Sammy finally started hitting the post. They were already a quarter of the way through the farmer's supply of cartridges but the hard bit was over. She could point the gun in a direction and make the shot move in something like that same direction. It wasn't exactly where she intended it to go, but it was no longer threatening to add another hole to her body. Other people's bodies, maybe. But Sammy would be fine.

Shooting stoned seemed to suit her. Where John Barton kept losing sense of time, looking at his watch only to find it had moved backwards from where he'd seen it last, Sammy seemed to loosen up. John moved up behind her. He would help her with her aim, his hands on her hips and shoulders, guiding.

'Helping. Just helping,' he whispered in her ear.

He wondered whether it was the blood of the hashashin that gave her these magical powers. She was quite small beneath him, her dark hair in his nose. He craned out his neck and licked her ear.

Here we go again, Sammy thought. The boy was insatiable. Sidling up behind her with a stiffy. Is this the countryside way?

She fired again. The boom was growing on her. The feel of being shoved. She'd learned not to close an eye, not even to aim. It was a pointing thing. Feel it, follow it, pull and *BOOM*! It was exciting, she supposed, in its way.

'Think I've got a chance at the title?'

'Mmm?' John appeared to be rubbing his nose on her head. 'Yeah. Definitely.'

'You're a pure bullshitter, John Barton.'

'But you like me,' he mouthed through her hair.

It was then that John Barton gave her a couple of thrusts. It felt like he was prodding to get her attention. Automatically, she turned to look. There, wandering curious into the clearing, was a rabbit. She saw its fluffy tail and mindless, black eyes and lifted the gun towards it.

'Don't,' John Barton whispered, backing off from her now and moving into a hunter's crouch, 'there'll be nothing left of it if you hit it with a shotgun. That thing's a twelve gauge. It'll be rabbit smoothie.'

'Then it'll be perfect for me!' Sammy laughed, pointing the weapon in the rabbit's direction. *BOOM*!

Against all odds, she hit it.

The rabbit blinked out of existence like a sloppy cut in old analogue film. One frame there was a rabbit, the next there was a very thin paste smeared five feet along the forest floor and, hanging in the air, a cloud of pink particles. It was, indeed, rabbit smoothie.

'WAheeeey!' Sammy screamed, thrusting the shotgun into the air and pumping her arm.

'I can't believe it,' John took his flatcap off, his jaw falling slack.

As they moved over to the meat stain, all John Barton could think about was her killer instinct; her sudden ability to hit a target when that target was alive and she didn't want it to be. Normally it was the reverse. The most hardened hunters are still better at the range than in the field. Something about pulling the trigger on a living thing should make you flinch, but it made Sammy better, clearer, more focused.

Sammy was thinking something else as they walked over. She felt no guilt for the rabbit. They were there to be shot, right? Why else would they put them there? No, it was that bad cut between the rabbit and the bloodcloud that kept playing back. After the initial adrenaline boost passed, she had realised just what that smear meant.

Twelve gauge. That's what she'd been hit it with. That was what this gun was and, if the report from the ballistics specialist was correct, that was the original size of the gun that hit her. If it hadn't been shrunk, customised, or... however they did it, she'd have been paste, just as the rabbit was. One frame would have shown Sammy Habib, reporter for the Bantz Testament, hot on the lead of another story. The next frame would have shown a kitchen slick with horror, air heavy with floating blood, and a jigsaw puzzle of bone and torn organs spilling out five feet along the carpet.

The two of them stood silently over the smashed rabbit. Their eyes quivered. They were wary. Death was there with them. It filled their heavy breathing chests and, panting slowly, they moved close to each other. They held each other. The blood had gotten on their boots.

At first they held each other softly, like they were consoling each other. Then, with her head held against the country boy's chest, Sammy decided that she'd done reflecting. It wasn't her style. If the gun was bigger she'd have been dead, but the gun was small. Smaller is nicer.

'Shall we go back to the tent?' he asked her.

Sammy looked left, then right, circumspect. 'Are we really as far out from town as you said?'

'There's nobody for miles'

'Right,' she grinned, 'then we're doing it here!'

11

It was the day of the contest. Every street in Avon Murray was strung with bunting, like they'd been attacked by a festive spider. Cars beeped hopelessly as crowds swirled around them. Traders yelled over each other. The local dogs had taken the opportunity to run free and form packs. One pack overturned a meat stand, another liberated the pet shop. Everyone was out. It was carnival day.

Sammy strode up the main street with the shotgun on her shoulder. She was alone. She'd left John Barton in the tent. He'd only get in her way. She was wearing oversized tweeds, borrowed from John. The competition required "sporting wear".

As she passed the pub a crowd of local alcoholics spotted her. It was a woman who first shouted. She was dark haired and looked to be in her twenties, but upon seeing Sammy, her face twisted up into that of an old crone.

'Tsurr!'

The rest of the crowd swivelled, pointed and laughed.

Sammy walked on, undeterred. She felt like she had grown over the past couple of days. She no longer needed to get angry when laughed at by the locals. After all, she thought, I'm Sammy-fucking-Habib, world famous reporter. She walked on without saying a word, quietly comparing herself to Jesus as she did so.

The shooting contest was in the park at the centre of town. The festivities opened with a football match. The teams consisted of two sets of residents, both of whose houses backed on to the park. The loser would have the shooting range oriented in their direction. There was everything to play for.

Sammy strode over to the sign-up tent as the game reached

penalties. A bloated alcoholic wellied the ball as hard as he could at the net, only for it to be saved by Mrs Mildred, the school's librarian. The ball bounced high off her face as she dived.

'Name?' the wizened official asked, running a finger down the sign-up list.

'Samra Habib,' she rolled the *r*.

'You what?'

He looked up at her. She was grinning at him. She knew what she was doing. He sighed.

'Just write it on the board.'

She leaned over and wrote, "Sammy Habib", then passed back the pen.

'There. Not so hard, is it?'

The official smirked. Okay, so not everyone in this town is devoid of a sense of humour. He turned and chalked SH next to a number of other initials on a rather complex diagram. It looked like the blueprints to something hydraulic, but was in fact the current tournament system.

'Right, Sammy,' he smiled, 'it appears that you'll be in the second set of shooters. Have you shot before?'

'Sure have,' she grinned. 'I've been shooting for a whole day now, and I'm feeling pretty good about it.'

She thought back over the past day, the shooting and the country boy who, admittedly, also kept her busy.

'Well... a whole day, on and off.'

'I meant in a shooting competition.'

'Oh, then no,' she admitted, 'but I've Googled it.'

'Googled it?' he raised a wry eyebrow, a wrybrow. 'Well, if you've Googled it then you probably know more about it than I do. The match is just ending and it seems we'll be shooting to the West, so you've time to grab a coffee and then we'll be on our way. The range is going to be just over there,' he pointed over to a sobbing footballer who'd just put the ball through his new double-glazing. 'It'll be three rounds of pigeons followed by straight-shooting with targets.'

'Pigeons?'

'Clays.'

'Oh,' Sammy scratched beneath her flatcap with the end of her shotgun. 'I thought I was in luck there. I love killing shit.'

She grinned and walked off. The official returned to his magazine.

*

Sammy wandered off to get a coffee. It took her a while, coffee stalls not being prevalent in the countryside. By the time she found a café her lips were cracked from swearing under her breath about lazy backwoods yokels. The coffee, when it did arrive, seemed miniscule. It was only the size of a small cup.

'This is a sample, right?'

'No, love, that's the small,' the coffee girl was incredulous. 'You asked for the small, right?'

'Yeah, but...'

A small never actually meant small.

'I think I actually meant a large. An extra-large, if you do them.'

'We don't,' said the coffee girl, ignoring her now. 'If you want another then go to the back of the queue.'

*

The competition began with a proclamation from a man dressed as a medieval jester. A woman dressed in multi-coloured tweeds then ran on with a comically oversized shotgun that fired fireworks. She shot them at the fool as he retreated. Neither the crowd nor the competitors were much impressed. It was merely tradition. As they took to their places there was no ceremony, just the word '*PULL!*'

There were six shooters and twelve clays in the air. Eight of them exploded into dust. The officials walked forwards and inspected the remains. Using some identification system that Sammy couldn't work out, the official's raised their arms and two shooters stepped away from their plates. Over the buzz of the crowd Sammy could hear one spitting "bullshit!" over and over. The official sighed and rolled his eyes.

The second round of clays were loaded and Sammy was interested now. She was trying to work out the complex arrangement whereby all of these shooters could take shots at their own clays while missing the others. The machines comprised of whirring rotors and a sling arm. As someone yelled '*PULL!*' she appreciated the synchronicity of the arms slinging, the unity of trajectories as projectiles crossed in the air. The only part not synchronised was the shooting. Everyone seemed to have their own method. Some unabashedly aimed for the machine itself, trying to get the clay on its way out. The majority tried to hit the clays at their apex, although that was hard to judge. And then, finally, there was one man who seemed to think it best to shoot just before the clay hit the ground. It was a bad technique. As the inspectors went out this time he was the only one sent off.

They were down to three and there was one round left of the clays before the targets. Sammy was reading from her phone. The clays were elimination rounds. Each round had a gold clay and a bronze clay. Miss one gold and you were out, miss three bronzes across the three rounds and you were out. It was actually fairly simple, she reckoned, although she still had no idea how they identified whose clay was whose. Either way, once she'd got through that round (there was no doubt in her mind that she would) it would be on to the targets.

The target was separated into points areas, like a dartboard but ten times bigger. Each shooter had three shots each. Of those who made it to the target round, only two would enter the showdown phase.

The showdown phase was different each year. Last year it was shooting from a moving vehicle, before that it was shooting while swimming and, in the legendary tournament of 1848, the winner was decided by who could shoot the other fastest. Some locals considered the showdown phase to have gone downhill from 1849 onwards. Sammy was nevertheless psyched up. What challenges would await her? Her confidence in her abilities was unshakeable.

She watched as the final clays were loaded. She imagined herself lining up to fire. What angle would she pick? What line of approach was best?

Then, as an attendant shouted '*PULL!*' she was yanked backwards by both shoulders.

'Hey!' she screamed, 'what the fuck's this?'

'Calm down, ma'am!'

It was a cop, she realised. They'd got her.

'Sergeant, get the gun.'

'You can't shoot me, you bastards! I've got rights!'

'No-one's shooting anyone, ma'am.'

The policeman was cordial. Too cordial, she would have thought, were she not being wrestled to the ground by a policewoman with some kind of super strength. 'We are investigating the case of a stolen firearm. This is simply a routine check.'

Sammy gave up struggling. She could feel the policewoman's knee pinning down her inner thigh. Bloody perv, she sighed.

'Well, officer, if that's what I'm supposed to call you…'

'You can call me whatever you like, ma'am,' he smiled, 'I've heard it all. Alan, can you run the serial number on this weapon.'

Sammy swallowed. She weighed up the benefits of causing a scene versus talking her way out. In this case, she reckoned, it was better to take the high risk strategy. Total confidence. After all, she had a competition to win, and then a mystery to solve.

She'd return with the kidnapped celebrities and it'd be a viral hit on Bantz, and then she'd have the last laugh.

'It's her officer!' it was the farmer, John's boss, of course. 'I told you! The other night someone broke in and took my guns and I just know it's her, officer! The terrorist!'

'Do I know you?' Sammy asked, ignoring the policewoman whose lips were now very close to Sammy's face.

'Please sir, let us continue the investigation and we'll call you when we need you.'

The officer gently pushed an open palm into the farmer's tweeds and watched his crimson features fade back into the gathering crowd. Whispers of 'terrorist' rippled in the air.

'Look, officer,' Sammy had decided that was the right term. 'That's my own gun. I brought it from home. You can check the serial number; it's registered to my gaff.'

'That's exactly what we are doing, ma'am, and if it turns out you're telling the truth then we'll let you be on your way.'

He looked around at the crowd and decided to look busy. He took out his notebook, 'and what exactly was it that brought you to this busy place on this busy morning, armed with a shotgun, ma'am?'

'Very funny,' Sammy spat back.

The policewoman on top of her was breathing heavily. Sammy hoped she was just out of shape.

'Don't you know that the Avon Murray shooting tournament is legendary, officer? I've travelled all the way from the big city to come and take part.'

'A likely story,' the officer smiled. 'I happen to be from Withington myself, ma'am, and I'm under no illusions about Avon Murray's level of visibility to the wider world.'

'Oy!' came a voice from the gathered crowd.

'Well, officer, if you must know...' Sammy smiled. She had almost decided to tell him the whole story; the shooting in the hotel, the escape from the hospital, the missing celebrities, tracking the shooter's gun all the way to Avon Murray, her final plan for getting into Reginald Gunsmith's and tracing the gun that shot her to its owner and revealing the sinister kidnapping operation once and for all... but then, thankfully quick enough, she realised that she was already wanted in connection to that first shooting and that there were no doubt twenty or thirty jailable offences that she had committed subsequently.

Goddamn full-time coppers. They couldn't understand the trials of the freelancer.

'What must I know?' the officer replied. Sammy realised that she'd just trailed off.

Just then, a bespectacled man in uniform, presumably Alan, walked up beside the main officer and passed him back the shotgun.

'Here you are, sir. I checked on the registry database and it's registered to exactly where she said it was. An office by the name of the Bantz Testament.'

'A religious organisation?' the officer asked.

'Yes, sir,' Sammy smiled, 'are you a Christian yourself, officer?'

'I am, for my sins,' he chuckled. 'Let her up, sergeant.'

Sammy felt the policewoman reluctantly shift off her. For all her strength, Sammy realised, she had been surprisingly tender. The sergeant passed her back her weapon and Sammy started laughing. Ah, the digital age! What wonders it contained!

'Sorry about the mix-up, ma'am,' the officer doffed his cap.

'No problem, officer!' she laughed.

The farmer could be seen in the background, snot running down his chin with fury.

As Sammy walked away from the mix-up, she realised it was time to take her place. The first round of shooters had gone and the leaderboard showed scores in the triple figures. They were going to be tough to beat, Sammy realised, but all the sweeter once she'd achieved her certain victory.

They took their places. Sammy was four along. It was a good peg. She was feeling confident. She looked back in her mind to the previous rounds she had seen. The airborne trellis of potential pathways seemed to stretch out in front of her. She lifted her gun and pointed it along one. Yes, she felt ready.

Then, before she could even gather her thoughts, she heard the sudden '*PULL!*' and the clays were in the air. Which were hers? She still couldn't tell. There was no way of telling! She felt her body move, the shotgun rise. *BANGBANG!* One bang followed the other. Two clays flickered out of existence. The air was filled with coloured dust. In the distance she heard the smashing of double glazing.

The attendants slumped out. They saw whatever it was that they saw and, pausing and scratching their heads, checking with each other, then shrugging, they pointed to the two shooters either side of Sammy.

Sammy beamed, adrenaline filling her system. She was doing it! She was winning! The two shooters either side eyed her with disbelief. She heard them muttering 'bullshit!' but didn't care. Next year they'd probably go back to banning women again.

She didn't know how she'd managed it, but somehow it just clicked. The same as when she'd shot for the rabbit, she felt something deep inside her calling out to kill. It wasn't a desire to kill, more like an instinct. Her side, still no doubt weeping blood beneath the sheep bandage, twinged before each shot. Maybe, she wondered to herself, getting shot had given her superpowers? It was like getting bitten by a radioactive spider, only with bullets.

'*PULL!*'

Without thinking, she smashed the next two clays out of the air. She was a shooting machine. Destiny was moving her. Sammy felt the breeze in her hair. She felt alive. The officials pointed to three more shooters. It was just her and one other!

The guy, it turned out, was Reginald himself, of Reginald Gunsmith's. He was an infamously good shot and an even more infamous cheapskate. He took part in his own tournament every year hoping to prevent others from getting the prize.

Their eyes met across the pegs. Reginald spat. Sammy, unimpressed and remembering the way he'd turned her out of his shop only a couple of days ago, snorted a vast ball of phlegm into her mouth and puked it onto the ground. It was meant to be a show of defiance, but was more like a cat puking up a hairball. Never mind, I'll let my shooting to the talking.

'*PULL!' BANG! BANGBANG! BANG!*

Reginald left a pause between his shots. Sammy shot rapidly, instinctually. All four clays burst from the sky. As clouds of primary-coloured dust floated gently down to the ground, the attendants nodded to themselves and the two shooters backed off their pegs. A five-minute break was announced while they put up the targets.

Sammy was through to the semi-finals.

*

Sammy found a piece of dry grass and sat down on it, cross-legged. She couldn't help but notice the crowd mumbling about her, eyeing her up. Ignore them, she told herself. The mission is what matters. Still, it'd be nice to shove her victory in their collective faces. She thought about the trophy (surely there's a trophy?) sitting on her nightstand, waiting to be pawned. Maybe she'd just throw it in a river. Fuck it.

She watched as the first target was hauled into position. Someone had put Khaki and Morland on the job and they'd managed to turn a relatively simple task into a Sisyphean endeavour. The targets swung forwards and back as they carried them, the weight moved around unpredictably. Sure enough, they both collapsed, the target falling over onto them. It rolled away. It was chaos, but the rest of the officials and attendants were buggered if they'd be the ones to do the job.

Sammy looked around the crowd. She picked out the faces she knew. Avon Murray was a small town and she had already turned everyone important against her. Maybe not "turned". Maybe they were already hostile to strangers, but she'd certainly done her part to encourage that hostility

There was Reginald Gunsmith, whispering now with the farmer, the two of them openly staring at her as they grumbled and spat. There was the gang from the pub, laughing and chatting with cans in their hands. Some also carried pints, presumably nicked from the bar without fear of repercussion. Then, who was that?

Sammy spotted a face in the crowd. It stood out, clear, it was all that she could see in fact. A dark complexion. He looked Indian. That in itself was enough to set a man apart in Avon Murray, but now, as he looked over at her, she could sense something else in him. Some intimate knowledge of her. Could it be?

'The baby,' she mouthed to herself. 'It couldn't be…'

But it was. It must have been. Or maybe, thinking rationally, the baby's father? The baby who had shot her. The one wearing a suit. The one who disappeared into thin air, leaving her open and bleeding on the floor. It was him. Or his father. She was sure of it.

The moment that her sureness registered, he moved. It was as if, in that moment, he knew that she knew. In the open daylight, unselfconscious, he started running away from her.

Without thinking, Sammy was running after him. She vaulted over the attendant who was arranging the shooting pins, barged past Reginald and the farmer, and sprinted after the running figure, her shotgun swinging from her shoulder.

She saw him reach the corner of the field. He looked back at her and panicked. Yes, she was certain it was him now. His eyes were focused. He was looking for an escape route. Stuck between choices, she gained ground on him, before, suddenly, he threw himself under a barrier and disappeared down a steep ditch leading to a brook.

Sammy reached the slope seconds later. She looked down to find him gone, only shifting soil and leaves marked his escape route.

She looked down. Looked back to the competition. 'Screw it,' she mumbled, then jumped down the slope herself.

She felt herself losing control, rolling and rolling and rolling. The slope was steeper than she thought. Muddier too. She lost the shotgun, hooked onto a tree above her. Her trousers tore at both knees. A branch scraped down her back. Her flatcap got caught in a patch of nettles and brambles. The plants scratched and stung her hands and face. By the time she landed in the muddy water at the bottom, she felt like she'd been worked over.

'Bastard,' she breathed, winded.

She looked around. Nothing. No sign. Her fall had been for nothing and, once again, she realised the figure had only been seen by her. A mirage. Passed from nothing back into nothing. She rubbed river water over her stinging face and said again, louder this time.

'*BASTARD! BASTARDS! BA-STARD!*'

*

'They gave you five minutes,' the official explained calmly. His face registered genuine disappointment. Of all the competitors to cause a fuss over rules, he'd least expected it from the Arabic girl. He had felt they'd had an understanding. 'The rules are the rules, I'm afraid. We can't make exceptions.'

'But you don't undershtand,' she sighed.

She was still partially winded, had no gun, and her clothes were dripping with grainy, silty, river mud. There was a stink coming off her too, and her face was bloated from nettle poison. Her lips were swollen.

'It wash important. Critical even! I had to chashe shomeone!'

'Whether you had to I don't know, but, yes, we all saw you run off after Mr Lund.'

The official scratched at his nose.

'What business you have with the man is no business of mine, but I'm afraid that running off in the middle of a tourney is classed under "disrespectful behaviour".

'Disrespe-'

'Please, miss, let me finish,' he pushed his glasses higher in order to read from a leatherbound rulebook. 'Leaving the tournament while it is in session and the competitor is still in play, brackets, whether for nefarious purposes or otherwise, close brackets, disrespects the sacred tournament and shall result in a lifetime ban.'

'A ban?!'

'I'm afraid so, ma'am.'

Sammy ruffled at the ma'am; had he picked that up from the cop?

'And I have also been tasked with informing you that you are double-banned from Reginald Gunsmith's. Also for life.'

'Double-banned?'

'Yes.'

'But... but... I was going to win!'

'I'm very sorry, ma'am.'

The official turned away. He lifted some papers to his eyes, perusing them intently. It was his way of signifying that she no longer existed to him.

Distraught, pissed off, Sammy wandered slowly away from the tent. She had blown it. The one big chance that had presented itself to her. It was gone.

Now what? She wondered. Would all the parts of the mystery stay separate forever? No resolution. No story. Nothing.

*

Sammy wandered the town for a bit. Where else could she go? The streets were deserted. Everyone was at the shooting competition watching Reginald win his own gun again. She moped down sidestreets and across abandoned parks. All the cobble and stone of the place seemed to her like the weight of years. The great pointless dead piled up on top of her where, just like her, they meant nothing. Why was she even here? Was it only for the story? Why, when Bantz had already cast her away, denied her three times, more, even?

She was swinging sadly on a rather pathetic swingset when John Barton sat himself down beside her.

'Want an icecream, chuck?'

'Chuck?' she mumbled, taking the ice cream from him.

'You're my little chucky egg,' he grinned, grabbing her cheek. 'Aren't yer? Eh?'

'Fuck off, John Barton.'

'Charming.'

He leaned back on his swing, licking his own icecream.

'I heard what happened, y'know?'

'I bet you did.'

'Went chasing after some rich bloke. Got disqualified from the tournament. Covered yourself in muck. A real gala day for you, eh?'

He laughed as she punched his arm.

'Well, I have to admit. I hadn't foreseen you getting anywhere near as far. I'm impressed, I really am.'

The two licked at their icecreams. Sammy finished hers and sat, kicking at the ground, while John Barton slowly crunched.

'Right,' John Barton announced, munching the last of his cone and standing tall. He reached into his bag and brought out a leather-bound book. 'You'll be wanting this, I expect?'

'What?'

He passed it to her and she opened it. It was the ledger, from Reginald Gunsmiths. All the details of every gun made since... she flipped to the back... 1926! If the gun that shot her was made in Avon Murray, and she was still certain that it was, then it would be in this book.

'Holy shit, Jonny!' her eyes were wide with disbelief. 'How?'

'Well,' he scratched at his neck, 'I figured that wherever it is that you go, you tend to er… bring the ruckus, as they say. So, I could almost guarantee that if you were at the shooting tournament, then the whole town would be there too, most likely in a state of shock. As such, I figured I'd borrow some of your kit.'

He rustled in his bag and lifted out Sammy's journalism kit; her mirrored card, safecracking tools and, lifting up his phone, she saw AlarmTrackr installed there next to something called SheepHerdr.

'So, you broke in?'

'Well…' he turned red, 'surely you have a better euphemism? Investigated perhaps… Negotiated a way in…'

'Oh you little slut!' she roared, leaping up to kiss him. Her muddy face rubbed dirt into his stubble. 'I'm going to make you ache tonight you beautiful bastard!'

'Jesus, Sammy!' John laughed as she dragged him away, book under one arm, his belt in the other. 'You're very welcome!'

'Quiet!' Sammy shouted. 'I have a plan!'

12

'Mr. Lund, he said...'

Sammy thought back to the words of the official.

'An important man, he said...'

'Are you mumbling to yourself again?'

John Barton was busy scrambling eggs with some foraged mushrooms. Ray Mears bullshit, Sammy had called it.

Sammy was fixating on an entry in the ledger. The gun had been purchased three years before Sammy was shot. It wasn't a miniature gun; she'd investigated the ledger six times front to back and found no evidence of any miniature firearms having been made by Reginald. Instead, this was a gun that came with a number of strange requests.

These were made stranger by a series of revisions across the years.

First, the gun was made entirely out of the same metal. The ledger even quoted 'exact elemental equivalency across all parts.' And then, eight months later, there was the inclusion of other metals, then plastics, then, six months ago, wood and carbon fibre. Whoever had commissioned the gun had had an aversion to complex materials which their three year stay in Avon Murray had clearly helped them to overcome. That man was Zane Lund.

Sammy had dropped the name immediately into Google. If he was on the gun registry and was known around Avon Murray as an important man, then he should at least have a LinkedIn. As it was, the internet showed nothing. She searched everything, legal and illegal. Even the birth registry showed nothing.

'Curiouser and curiouser,' Sammy mumbled, stroking her chin. 'It seems that our man, Zane Lund, has done a deep clean. No web presence whatsoever.'

'I had an uncle once who wasn't on Facebook,' John shrugged. 'I don't know what happened to him. Presumably he was cut out of everyone's lives and now wanders the Earth alone.'

'Shut up John.'

Sammy was thinking.

She was sure that this was her man. Zane Lund. Seeing him that afternoon at the shooting competition, his face was still fresh in her mind. He was almost identical to the baby that shot her. Could he really be the boy's dad? Maybe the shock had turned Zane Lund into a baby in her mind? It wouldn't be the first time Sammy had been sent strange messages by her biological clock. Whatever the explanation, she had known when she saw him. She knew that this was the man. Now he'd turned up in the ledger, the thing she'd dragged herself out here to find, and he was a non-entity on the internet. The more she thought about it, the more certain she was that this was the man.

'Right, grub's up,' John called. 'Blender out.'

Snorting, Sammy held out her blender for John to pour the eggs and mushroom into. He'd added some ham as well. Luckily Sammy had never cared much for food, otherwise she might have felt bad about never being able to eat it again.

'John, you're from the sticks…'

'That's the nicest way you've ever phrased that, Sammy. I think you're starting to take a shine to the place.'

'What would you do,' she ignored him, 'if you needed to find someone.'

'We have the internet in Avon Murray, Sammy.'

'To an extent.'

'That's fair.'

'So,' Sammy slugged back some eggshake, 'on the three in five days when your internet is down, what do you do?'

'Well, Sammy,' he spoke slowly, exaggerated, as if to a child. 'There are these things called words, and if you want to, then you can take them off the internet and write them on things called paper.'

'Of course you'd turn this into an opportunity to virtue signal about your books… I keep telling you John Barton, reading is for losers. It does give me an idea though, so thanks I guess.'

'No problem. I live to serve.'

He watched her walk away, phone to her ear, leaving a pile of egg-covered cups and blender parts behind her.

*

'Pick up, you old bastard…' Sammy was tapping the phone with her finger, listening to the dial tone repeating.

She heard it pick up and, before she could say anything, her photographer Jonny's voice was in her ear. 'I'm not speaking to you.'

'Jonny, please, you're my only hope.'

'I'm not speaking to you. I'm not even going to say your name.'

She knew he'd never hang up.

'It's been a shitshow around here since you… evaded capture. The police are probably listening in right now. Bantz have halved my hours so I'm back to delivering pizzas three nights a week. Jesus, Sammy, was that a Star Wars reference?'

'It might have been. It depends on whether you're willing to help me out.'

'I don't know what you mean… are you trying to pay me with Star Wars references?' he sounded incredulous, but he hadn't put down the phone.

'Come on big daddy Yoda. The galaxy needs your help. I need you to break into Bantz and find our old back-ups. The ones from before the great GDPR datawipe. The last living records of the free internet. You know the ones, Obi Wan?'

'Break in? Sammy, I work at Bantz! I don't need to break in!'

'Then you're halfway there already.'

Sammy hung up the phone. She stood for ten seconds, waiting for her confirmation when, yes, she saw he was ringing her back. She declined the call. God, Jonny was so manipulable. Now she just had to sit back and wait.

*

Half an hour later, Jonny called back. As predicted, he had gone straight to the Bantz offices and taken the back-up drives out of storage. The drives were thin slices of internet frozen in time. No-one had quite known what they were for and, legally, Bantz could be fined out of existence for keeping that amount of data stored. In the post-GDPR era, all online information had to be legally justified or else be deleted. Instead, these back-ups were piled high with racist jokes, celebrities' home addresses and thousand-page blogs about Barack Obama being a Muslim Satanist. If Bantz didn't cycle through upper management faster than a weathervane in a tornado, someone might have noticed the back-ups and had them wiped. As it was, Jonny now had them on his desk, and Sammy was guiding him through a tangle of myspace pages and early, unsourced Wikipedia articles.

'Okay, Jonny, send them through.'

Her phone filled with old pictures of Zane Lund. She looked at him. No more than seventeen. His eyes were bulging and he was wearing a Slipknot hoody. Yes, she knew now. She knew what she was dealing with.

Zane Lund had dropped out of MIT after his driver plugin for a lesser-used web design widget made him $300 in a month. He was an acolyte of Bill Gates and Steve Jobs, a wannabe tech entrepreneur who had very little patience for the tech part. After a few months back in his mom's basement, he secured a place on the vocaliser team for Crazy Frog. He toured with the band, keeping their vocoder running and improvising new synth plugins that allowed the Frog to speak directly to the crowd. After a bit more tinkering, the Frog could even respond, albeit in a broken and distorted manner, to interviewers.

It was with the development of WaitBnch that Zane Lund finally found his footing. It was a totally integrated system connecting small businesses in the West with Indian sweatshops. He had needed to reroute some IPs and drop some fairly major backhanders to tech-friendly politicians, but it was all worthwhile when he made his first ten million. WaitBnch was followed by WaitBnch Micro, also known as Home.ly, which reversed the distribution pattern and connected Indian corporations to a network of Western freelancers. There was an integrated race-to-the-bottom feature which resulted in a number of highly successful marketing campaigns being conducted for bargain basement prices. It turned out that Western freelancers, pampered by sufficient gamification and an endearing UI, would work for the same rate as sweatshop workers, and were not only happy, but bragged about their jobs on social media, depicting them as a luxury lifestyle choice.

Appearances, Lund was coming to learn, were everything. Intention, nothing.

It was after the success of these two services that Zane Lund was finally welcomed back by his family. In business terms, this meant the integration of Zane's company – Turbo Wombat Inc – with the wider Lund Corporation. The Indian megacorp, headed by an established Pakistani dynasty, backed by Chinese and American investment, had been syphoning off funds to send to Zane all along. It was only post-Home.ly. however, that Zane was brought fully back into the fold, taken to the barbers and the tailors, and then outed as a fully-fledged tech messiah. With circular glasses and a turtleneck/blazer combo, he was ready for stardom.

'Fucking hell,' Sammy mouthed as Jonny livestreamed the backup's files onto her phone. She waded through pages and pages of interviews, thinkpieces, and share index reports; all of it making Zane Lund out to be the next huge thing. If he didn't have the exact same face,she'd have no idea what he was doing here. Tech billionaires don't come to Avon Murray. The screen kept on rolling. More and more information. And then…

'And then it just stops.' Jonny's crackling voice came through her screen.

'Just stops?'

'Yup.' She could hear him nodding (he had a very heavy head) 'And then there's nothing new on the next backup or the one after that. Then we're on to the 'right to be forgotten' era and all of this stuff, what we've just been looking at; that all goes away then too.'

'So it was a wipe?'

'Yep.' Jonny closed down the screenshare. 'Please don't make a joke, Sammy. It's half nine and I'm not in the mood.'

'Just another turd,' Sammy smiled, 'wiped off the ass of the internet.'

'You're so gross.'

'That's all I needed anyway, Jonny. Kay-thanx-bye!'

'Wait, what about-'

But she'd already hung up. She was fresh on the trail again. She had four windows open simultaneously, each one straining at the poor internet. Nevertheless, she would find him. She was sure of it.

So, you made your millions, Mister Lund, and proved to your family that there was indeed something in this whole internet game. But then, Mister Lund, you disappeared at the height of your fame. What, Mister Lund, is it exactly that you are hiding?

'You're mumbling again.'

John Barton walked up to her. she had been mindlessly circling, taking tiny footsteps along the edge of the clearing.

'I'm busy…' she mumbled.

She had a number of registries cracked and mirrored in servers out in Iceland. She was searching through them now. Mostly property transactions, purchase orders, planning permissions. Stuff that most people and even most government workers didn't know was backed up and collected into databases. She felt arms around her and breath on the back of her neck.

'Goddamnit, John Barton. Are you naked?'

'Aye,' he whispered into her ear. 'Now, are we going to celebrate our successful day, or what?'

'Mmm.'

'Come on. We rode horses, almost won the shooting competition, did some breaking and entering, located your gun and found the man who's behind it all. I think that calls for some sort of celebration.'

'Probably.'

Sammy blinked out of her trance. She span around, out of his arms and slapped him in the nethers.

'But it'll have to wait. Get your bloody pants on. We've a ride ahead of us.'

John Barton looked wounded, perhaps more from the slap in the balls than the idea of a protracted ride at dusk, though it was hard to tell. As he limped back to the camp, Sammy ran past him, spanking him hard.

'Come on, John Barton! I'm going to start taking the bloody tent down. If you don't hurry up, I'll roll your pants up and throw 'em in the river.'

*

Using her intel, Sammy tracked down a square kilometre of land that Zane Lund had purchased in the area. The ledger from Reginald Gunsmiths listed Lund's address as "unlisted". Technically this wasn't legal, not on a gun registry, but then disappearing was something of a speciality for Zane Lund. He couldn't hide land purchases though, and Sammy had found a considerable tract of land bought up just over three years ago in an area called Fallow's Creek.

Anything but fallow, the creek was totally overgrown, hidden from prying eyes. Local legends said that its real name was Gallow's Creek, and it was where the people of Avon Murray used to take the possessed to hang them. It was far enough away from town that they wouldn't hear the screams of the damned as they came to reclaim the bodies.

It was an hour's ride from where they'd pitched their tents and, having packed everything up, they left at just gone 10pm. The horses were spooked in the dark, as was John Barton. It was only the manic glint in Sammy's eye that drove them on. She dragged herself out of a hospital bed to be here, John Barton reminded himself, nursing his wounded pride and spanked testicles. If the threat of death couldn't slow her down, it was unlikely that he could either.

*

When they finally arrived at the Creek it was past midnight. The air was still. A thin haze hung over the twisted foliage and, difficult to make out in the cloudy night, a sheltered compound could be seen at the base of the valley. A road ran up to it, ending at a wall. Sammy presumed the wall slid back or lifted up as, looking down over it, she saw a winding path leading around a wildflower garden and up to an ornamental front entrance. Where the rest of the compound was flattened concrete, looking like a stealth fighter or other piece of military emplacement, the entrance was instead a mix of neon-blue light and white plastic.

Soft lighting gave the place a calming aura. It was welcoming. It oozed luxury.

'We're pulling up here,' Sammy whispered, falling off her horse. 'You alright?'

'I'm fine,' she whispered from the ground. 'Tie up the horses and then set up camp where we can't be spotted from the road. Make sure not to use any torches or open flames. I'll stay here and keep watch.'

'So, let me get this right?' John Barton leapt effortlessly off his horse and took Sammy's by the reins. 'You'll lie here in a bush while I do all the work in the pitch dark?'

'That's pretty much it, yes.'

She opened a binocular app on her phone and started peering towards the door.

'You make it sound like I'm doing nothing, John. When you and I know that my work is, in fact, much more important than yours.'

'Thanks, Sammy.' John led the horses off to set up camp. He'd hide just behind the ridge. That way he could guarantee they'd be invisible by morning.

Sammy settled down into a long night of watching. It didn't take long for her to work out her pattern. She'd start by looking without seeing, letting her eyes take in the whole undifferentiated dark. That way, if there was any movement at all then she'd have a chance of picking it up. From there she ran the binoculars slowly and meticulously down the road and then back up it again. No vehicles appeared, but if they did then she'd be onto them. She did a few minutes surveying the whole scene again before turning the binoculars onto the entrance and the wildflower garden. Maybe there'd be some early morning visitors, or perhaps a patrol? Finally, she would search the whole roof of the compound, its many angular concrete walls, just in case snipers were positioned there.

Would there be snipers? Who knew? Probably. Why not? She had a pattern established anyway, a patrol route for her eyes. Now she just had to keep it up until morning.

*

'Coffee?'

By the time the morning came Sammy was bleary eyed and although still awake, she was now snoring audibly. John Barton crouched down in the bush next to her and noted that she was, once again, covered in mud.

'I've worked it out, John Barton,' she whispered, slightly manic. 'I know how it all works. Only thing is, there's no way in. Not for sneaking. That I'm sure of.'

'Have your coffee and take us back to the start,' John muttered, passing her a travel mug. 'I'm not reading you.'

'I snuck up there, in the night,' she slurped at the thick black brew. 'I reconnoitred it. They didn't see me. There was no way, I was too stealthy.'

'A real solid snake,' John smirked.

'Enough about your night-time obsessions, John Barton.'

She was awake enough for giving him shit at least. 'I found out that it's a celebrity resort. Though obviously it's not a resort, but that's what it calls itself. Who knows what goulish things go on in there. It's called Lund Acres. Crap name. There's no way that this place is more than an acre. Anyway, that's what it's called and that's what they say they do.'

'Right,' John slurped and she slurped back. 'So where does that leave us? What's going on?'

'Something bad. I'm certain of it. But exactly what, I just don't know.'

'And…' he hesitated to ask. 'What is it that we're doing now? What's the plan? Sleep, hopefully,' he added. 'You've been up all night.'

'I'll sleep when I've had kids.'

She lifted her phone with the binoculars app again.

'This stuff's more important. And as for the plan: well, it's not something I'm proud of. But I think it's time that I called in the big guns.'

Without warning she passed him her coffee, letting go before he had time to grab it, splashing it all over his trousers. She was already striding up to the top of the creek, her mobile in her hand, searching for signal.

*

She barely heard the dial tone before the phone was picked up.

'Yo, this is Marley. Got news?'

'Ey up, Marley. It's Sammy!'

'Sammy?'

'Sammy Habib, I work for you.'

'Not any more you don't, Sammy.'

She could hear his shiteating grin coming down the line.

'You're a wanted criminal, yah? We don't employ those at Bantz. Only the unwanted sort, you get me? Anyway, darling, what can I do for ya?'

She hated Marley, but he was the only person at management level who seemed to have any staying power. He'd been in the job for four months, beating the record set by the previous incumbent by three months. In Bantz years he was almost at retirement.

'This whole being on the lamb thing, Marley; it's bringing me down.'

'I can tell, babe. Your voice is shot to shit'

'I know, tell me about it.'

She laughed a smoky laugh. It echoed in the trees like a dying bird.

'Anyways, think Bantz might shoot me some expenses? Got this niche retreat all picked out. Lund Acres. Real nice. Celebrities-'

'Celebrities?' Marley did his strange, drawn-out, buh-huh-huh laugh down the phone. 'I like your thinking, Sammy. All those police chases really bad for the anxiety, yeah? Might as well take a load off. Churlish not to.'

'Exactly. Lots of celebrities, maybe topless, no biggie. You know how I like to whip 'em out, Marley. All about that nature girl shit. Get us on the guest list anyway and I'll send you my holiday snaps. Sound like a deal?'

'Lund Acres, yeah?' She could hear him rolling a holographic mouse around on his desk. 'Well, Sammy, it's pricey stuff. Dark web exclusive, get me? I'm going to want a hella good slideshow when you get back, yeah? I'm talking like Kylie-Minogue-doing-butt-stuff tasty.'

'Kylie Minogue's old, you creaky old man,' she laughed. 'Don't drop those retro references around Duncan or you'll be mailing your CV to Country Life. Anyway, I've got a new shooter with me. Jonny's busy rubbing his pennies together for warmth like, after you cut his hours. No get up and go, Marley, not like us. The new guy's solid anyway, you'll like him. Name of John Barton. Sort him a ticket too, yeah?'

'No can do, sweetie. Can barely justify getting you in, there's no room for your new gigolo. Sorry, babes.'

'He's not a gigolo.' She broke character. 'He's my photographer. He's essential.'

Then Marley broke character too.

'I don't care if he's Ansel Adams, Sammy. He's not getting a ticket.'

You don't want Marley breaking character, Sammy thought, without his irony he's an irredeemably evil bastard. She swallowed, sighed and spoke again, curling her hair around her finger.

'Sure thing, daddy-O. Table for one it'll be then. Who knows, maybe I can seduce some young, hip celeb like Kylie or Madonna or Doris Day… Nice Ansel Adams reference by the way, nerd. And thanks for the free money.'

'Stay radical, bitch.' His strange laugh honked down the phone again. Before hanging up she could hear him singing to himself; 'Breaking the law, Breaking the law…'

*

As she strode down to the makeshift camp she found John Barton frying up sausages. Why was it always sausage with him? She went straight to her tent, pulled out everything she needed – mostly phone gear – and pushed it into a backpack. The rest of her clothes, toiletries and John's first aid kit she left in a mound on the floor of the tent. She re-tied her shoes, stepped out of the tent and slung the pack onto her back.

'You want anything on these?' John asked her, his eyes on the pan. 'No ketchup I'm afraid, but we've brown sauce and some mustard.'

'I'm alright,' she stood stiffly, facing him.

'You need to eat, Sammy. You've been up all night.'

'I know, John Barton, but I won't be eating here.'

'You what?'

He turned to look at her. It was the first time, he realised, that she'd actually looked at him for any protracted length of time. She wasn't looking at her phone. She wasn't eyeing up the surrounding neighbourhood for criminal opportunities. She wasn't closing her eyes in ecstasy, which, he remembered lovingly, was the other way he'd seen her. No, she was staring right at him, her face fallen, serious. Too serious to really believe it was the same woman he'd known all this time. All these, well, three or four days…

'I'm going in to the compound, John Barton, and you're not to come with me.'

She could barely face it, seeing his incomprehension.

'This is what I came here to do. I really appreciate everything that you've done for me and-'

'What?' his heart sank, he couldn't hear. 'What are you on about, Sammy?'

'It's hard, John, I know. It's a bastard. But it's life. Life's a bastard.'

'What does life have to do with anything?'

He didn't get it. His brain wasn't letting him get it. His heart was rolling over and over in his chest.

'It moves on,' Sammy choked up. 'Life does. It finds a way and everything.'

'You're talking barmy,' John Barton called out. 'You can't just walk off. After all that we've… I've… Well, Sammy, what can I say? I think I love you!'

'Oh fuck off, John Barton!'

She felt herself crying. She turned and ran. She sprinted down, blindly into the foliage. She could hear him rise up behind her, wanting to run after her, but he had the pan and stove to look after, he had his things that tied him down. She would run, she could run. Nothing kept Sammy Habib down. Nothing tied her down.

Goddamnit, girl! You're a freelancer aren't you? You run and you run and you never stop fucking running until your legs wear down to bloody stumps and you're dead on the ground. Just – keep – running…

…and never look back.

*

When she reached that glowing front door, the one she'd been staring at all night, she was distraught. Tears ran down her face. She couldn't breathe. She was covered in mud and, once again, her face and arms were torn up from brambles and swelled with nettle stings. She had lost any sense of propriety. She couldn't hold herself together. What the hell was she going to do now?

The door swung open. Two beautiful women walked out to her. She was slumped on the floor. She looked up at them. They put a heavy fur coat around her shoulders and directed her in through the doorway.

Inside there was a small, incredibly neat man. He barely

registered Sammy's collapsed state. He'd seen it all before. It was normal. Instead, he walked to her, slow and precise. His heels clicked on the marble floor.

'Miss Samra Habib. Welcome. We hope you enjoy your stay at Lund Acres. Don't worry about your appearance. Our first pleasure will be to give you a full makeover, ready for entering the resort. Your employers phoned ahead and let us know that you were running around in the bushes. We had sort of wondered what you were doing when our cameras picked you up last night but never fear, we don't judge. You're in safe hands now. You can finally relax.'

She felt herself directed to an ipad. Her name was written there next to the description, 'world famous journalist.' Through her tears, she smiled. She pushed her finger into the registry and the screen turned green. With that, the neat man turned and walked away, his heels clicking on the marble.

Sammy was led away by the two tall women. She noticed they wore lab coats. She gave herself up, let herself be directed. The door closed behind her and she sniffed. 'I'm in. I made it.'

13

'We've taken your clothes to the laundry. You'll get them back once your stay with us has come to an end. We ask that all of our guests wear the robes provided. They are made of pure silk and optimised for your comfort. Lund Acres is a place of abundance. Here you can cast away the restraints of your busy life and live free. You may find the robes unusual at first, but they'll soon feel like you're wearing nothing at all.'

'Creepy,' Sammy muttered to herself as she was escorted out of a warm Romanesque bath by one of the two tall attendants. The other approached with a towel, as if to dry Sammy off.

'It's okay.'

Sammy made a grab for the towel. No way she'd be having these six-foot-four Barbie dolls rubbing her down. The robes were intimidating enough. Gleaming white with thin lines of turquoise piping.

I am immediately going to spill pasta down the front of that.

'If you would like privacy, Ms Habib, we can deploy the modesty curtain?'

'Deploy? Erm, I mean, sure thing!'

They must have clocked her holding the towel up. Did rich people enjoy having staff look at their naked bodies? Was she going to be dealing with this kind of thing the whole time?

'As you command.'

One of the women smiled, adding a small bow. The other made a swishing motion in the air and a hologram suddenly blinked into existence. It was being projected onto the steam from the bath. Sammy noted it and nodded. Impressive. With a flick of a wrist, the modesty curtain was initiated. A series of glass panels extended from the floor, reaching Sammy's neck height and then stopping. With a slight fizz, they frosted blue.

Sammy was impressed. The mix of art nouveau and Space Odyssey stuff ('tech-nouveau'? Is that what she'd call it in her article?) came off as smug, but deservedly so. Like it had earned the right to be insufferable.

The two attendants, for their part, saw only a grumbling head bobbing up and down. The occasional flail of limbs silhouetted behind the curtain. They'd spent the morning feeding, bathing, massaging, sewing up and generally pampering their new client. The gunwound had surprised them, but they kept a consultant surgeon on staff at all times who was able to reinforce the loose stitching and temporarily graft a layer of artificial skin over it, replacing the sodden and stinking sheep bandage. Diagnosing her with acute fatigue, they gave her a series of vitamin injections. These may have accounted for the vigorous motions displayed behind the screen.

'Wait a minute!' Sammy shouted over to them. 'Where are my pants?'

'Your..?'

'Underwear!'

'Oh, there is no underwear, Ms Habib. It is our fault. We should have explained. The robes are designed to take account of your natural body shape. Underwear would merely add an unwanted layer of restriction.'

'Fucksake.' Sammy sighed as she slid the pure white folds down over her. 'This is some hubristic shit right here. Keep me away from the curry is all I'm saying.'

As soon as she had put on the final item of clothing, a pastel-blue stole that made her look like a space-priest, the glass immediately defrosted and fell back to the floor. The two attendants smiled sweetly at their new and improved, temporarily clean, guest.

'How did the glass know to fall then?' Sammy asked as they took her by the arms and led her away. 'Were you watching me on a camera the whole time?'

'There are no cameras, Ms Habib. You needn't worry about that. Cameras are forbidden in Lund Acres. It was purely machine learning. You'll find that machine learning is used extensively throughout Lund Acres to optimise your relaxation experience.'

'Machine learning, my arse,' Sammy smirked.

Her face then fell as she realised that, based upon the modesty curtain experience, the machine had undoubtedly now learned her arse. It could probably pick it out of a line-up of a million different arses, or 3D print a perfect replica of it. Grim.

*

They led her down an ornate corridor, more tech-nouveau. Ornamental wires spiralled, integrated into wooden support beams. The wall was painted with twisting branches and frail leaves, all overlapping and hosting tiny, glistening bugs which, looked at carefully enough, were actually LEDs indicating system functionality. Like Rivendell with a modem, Sammy thought.

They paused at a perfectly circular door.

'Before we enter Lund Acres,' one of the attendants said, (Sammy still couldn't tell the difference between them) 'we ask that you place all of your electronic equipment into secure storage.'

'Do not fear,' she had seen the panic in Sammy's eyes, 'there will be electronics made available to you upon entering Lund Acres. We must request, however, that your personal equipment is left here.'

'Why?'

'Decompression,' they replied in unison.

'What?'

The first opened the door and gestured. It was clear she'd rather Sammy keep moving and find out for herself rather than persist with questions. They never had this problem with models, pop stars, actresses and the like. Their usual clientele simply adopted the part allotted to them, no questions asked.

Sammy, by contrast, panicked. She grabbed desperately at her electronic equipment. She turned back to the Barbies and shut the door.

'Just making a private call, ladies. Gotta shut you out. Cheers, love. Cheers…'

She saw them roll their eyes as the door sealed.

Okay. What next, what next? Sammy's head filled with a rushing sound, all the blood trying to get into it at once. She could call John Barton, apologise, try and explain… Or she could send out a series of tweets, tag her location, see if she could get the police out here. Surely that would be more sensible than this James Bond act? Damn, which one? What to do?

There was a wall of lockers. A single one was open. This was where she was to deposit her gear. Her sweet, sweet electronic eyes and ears.

She felt inside the locker and knocked at the plastic door. Something told her it was lined with lead. Once the gear was inside it was truly off the grid. She was truly off the grid.

'Nope!'

Sammy intuitively knew that it wasn't happening. She only had a couple of minutes. She didn't know how, but she'd get her phone in. She had to.

She patted at her robes. Nope, no pockets. Of course not. She ran her fingers along the edge of each piece of fabric hoping to find a weakness in the lining. No, each was a single piece of silk. There was no lining to speak of. Damn. Looking at the table of equipment she had a brainwave. She unwrapped her headphones and tied the cable around her middle. She would make a cradle for her phone. She only had to get past security, after all. Then she'd find a place to hide it. Maybe find a bag. Wrapped up in the headphone cable, she realised it wasn't as long as she'd hoped.

She tried a few tying methods but each time her phone fell through. So strapping on her phone was impossible, then.

No pockets, no strings. She held the phone in her hand. She needed to get it in. She measured its width between finger and thumb. Would she dare to try it prisoner-style? It was quite a large phone. It'd be a stretch…

Then, as she was rubbing warily at her body, she remembered her recent surgery. She opened her robes, pulled off the headphone cable that was still wrapped around her, and inspected the piece of skin they'd just grafted onto her an hour ago. Now, she thought, what did the consultant tell her? This wasn't to replace her real skin, but merely to protect it. Her real skin, with the new stitching, was secure beneath this layer. This was an extra layer which, once the first layer was healed, could safely be peeled off.

In the meantime, she also remembered, it would feel just like real skin, with all the pain and pleasure receptors of normal skin.

Okay, Sammy thought, I've worked out how to get my phone in. All it entails is tearing open my own skin and I'll then have a perfect, hermetically sealed, phone-sized pocket in my torso.

'Fuck me,' she whispered to herself, her breathing heavy with the realisation. 'Am I really going to do this? Do I really care so much about this piece-of-shit story?'

*

The door too was lined with lead. An extra precaution against phone signal leaking out of the lockers. Thanks to this, the two attendants stood waiting outside couldn't hear Sammy screaming as she tore a hole in her flesh with her car keys.

Thankfully, being an artificial graft, there was no blood.

Sammy reappeared at the door with a demented smile.

'Are all your electronics securely stowed?' they asked her.

'Absolutely!' Sammy grinned, her teeth clenched. 'And the tray tables are stowed in the upright position and everything!'

'Then we shall proceed to decompression.'

She found herself guided back along the corridor, an arm in each of the tall attendants', making her feel like a naughty schoolgirl. They turned a corner and passed a tasteful mural of a stoat. It was carrying a circuit board and riding on top of a deer with aerial antlers. Cheesy, Sammy nodded, but nicely rendered. The deer was staring on to the end of the corridor where a series of wrought iron twirls hung from a hatch.

'Through here–' one attendant began.

The other continued, 'is decompression. It is a quick, painless and routine process whereby your alignment is readjusted, desynchronised from your stressful everyday life and resynchronised with the stress-free world of Lund Acres.'

They opened the hatch and Sammy could see that the interior was bright white. There was a small cube in the centre which could be either a chair or a table, or maybe an exhaust chute. The rest was featureless and bright. The two attendants, finally revealing their impatience, pushed her into the room by the shoulders. Sammy turned back to see them sealing the door.

'Why did you say 'painless'?' she shouted after them.

The hatch sealed with a thoom sound. The air sucked out, leaving a totally still and silent space.

'All I'm saying is,' Sammy shouted into the blank air. 'Maybe don't say 'painless' next time. It makes me very conscious of the fact that this will probably hurt a lot!'

There was no answer. Ten seconds of silence passed and then she heard a clicking from the rear of the room. Was it opposite the hatch? She couldn't remember where the hatch was. Where had the hatch gone?

Instead, the clicking turned to whooshing, and the whooshing to a clicking-and-hissing sound. Then, like a car boot opening, the entire wall slid upwards to reveal a bright summer's day. They were in the middle of a market square. The houses looked Grecian, the shop fronts French. There was an ornate fountain in the centre of a cobbled square, and small groups of tall and elegant robe-wearers swished through the streets arm in arm.

Sammy stepped out of the decompression chamber and felt the warm sun on her face. The sky above was startling blue, with faint wisps of cloud like dabs from an impressionist's paintbrush. The Barbies had been right; the sun poured through her robes like she was wearing nothing at all. She looked back at the swaying robe-wearers and saw how clean and tanned they all were. Some were tall and athletic, others short with big heads and highly photogenic smiles. She'd seen many of them before. She had given their movies bad reviews and put together slideshows about their cellulite. Between the celebrities moved servants. The servant's robes mimicked their client's white-lined-with-turquoise colouring, but they were inverted. They wore instead a complementary turquoise-lined-with-white. The servants, Sammy noted, weren't carrying anything. They were even smiling what looked like real smiles. They too were tall and handsome. The only difference Sammy could make out was the servant's ability to conjure holographic UIs from thin air. She saw a girl open one and, as if to prove her point, dial in coffee orders for two young Formula E racers.

'What is this place?' Sammy spoke aloud, adding in her head, and how the hell does it fit into that tiny concrete compound?

'Welcome to Lund Acres,' came a soothing voice from behind her.

Sammy turned. 'Bloody hell! Another one!'

The six-foot-four blonde beauty ignored Sammy's comment and swept her arm out across the square.

'Here you'll find everything you could possibly desire. Your wildest dreams can be fulfilled. Anything you wish for will be brought to you within minutes. All you have to do is speak to one of our allocated guardians. You can identify them by the blue colouration of their robes. Everything here is free and you are welcome to as much of it as you like. If you desire excess, we can provide excess. As you will soon discover, however, excess easily granted holds no real pleasure. We find that once our guests are settled in, all they really desire is tranquillity, privacy and politeness.'

'Politeness?'

'Oh yes, Ms Habib,' the guardian smiled, 'we find politeness to be one of the truest of all life's pleasures.'

'Fuckin' eh?'

'Indeed. Now, if you'll care to accompany me, Ms Habib, I shall provide you with a tour of the facilities. Well, an indicative tour at least,' she laughed, 'we have the agora you see, where we are now, and the accommodation district comprising of both luxury towers for the vertically inclined and regal estates for the more traditional. The leisure district sits just beyond those trees over there and caters for tastes both intellectual and carnal. If you desire experiences not permitted by our current laws of physics there is also the VR centre, where our team of in-house experiential designers can procedurally generate entire universes more to your liking...'

'Like a videogame, right?'

'Sort of.'

This guardian seemed less robotic than the other two. Sammy quite liked her. As they passed a bistro where an aging rockstar sat drinking with his family, Sammy realised the sheer scale of the place. They had turned a corner to reveal seven vast towers in the distance, the space between gleaming with white buildings, terracotta roofs, golf courses, forests and landscape gardens. The guardian was still describing the facilities. Sammy felt like it would go on for quite some time.

'...and then there are the hiking zones, particularly popular with families, where pets are made available to accompany you on walks and you can bathe in many waterfalls and warm pools positioned at strategic locations around the mountains-'

'You guys have… mountains?'

'Only six so far, but we're currently expanding our provision. We hope to have twenty-eight by next year.'

She laughed. She sounded more casual now, more human; less like a weird cultist.

'We've been surprised by the level of interest! Who knew people loved climbing mountains so much!'

'Crazy!' Sammy smiled back.

This is fucked up, she was thinking. Is this like a Tardis, or what? Is it a vision? She couldn't remember putting any headgear on, and VR wasn't usually this convincing. Had they drugged her? Well, they had drugged her, she had watched them put the needles in, but was there more than just vitamins in those syringes?

But then, Sammy had done plenty of drugs before. What drug could accomplish this?

She needed to get a photo. It didn't matter how. She needed to get a photo and, ideally, send it out with some sort of location data attached so Jonny or Marley or John Barton or someone could tell her where the hell this paradise was supposed to be? It couldn't possibly be on the outskirts of Avon Murray. It couldn't even be in the North. It just couldn't!

They passed two teenage girls. One of them Sammy recognised as a friend of the once-missing Mel Ditty. They were striding down the cobbled road naked, giggling and eating some excessively shiny apples. The guardian was still talking.

'You should note, Ms Habib, that Lund Acres does not comply with the restrictive laws of the UK Government. Drugs are legal here, as are weapons, should you want weapons, and public nudity is actively encouraged. You'll note that the robes you are wearing feel like you're wearing…'

'…nothing at all. Yes, I've noticed.'

Sammy was gazing around for some excuse to lose her guardian.

'We have very few rules here, Ms Habib,' the guardian smiled. 'You'll find us an exceptionally liberal people.'

As if in response to the guardian's blissed-out smile, Sammy felt a sudden strange clattering inside her robes. She wriggled and slapped at her body. It was like a crane fly was stuck in there, up against her skin, near her wound.

'Argh!' she yelled, too rocked by internal bug-panic to manage words.

'What is it, Ms Habib?' The guardian looked concerned.

'It's a bloody...' she swatted at herself, feeling the wriggling working its way up around to her back and up towards her neck, 'a bloody spider or a... crane fly or something? It's stuck in my robe!'

Whatever it was, it reached her neckline. It was then that she felt two tiny hands pulling back her robes. Two tiny feet kicked off from the back of her neck. Then, she saw it: a tiny woman. She flew on long, golden wings and she was wearing the turquoise robes of a guardian. She was only about six inches high, with a large afro adding another inch on top. Sammy noted that the robes definitely worked better on a darker complexion. The tiny dragonfly lady looked like an emissary from a more developed future. All the white people she'd seen so far had looked like cultists on a cruise.

From nowhere, another guardian stepped forward. He held out a small disk in his muscular hand, a tiny podium standing in the middle of it. The tiny flying woman glided elegantly down onto the disc and took her place at the podium.

'Captain Adisa,' the guide saluted her tiny comrade. 'I was just giving Ms Habib a tour of the facilities. She is newly arrived this morning.'

'I know,' the Captain replied, her voice deep and authoritative, her accent Zimbabwean. 'She is carrying a camera.'

'A camera?' the tall woman was shocked. She turned to Sammy with a betrayed look. 'Is this true, Ms Habib? Have you brought a camera in to Lund Acres?'

'It's not a camera,' Sammy said. 'It's a phone.'

'A camera phone!' Captain Adisa corrected her.

'Who calls them camera phones in 2028?'

'Mrs Habib,' the tall guardian put a hand on Sammy's shoulder. 'I'm afraid that you have committed a violation of the Lund Acres judicial code. As much as it pains me to say it, I'm afraid that we will have to ask you to leave.'

'Take her!' Captain Adisa ordered, rising into the air on her golden wings so the muscular guardian could lunge at Sammy with both hands.

'Woah!'

Sammy wriggled out of the way. She knew this place was trouble. She could smell it when she came in the door. Sometimes trouble smelled rank, but more often it smelled like too much soap. Not waiting for the hulking guardian to regain his balance, Sammy thrust her fingers into her skin-pocket, roaring with the pain of it. A flash of bright light shot into her brain as she tore her phone out. Its screen caught on her gunwound stitches on its way out.

'Seize her!' She could hear Captain Adisa shouting, although without her podium it sounded like the cry of a falsetto ant. 'She must not escape!'

'I have no plans to escape!' Sammy shouted back.

She pushed one hand out towards the guardians, warning them back. The other was poised over her phone.

'One false move and I'll tweet!'

'What?' the blonde guardian asked, still hurt and baffled that anyone would think of breaking the rules.

'Every tweet I send is loaded with location data, a timestamp and an encrypted stamp of personal verification. The police have been watching my feeds around the clock ever since I got this stupid shotgun wound, thinking I'm some sort of criminal. All I have to do is tweet – random letters and numbers, emojis, epic memes, anything – and they'll be down here before you even have time to set up a tripadvisor page,' she wasn't sure where she was going with that last bit, '…and, I can tell you, you're going to be getting some bad reviews!'

That'll do, Sammy reckoned, it was sort of witty, provided you didn't think about it too much.

The guardians had frozen in place. Sammy held her thumb out, hovering it over the 'SEND' button. She noticed that other guardians had appeared now, surrounding her. Responding to the Captain who had landed on his shoulder and was whispering into his ear, the muscular guardian took the podium-disc back out and held it up to Sammy. The Captain flew down to it, landed elegantly, and remounted the podium.

'Okay,' she began, 'you have us. Now, what is it that you want?'

'Nothing much,' Sammy straightened up. 'Just an interview with Zane Lund.'

There was a sharp intake of breath from the circle of guardians. The woman who had been her guide only a moment before raised her hand in shock.

'Oh, don't be so dramatic!' Captain Adisa laughed. 'Get a hold of yourselves! If Samra Habib wants to speak to the boss, then she can speak to the boss!'

She laughed again as many of the guardians' faces burned red, embarrassed by their own melodrama.

The Captain continued. 'And you, Ms Habib. I like you! You don't take any shit. It is commendable in a woman. Come, I shall take you to the man you wish to see!'

And with that, the Captain rose into the air on her golden wings and led Sammy past the baffled guardians, down the cobbles, toward a distant tower.

14

The tower was a masterpiece of spiralling white wood and pale blue light. Its geometries seemed impossible. How could it so easily defy gravity? What power was in it that could overcome the basic desire of all stuff to fall groundwards? The extreme delicacy of the support structure, the subtle majesty of the interiors, all visible through four-storey panes of glass, left a weird taste in her mouth. It was like CGI. Like a big toy.

Sammy was led into the tower by Captain Adisa. She made an effort to follow the miniature Captain's erratic flightpath. She was flanked by two guardians. There were no extra security in the tower as such, although she had the vague sense of machine eyes perving on her, ticking off her bits on some horny database.

The lobby was like a cybernetic hunting lodge. Clearly the peaceful murals of electronically-enhanced wildlife were not enough for Zane Lund. In their place were chairs and rugs, wall-hangings made from animal parts. Zebra-skin throws lay on ox-hide chairs. A lion-skin rug roared underfoot, defending its territory from an animatronicised bear who leaned out, offering to take guests' robes. A stuffed alligator revolved in the air.

As she looked up, Sammy realised that every floor hung loose independently. You could see all the way up to the penthouse through the tower's jenga-like structure. Now that definitely shouldn't stay up.

They marched past the receptionist. She opened a floating UI and flicked a couple of switches. The bookcase that Captain Adisa had been flapping aggressively towards slid open, revealing a lift. It was lit in deep blue. As they stepped in, Sammy noticed it came with a blacklight. The guardians around her lit up like Tron characters; the white piping on their robes outlining them in negative. Sammy, by contrast, glowed like a toothpaste advert. As she grimaced, she realised her teeth were probably neon white too. She sucked on her gums instead.

'We are here,' Captain Adisa announced. Without amplification her voice was tiny and shrill.

The announcement was enough, however. The lift door swept open to reveal a huge penthouse floor. It almost empty but for a desk and two chairs. These were positioned on an implausibly long balcony, stretching out into the air twenty-five feet from the main building.

'We're going out there, right?'

Sammy jerked her head in the direction of the dangerous desk. A guardian nodded. Sammy pulled a face.

'Looks bloody lethal.'

'Keep walking!' the Captain shouted. 'Do not be a coward!'

'Alright, alright!' Sammy followed. 'It's aright you being missus Big Balls when you've got wings. One gust of wind and I'm dead.'

Thankfully, the air was calm. Almost too calm, Sammy thought, narrowing her eyes. As they approached the table, it narrowed so that they could only walk single file. Sammy wanted to reach her hands out, images of tightrope walkers filling her brain, but fought the urge. Zane Lund had made it very clear that appearances were important to him. If he wants to live in a Roger Dean painting, Sammy thought, more power to him. She'd humour him, for now.

As she approached the desk, the two guardians behind withdrew. It was just her and the tiny, flying Captain. The top of Zane Lund's head rested on the back of his chair.

'Are you going to rotate menacingly?' Sammy asked, sitting down in her own chair, not waiting for an invitation.

Slowly, menacingly, Zane Lund rotated his chair around

until he was facing her.

'Why, Samra Habib, I don't know what you mean.'

'Well, you just did it, so…'

'Is a man not entitled to some melodrama every once in a while?'

'I suppose,' Sammy shrugged.

Even in her glistening white robes she felt scruffy, underdressed. She noted that he wore a three-piece suit. Lund clearly wasn't a fan of feeling naked either.

'They tell me, Samra Habib, that you smuggled a phone into my resort by concealing it within an open wound.'

Sammy nodded. As she studied the man's face she noted the slight twitching under his left eye, the studied nonchalance. Yes, she told herself, this was the man that shot me. I might have seen a baby, but it was this man. No doubt.

'I have to say that I find this very impressive, Ms Habib. Such a level of commitment should be greatly rewarded, we should hope?'

'What can I say?' Sammy shrugged. 'I'm a sucker for Candy Crush. Take it with me everywhere, like. High scores to beat. Yeah man,' she folded her arms, 'I just gotta have my Crush, y'know?'

'And a comedian too!' Lund laughed.

It wasn't quite an evil laugh, but Sammy could tell he'd been practising. Maybe he had a laugh coach. He came across as the sort of man who would.

Sammy noted the man's youth. The photos she had last seen of him were, when? Five, ten years ago? If anything he looked even younger now. There was not a wrinkle on his face and, other than two patches of grey at the temples, his hair was jet black. Sammy got the impression that he dyed in the grey for gravitas. He radiated focus, which is another way of saying that he leaned forward a lot and didn't blink. Only vast wealth, Sammy thought, blinking, or vast stupidity, could give a man that level of control over his eyelids. He might have dropped out of uni, but Zane Lund seemed anything but dumb.

'So, Samra-'

'Look, can you just call me Sammy?'

She was tiring of his whole supervillain act.

'Sammy?' He steepled his fingers. 'So, you wish for informality?'

'I wish, mate, for you to just use my name, alright?'

She was surprised at how pissed off she was getting.

'You drag me up here like this is all some brilliant scheme you've been working on for years. "Finally!" she was doing the voice of a Bollywood villain, "I have you in my power!" When you had no idea who I was until about ten minutes ago. If your pervy flying midget hadn't have been scampering around under my clothes you'd still be none the wiser now! Where is she, by the way?'

Sammy looked around, twisting in her seat, but could see no sign of the Captain. Lund had leaned back in his chair, his hands on his lap, slightly pouting.

'Pixie has gone to... recompress.'

'Pixie?'

'This is what I call her,' Lund smiled, revealing the work of an evil smile coach. 'She is my Pixie, and she makes my wishes come true, you see? I warn you, however, she is no Tinkerbell to be trifled with. Pixie was the leading mercenary operating out of the Congo. Part of the conflict – still ongoing – concerned the possession of certain... elements essential for our operations here. She understood the importance of those in advance. She has a PhD in biochemical engineering from Cambridge, and she kills without mercy.'

'Good for her,' Sammy swallowed. She turned back in her chair again but saw no sign of the deadly doctor. 'Not bad for a woman who's only six inches tall. Puts my limited achievements into some sort of perspective.'

'You are being flippant, Sammy Habib. You consider it an endearing quality but it merely reveals your lack of seriousness. I am beginning to doubt my capacity to work with you. You are beginning to try my patience.'

'Oh, am I?'

Sammy gave up her search for the Captain and turned back to him.

'Well, Mr Lund, I found it very trying to lose a few feet of my small intestine when they were splattered up the walls of the Manchester Hilton. I do, indeed, find it rather a bore that I'll never eat solid foods again. But, Mr Lund, what I find far more trying than all of that, is the existence of an entire fucking utopian civilisation held in a far-too-small, desperately secret compound on the outskirts of Avon-nowhere-Murray.

'Now, I don't want to cast aspersions, Mr Lund, but it appears to me that this shit must be pretty far from kosher otherwise your face would be plastered across the front pages of every website in the world… and print newspapers too, if they still exist.'

She noticed his eyes light up at the sound of news, of fame.

'There's a lot of questions that I want answering, Mr Zane Lund. Too many, in fact. And I do find that these questions can be so very, very trying…'

She placed her phone on the table.

'That it might be best to bring the police in here to sort it all out for me.'

'I see…' Lund closed his eyes.

Somewhere in there, she could tell, he was still thinking about fame.

'Well, Sammy… perhaps I can offer you something in the way of an explanation? Perhaps this will provide you with solace at this most trying of times.'

'Yes,' Sammy smiled, initiating the hidden switch that turned on her phone's voice recorder. 'Some explanations are, I think, in order.'

'Where would like me to begin?'

'Where are you keeping the kidnapped celebrities?'

He snorted. She had gone in hard. Too hard.

'No-one has kidnapped any celebrities, Sammy. Our guests come here of their own accord. Everyone is treated equally here in Lund Acres, both guests and guardians alike. Life is plentiful here, there is enough for everyone. Of course, with our price point, our exclusivity, our guarantee of total discretion, we do indeed attract what you call celebrities, but to say that they have been kidnapped is highly inaccurate.'

'Then what happened to Mel Ditty?'

'I am not at liberty to divulge information regarding any individual guest.' Lund leaned in, 'but I can guarantee that anyone who leaves Lund Acres unsatisfied does so on account of their own psychological weaknesses. What we provide here, Sammy, is a Garden of Eden. Some of our guests, I am sorry to say, are not yet... emotionally sophisticated enough to experience its benefits in moderation.'

'That may be so, Mr Lund, but what about the party?'

He blinked.

'You know the one. That night. My guts on the wall. Ring any bells?'

'I do not know to what you refer, Sammy.'

Blink-blink-blink went Zane's eyelids. Gotcha. She could see him swallow. Centre himself. So he has a media training coach too? How nice for him.

'I can't say that mistakes don't happen. We provide very clear instructions to our guests as to the regular procedure of retrieval. Not everyone, Sammy, turns up in the bushes outside like you do. No, we offer a premium service. You wait at a set location at a set time, unaccompanied, and we will extract you. It is safe and it is clean.

She could sense a quiet anger boiling in him now.

'If someone decides to schedule a drug-fuelled orgy and invite every famous person in Manchester to come to their extraction zone, all of them bringing armed bodyguards, then NO, Sammy, we cannot guarantee their safety under such conditions! There is not an organisation in the world that could!'

'So you killed them?'

'Sammy!' He yelled. 'Why are you fixated on these... these

frivolous details?'

'The hole you blasted in my guts might seem an insignificant detail to you, Mr Lund-'

'I did not say that it was insignificant, Sammy!'

He rose from his chair now and began pacing, gesturing. It was an impressive feat for a man on a very thin platform thirty stories up.

Walking in the air, he ranted, 'I said that it was frivolous! Frivolous! In that it is frivolous to talk of such things when our technology has not only solved them, cured them, made them a simple matter of repair, but it, our superior technology, has surpassed them, surpassed such banalities as repair and maintenance. Do you simply not see, Sammy, how frivolous your questions are when I possess, here, within my mind, the knowledge that will remake the world? It will remake it, Sammy, not once, but a million times over! Lund Acres is not the main issue here, Sammy, and celebrities certainly aren't. Our technology, Sammy; it can give every man, woman and child their very own universe.'

A shiver ran down Sammy's spine. She was used to tech bullshit. She'd seen her share of TED talks. But this felt like something else. She could see, burning there in the man's eyes, not only a faith that what he was saying was true, but a certainty. He spoke as if he had seen it, lived in it every day. He was frustrated because she couldn't even conceive of it.

'But what is it?' she asked, 'what are you talking about?'

'Pixie!' he clapped.

Sammy turned in her chair but found a hand already on her shoulder. She looked up to see Captain Adisa, seven-feet-tall, her wings folded behind her like huge golden banners. She leaned down and dropped a heavy object into Sammy's lap. Sammy, her heart racing, picked it up.

It was a sphere, perfectly smooth, about the size of a cricket ball. Inside was a dark mass, swirling. She held it to the light and gazed inside.

'That object, Sammy,' Lund announced, 'which you are holding in your hands. That bauble. That is a solar system.'

'What?'

'A complete and functioning solar system. A binary star surrounded by six planets. Two habitable, one explorable, three that are there primarily as ballast.'

Sammy stared deep into the darkness of the sphere. She could see nothing, only tiny specks floating around. But what they were floating around... that was, absolutely, undeniably, a real binary star. It was the size of a pinhead.

'And this...' Lund wasn't done. Captain Adisa placed a metal box on his desk. 'Thank you, Pixie! This...' he lifted out a slimy and gelatinous sphere; 'this is a white blood cell.'

Sammy didn't know what to think. She listened to her own breathing. The blood rushed around in her head. A head filled with white blood cells, presumably.

'Here!' Lund held out his hand. 'Pass me the solar system.'

Sammy looked down at the stars and planets and seemingly endless space that she held cupped in her hands. She couldn't move with it. She was transfixed. As if viewing the scene from outside of her own body, she watched as the Captain plucked the solar system from her hands and carried it over to Zane Lund. Lund, lifting the solar system briefly into the air to admire his handiwork, turned back to the white blood cell and dropped it in.

The solar system sank into the white blood cell. It was visible for a moment, a black patch sinking into a cloudy puddle of milk, and then, seeming to burst, it disappeared.

Contented by the look of pure horror on Sammy's face, Lund took the white blood cell in both hands and lifted it above his head. He walked to the edge of the balcony and launched it off. Standing on the precipice, he watched it fall like a naughty kid.

Pixie rotated her arm in the air, opening a holographic UI. She opened a window and hit a button requesting a clean-up crew.

Sammy thought she heard a splash hundreds of feet below her.

Zane Lund returned to his chair. He stared at Sammy, and Sammy stared back. After a quiet moment passed, he spoke.

'I call it the size tool.'

'The size tool?'

'A device for resizing any given object. You simply select the size tool, select your object, drag and click. Any object can be any size.'

'But... how?'

'Do you have a PhD in physics, Sammy?'

'No.'

'Then you're going to struggle, aren't you?'

He said it without malice. His voice showed a genuine desire for her to understand.

'Let's just say that we began with pure elements. The laws of physics provide no definitive reason for things to be a certain size. It is a matter of relativity, you see, and until now we understood that to mean that, although things might be different in a different universe, in ours we did things a certain way. It was, we thought, a way that we were stuck with. Are you following me so far, Sammy?'

'Sure,' she nodded. If she wasn't, then her voice recorder was.

'Well, this is where the real discovery comes in: uridium. It was Pixie that first brought it to the attention our agents in the Congo. Her soldiers located a vast quantity of it abandoned by previous mining operations. Nobody, it seemed, knew what to do with it. One day there would be vast mountains of it. The next morning, where once the pile had been, there were only specks of it left lying in the dust. Anything it touched would rapidly distort too. Uridium is an interdimensional element, you see. It is not bound by the arbitrary figures defining our own universe. It exists between many universes simultaneously, or so we theorise. At the very least, it is detached from our own.

'When Pixie found it, the miners considered it cursed. Raw

uridium, you see, will affect every element differently. We saw a miner wash his hands in water contaminated with uridium. His skin grew to such a size that it rolled off his hands like custard. His tendons shrank by half, snapping every bone, as his muscles appeared to disappear completely. An autopsy later revealed that they had shrunk to the size of an ant.'

'...and you are... what?'

'You are impatient, Sammy. I am almost there. You see, it took us a very long time. Two and a half years. That is an age when it comes to tech. But, holed up here in Avon Murray, Lund Acres, whatever you wish to call it. Here, in secret, I learned how to manipulate uridium, how to bend it to my will. Once I had done this, Sammy, then all I needed was a catchy name. Then I could change the history of the world forever.'

Sammy swallowed. 'So, you picked the size tool?'

'Yes,' Lund smiled, 'it is catchy don't you think? Sort of benign, even mundane. 'Hey honey," now it was Lund that was doing voices, "fancy a swim?' 'Sure thing, darling, I'll just put a bowl of hot water in the garden, select the size tool, and we'll have an Olympic-sized swimming pool before you've even got your swimsuit on!"

'It's a nice idea...'

'Give me some credit here, Sammy!' He was jovial now. Explaining his invention had made him giddy. 'It's a bit more than a nice idea!'

'So Lund Acres... this is?'

'In the measurements of the regular world? A four-foot cube sat in the smallest room of the compound. Of course, 'regular world' will soon be a redundant category...'

Sammy bowed her head. She was trying to think of a question, but the vastness of what he was saying pushed everything else out. She felt a slight breeze across her nipples. 'One last question, Mr Lund.'

'Anything you like, Sammy.'

'Why are you so keen on everyone being naked at your resort?'

'Naked?' He laughed. 'You mean, with the robes? Why, that's purely for comfort. You see that our guests enjoy it.'

'I have seen that,' Sammy replied, leaning forward, consciously moving her mouth closer to her phone; 'I've seen a number of top celebrities walking around here naked. Stark, bare-ass naked. Is this something that your size tool offers too, Mr Lund?'

'It is not its primary function,' Lund laughed, 'but there is a reason why our trial society here at Lund Acres embraces such permissiveness. You see, Sammy, privacy is a very twentieth-century concept. For the vast majority of our time on this planet, humans have done exceedingly well without it. In India it is still very much a rarity that one can expect to have privacy. It is antisocial, don't you find? It leads to neuroses. No, I think that our future society will soon overcome its attachment to so-called privacy. We will live in public, Sammy. We will be happier for it. Nudity is just one element of this.'

Sammy leaned forward and picked up her phone. She coughed and, raising one hand to cover her mouth, she switched off the voice recorder with the other.

'I am glad we had this conversation, Sammy Habib.' Lund smiled. 'I am glad that you got everything you needed.'

'What do you mean?' she asked, adding a few more coughs.

'You just stopped your recording, yes? You have a terrible fake cough, by the way. If you would like a recommendation for a fake coughing coach, I know a very good woman.'

'I don't what you're on about, mate.'

Sammy stood up and started to cram her phone in her pocket only to realise she didn't have any.

'I am quite happy for you to leave, Sammy. I had been wondering when a journalist would stumble on our research here. I have been mentally preparing myself for the inevitable interest.'

He smiled in a way that demonstrated hours spent before a mirror; a photogenic monstrosity.

'I can only congratulate you on getting in here before anyone else. You are persistent, Sammy, and I like that. Your trick with the phone was inspired… heroic even.'

He stopped smiling.

'You are free to leave whenever you like.'

'You won't try to take my phone?'

'No.'

'That's good. Because I've just backed up our conversation to the cloud and sent an encrypted copy to a secure location.'

'Good for you.'

He seemed to have lost interest in her now. As she turned to walk away, Pixie leading her onward, he added, off-hand, 'Oh, and by the way, you will be amazed at what the size tool means for medicine. Pixie, on Sammy's way out, can you please book her in to see the microsurgeons? They will repair all that unfortunate shotgun damage. You'll be good as new, Sammy. Better, in fact. They'll give you a full tune up. You'll feel ten years younger.'

'I'm only twenty-six!'

'Hmm…' Lund rolled back in his chair, his fingers steepled.

He looked out over his creation and reflected on how ugly life had been before the size tool, and how beautiful it would be after it.

Pixie put her arm around Sammy's shoulder and led her away.

'Why is everyone so tall around here?' Sammy found herself wondering. 'Oh, of course…'

*

Back at the farm, John Barton wiped the tears away from his eyes. He'd just tied up the horses and walked past the farmer. The farmer stared furiously from his window. John opened his front door and hung up his coat. The sofa was still covered in all of their crap from two nights ago; plans, books, clothes, food and bedding. How had a woman broken his heart who, just over a week ago, he had not even met? How could he possibly feel so hollow? So drained of life and meaning?

He checked his phone. It had been dead for the past hour. Sammy had monopolised the charger, of course. He cleared some space on the kitchen worktop and plugged it in. It beeped. It came to life. He watched the Vodafone logo flash across the screen and then felt it buzz.

NEW MESSAGE:
SAMMY (PUB)

15

'So...'

Sammy was sat on John's sofa. For once, there was no television or radio on, nor was she looking at her phone. John was in the kitchen. Sammy could hear things steaming and boiling in there. She'd explained the situation. Well, as much as it was possible to explain something like that.

Now, she sat in silence. She waited for him to bring up the inevitable.

She heard him chop some more vegetables. Jesus Christ, what is he making? Surely he's already chopped every vegetable in the house three times over?

Then, she heard him sigh.

'Well, it would have been nice to have seen it...'

'Oh right, like that, is it?'

Sammy bolted out of her chair and marched over to him.

'You're going to be a little bitch about it?'

'About what?'

He chopped another carrot.

'Put that knife down! And you know what. You know there was no way I could have taken you in with me. You know that. Now you're giving me this whole sad puppy shtick... I honestly don't know where you're getting it.'

'Oh, so you don't know now?'

John turned. He pointed a half-chopped carrot at her.

'Well let me tell you, Sammy. I ran around after you when you were bleeding out on my sofa. I alienated everyone I knew around here. I broke laws for you. Why? Do you think it might have been because I like you?'

'I know that it's because you liked me, John,' she put her hand on his half-carrot. 'You made reaching that conclusion pretty much unavoidable.'

John Barton grimaced. He pulled his carrot away and threw it back in the fridge. Turning to the stove, he stared intensely into the boiling mush of potatoes and meat.

'You knew that I liked you, Sammy. And I'm pretty sure that you liked me too.'

'Of course I did... do, even-'

'Then why did you leave me that way?'

'It was for a job. It was only for a day.'

'I didn't know that, did I? And you didn't know that either, at the time. For all we knew you were going in there never to return. You were going in to find what you had been looking for and, if you found it, I'd never see you again.'

His eyes were welling up. He caught his breath and swallowed. As he spoke his voice cracked. 'You were crying. I saw you. And I was too. We knew it was the end.'

'Oh, grow up, John!

Sammy stepped away, her own voice trembling.

'It's the twenty-first century. Things can't happen like in the movies. I mean,' she felt a tear rolling down her cheek. She brushed it off.

'Sit down, Sammy.' He wiped his eyes with his sleeve. 'I'm cooking.'

'It doesn't have to be over, John.'

'It already is.'

Holding her middle, Sammy paced slowly back to the sofa. She couldn't understand where these feelings were coming from. She'd barely known the boy a few days and here they were, arguing like they'd been together for months. She had never felt this bad about a guy before. She had hurt him. She knew she had, and telling herself that it was just business didn't seem to dull that ache. It had always worked before. Now it didn't.

She sat down and rubbed at her middle. Maybe these feelings were just the result of her tune-up?

Her gunwound was entirely healed. The microsurgeons hadn't even left a scar. Not only this, but while she was under they had trimmed back her body fat and massaged her muscles. Where once there was what she endearingly referred to as her beer gut, her hand now rested on rippling abs. Her head, too, was clear, and she was full of energy. All of this within half an hour. For Sammy, the applications of the size tool were only just sinking in.

Something in her belly was rolling over and over. She caught herself sighing. Jesus, Sammy, you're like a sixteen-year-old kid again, breaking up with your first biker boy. Gross. Trying to keep her mind occupied, she flipped open John's laptop and opened up Word.

After they had released her from Lund Acres her electronics were returned. John's tweeds were returned to her, laundered, ironed and seemingly recut to fit her. She had set out marching. The walk would take her the rest of the afternoon. The trip to Lund Acres had only lasted a matter of hours after all. She had arrived back at John Barton's flat by sundown.

In the meantime she had carried her Mueller-Kueps as she walked, rolling the buttons around on the ball and bashing out a first pass at her article. The story of Lund Acres and the size tool would be a long one. She'd make sure that Marley gave her a special dispensation. Ideally, it would be three times the length of the average Bantz article. She might even hit 1,500 words.

It was this article that she compulsively read back to herself as she sat there on the sofa. It was compact, she realised. Maybe too compact? If you tried to skip you'd soon get lost. Still, if you wrote long sentences nowadays, you might as well be an academic; which is to say, entirely unread. Sammy had hated uni.

She caught another typo. Broke a sentence in half. Clarified another. It was almost there. They would, of course, have to fill out the majority of the page with images. Sammy hadn't managed to get any while she was there, but that was never much of a problem at Bantz. They had a whole team who could photobash that stuff together in half an hour. The main thing was the recording. Should she suggest embedding it? On the one hand, it would make her seem like a badass investigative journalist – the kind that wins awards – but, on the other, Zane Lund did not come out of it well. Listening back to the recording, Sammy was shocked at the undiluted malevolence carried in his voice. In person he was intimidating, but on the recording he was hellish. Embedding the audio would guarantee that she would never have access to him again.

It was a dilemma. Definite fame now, or possibly more fame later? She could guarantee that this wasn't the end of the size tool coverage. Lund might be a bastard but he had claimed to respect her. If she made him look good now, she could barter it for exclusive access later on. But then, maybe the story was big enough to win a Pulitzer on its own? A hard decision. Pulitzers don't pay the bills. Meanwhile, Zane Lund clearly does.

*

'Grub's up!' John called from the kitchen.

Snapping out of her reverie, Sammy realised how hungry she was. She clicked the laptop closed and slung it off the table.

'What is it?'

John looked at her astounded. 'Hot pot!'

Sammy was confused.

'I thought you were from here? Lancashire hot pot, right? Spuds and veg and meat, with a suet crust on top. Served, as all food should be, with buttered white bread on the side. Reet grand, eh?'

'Somehow, John Barton,' Sammy swirled her spoon around in

the mush, 'this delicacy has not yet made its way into the city centre.'

'Ah, you're missing out,' he mumbled through a mouthful of crust. 'You can keep your falafels and your wholemeal rubbish. This is the real stuff!'

'I see.'

She opened her mouth and put the food in. She hadn't eaten for so long that she'd forgotten how to chew. As her jaws moved back and forth, reminding themselves of their old habits, she was surprised to find the hot pot quite pleasant. A series of images, unbidden, filled her mind with pastoral landscapes, kids in the farmyard and a burly, grey-haired John Barton holding her in his arms.

'You like it?' he asked.

'I do, yes.' She smiled.

'So,' he leaned forward, his elbows on the table. 'You say this machine can make any object any size?'

'Pretty much.'

'And so...' he sucked a lump of beef off his spoon. 'So that means that if we have something then... we can make as much of it as we want?'

'Sort of,' she crunched a black chunk of onion, 'it'd be the same amount, but it'd be bigger. Which, arguably, is the same as having more of it, provided it's simple stuff like gold or... hot pot.'

'Infinite hot pot.'

'It would depend on somebody actually wanting it, John Barton,' she snorted. 'Of course, it'll also depend upon who can afford access to it. The sort of people who eat hot pot are unlikely to be at the front of the queue.'

John thought about this for a moment. His eyebrows furrowed.

'But, that's not right! We have a machine here that can make stuff plentiful for everyone. It could end world hunger, stop poverty. I'm guessing it can cure a bunch of diseases and injuries too. How are you even going to charge for that, if everyone can have as much of anything as they like?'

'They'll find a way,' Sammy laughed cynically, 'they always do, John. I remember the same shit with the internet. This would be before you had it out here. You only got electricity in the year 2018, right?'

John frowned.

'Everyone thought like you at the start. Free information, wow! That'll mean no more governments or corporations! Free everything man! Well it didn't work out that way, did it?'

She spat out a bone.

'First the corporations came in, and instead of everyone having their own website, we all got profiles set up on their websites. Then the government came in, regulated it all to fuck. Then the corporations came in again, teaming up with the government, and now there are regulations for the little guys and loopholes for the big guys. Everything we say and do is monitored, while they get to run wild. Same shit happens with everything, John Barton. It's the way of the world.'

'Well I think it's bloody shameful,' John was soaking up the last of his melted meat with a fistful of white bread. 'I know people, and people won't stand for that. You just watch, Sammy. I don't think this size tool thing can exist in the world that you've just described. The world will have to change to accommodate it.'

'I don't doubt that.'

'And it'll change for the better.'

'I do doubt that.'

'Right,' John set down his bowl. His spoon rattled with the force of it. 'If it's all so corrupt then what are you, then? Big city reporter coming and telling us all how it is? What are you doing to change it, eh?'

'Change it?'

She set her bowl down too. She hadn't finished but she felt full. The first time in days.

'Why would I want to change it, John? The world's fucked. It has always been fucked and it will always be fucked. All these devices that improve things; you think we'd do that if the world was fine? Why?

'Someone would do it. Scientists…'

'Your problem, John Barton,' she was angry now, irrationally angry. 'Your problem is that you've never fucking tried. You're an average sized fish in a tiny pond and you're satisfied with that. Well, I'm not. I don't want to sit around and wait to die. I want to accomplish something! And you only do that by sacrificing everything. Everything, John! That's what you have to do if you want to do something worthwhile, something lasting. Any fucker can sit around happy, John Barton. Few are the people who will reject every last bit of human warmth and comfort and softness and… and just fucking make something happen!'

'You don't mean any of this, Sammy.'

He was shaking his head. She realised she had stood up and was looming over him.

'If you meant all this, Sammy, you'd be mad.'

'I am fucking mad, John Barton. I'm mad at you! I'm mad at your complacency. I'm mad at the fact that I really fucking like you and yet I know that as soon as you're asked to put up with anything that you don't like, anything that intrudes on your comfort, then you're going to fucking bail! I can't be forever held back by you John. You're a drag! What you can't seem to understand is that nothing is free in this world, John, nothing! Least of all you and I.'

'So that's the thanks I get, then? That's all that the gracious Sammy Habib deigns to grant me, is it? I save your life, you got your fuck out of me and now you're off?'

'You say it like it's special, John. You say it like it's rare. What you don't get, John, is that this is every day for me!'

He scowled. She knew this wasn't true, but she kept pushing.

'You're just so bloody parochial, John Barton… and I'm not. I'm too big for this place. This story is too big. It was never going to work.'

'What was never going to work?'

'You know, John.'

'Oh, I know. I just wanted to know if you knew.'

'I know.'

'I'm pleased to hear it.'

His face was sour. Not sad anymore. Just angry, like Sammy.

'I'm pleased that you took the time to notice that we were falling in love. That you took that precious time out of your busy bloody schedule.'

There was the sound of a 4x4 pulling up on the gravel outside, followed by a horn beeping. Sammy's head sank. John looked to the curtains, closed now. He went to peer through them.

'Who is this now, eh? Is this you again?'

'It's Bantz,' Sammy sighed. She lifted her bag to her shoulder. 'Bantz Testament. They sent a car.'

'Right.' John clenched his fist and shook his head in frustration. 'So I take it that you're not staying the night then?'

'I never said that I was, John.'

'Well, forgive me for presuming. It's just that it's half nine at night now and-'

'And it's two and a half hours back to Manchester, and we have a midnight deadline on tomorrow's front page.'

'Fuckssake, Sammy.'

John Barton sunk down into himself. He let out a noise like a slow puncture. He was beaten.

'I'm sorry, John Barton.'

Another beep came from outside, more impatient now.

'We're just from different worlds, us two. I'm a big city rat, and your my little country mouse.'

She stroked him beneath his chin. She could feel his stubble and his breath soft on her hand.

'Can I have a last kiss before you go, Sammy?'

She sighed and moved to the door.

'Fuck off, my sweet John Barton.'

She blew him a kiss. He caught it and looked at his hand. By the time he looked back up, she was gone.

*

As Sammy Habib, freelance journalist, watched Avon Murray shrinking in the rearview mirror, she asked her driver to turn off the news station. There'd be time enough for all of that in a couple of hours. For now, she wanted to look out over the rolling hills and try to remember the North as it was. Everything, she knew, would change. Soon.

Book
Two

1

The world changed. The news broke the morning after Sammy returned to Manchester. At first, people didn't believe it. Some considered it satire, although its exact target was hard to discern. Tentatively, other news organisations began to run the story. By the time it hit the BBC front page the race was on. Everyone wanted to find Lund Acres, and to meet the man himself.

At midday, the Lund Corporation tweeted a set of coordinates. By 2pm news companies across the world had gathered at the compound. They were led, en masse, to "decompression", now openly referred to as the size tool. They were shrunk down and taken on a tour of Lund Acres. Livestreamed on every channel, the world watched. Then, at the culmination of their tour, they were addressed, at the foot of his personal tower, by the man himself: Zane Lund. The world watched as he took his place at the podium.

'Ladies and gentlemen, xim and xir, I welcome you all to the new world. It is a place without sickness, and without pain. It is a land of plenty. It is a paradise. I have created this for you, and I trust that you will use it wisely. The new world is yours!'

As the assembled journalists broke into applause, Zane Lund lifted a cricket-ball sized solar system above his head like a trophy. Sammy, watching from home, wondered just how many of those bloody things he had lying around. Zane Lund then stepped back and descended from the stage. As he strode away to his tower, flanked by guardians, Captain Adisa stepped forward. In her deep-voiced, martial tones, she announced;

'The bidding on the first size tool begins at sixty-eight billion dollars.'

With that, she too stepped off the stage. She opened her golden wings and launched herself into the sky.

The journalists did not clap this time. Instead, the world's viewers were treated to the sound of confused mumbling. In living rooms and pubs and offices around the globe similar conversations were happening.

'He said it was a new world!'

'You heard that woman. Sixty-eight billion dollars? Sounds very much like the old world to me. The rich get richer!'

'It's not right. A thing like this should be for everyone.'

'Aye. A public utility. Free to use. Free!'

By 5pm crowds had started massing in capital cities. Their placards revealed a mix of feelings. Alongside those who demanded size tools for all were those who considered it dangerous, an aberration. They wanted regulation, or better, that the size tool be destroyed and the research behind it forbidden. Speakers began addressing the crowds. Marxists against the size tool. Christians against the size tool. Feminists against the size tool; hasn't male sexual insecurity gone far enough?

The protests were loud, but they were spontaneous. They had no direction. As a prominent clinical psychologist described it on the news; 'this is the world coming to terms with itself. A new reality is being born and our old realities are dying. What we're seeing here are the seven stages of grief. These bloody neo-Marxists are stuck on anger and bargaining.'

As is so often the way, the media circus surrounding the protests provided useful cover for the power plays going on behind closed doors. The Lund Corporation had already been swamped with bids for the first size tool. Once the price hit a hundred billion, it became clear that the only serious bidders were the militaries. They arranged an international conference to be held at a luxury ski resort.

Lund Glacier was located in a two-foot-square box in a

shipping container in the North Sea. It was fitted with a set of hydraulics to keep it still in even the roughest waves. Generals, admirals and defence ministers from around the world were dropped in by helicopter. There they experienced the size tool first hand, stepping in to a neon-blue and blacklighted shipping container and stepping out to a winter wonderland. Before they sat down to dinner the bidding had already risen to $180 billion.

*

Sir Tallow-Wansworth Mosley sipped at a vodka martini. His olive was stuffed with thousands of tiny olives which, he had been told, were themselves stuffed with the same again. He sneered and rubbed at his teeth. He was sure that some of the ruddy microscopic blighters had leaked out into his drink. All very ostentatious this size tool business. All very gauche, he thought.

A young staffer with slicked back hair leaned over to him. They were stood on a wooden balcony overlooking the ski resort, supposedly enjoying their aperitifs and mingling, although no evidence of mingling could be found. Each nation's representatives were keeping to themselves, strategising. The oversized, Wagnerian mountain range that stretched out before them was entirely ignored.

'I don't see why we all have to wear these bally white robes,' Mosley was saying, 'it's damned nippy out here and we're walking around in nightgowns. Feels like I'm bally naked! Is that breeze going up you too, Smythe?'

'With respect, sir, I'm not even sure why we're here,' the staffer moaned, sipping an orange juice. 'We all know Britain can't afford the prices they're asking. We can't compete with the Americans. Certainly not with the Chinese.'

'Yes,' Mosley reflected, 'they do have an awful lot to thank us for, don't they? And don't forget the Indians, dear boy. Taught 'em everything they know, we did.'

'Sir, with due respect, the Empire is long over.'

Mosley cracked a boozy grin.

'Never say never, old boy. We English have our methods. Once ruled a quarter of the globe, we did, with only one colonial officer to every thousand natives. Says a lot for English charm, eh? English cunning…'

'Do you have a plan, sir?'

'Not as of yet, Smythe,' the home secretary paused to sip at his martini. 'But get me another one of these and we'll be halfway there. If his maj wants a size tool, we'll bally well get him a size tool, come hell or high water.'

'But, home secretary, even if we could get a size tool, would that even be wise?' He lifted a martini from a passing guardian. 'What about all the protestors?'

'Protestors? Pshh!' The home secretary blew a raspberry at the concept. 'All protestors are good for is keeping the secretary of defence busy while I'm out here in the real thick of it, eh? Far as I'm concerned, the more protests, the better. You know they protested my moustache?' He stroked the toothbrush of bristles nestled under his nose. 'It's just some bally facial hair, for godsakes. Chaplin wore one!'

'Yes sir, Chaplin did wear one, sir.'

Smythe bowed to the elder statesman. No one really knew why the home secretary was so attached to his Hitler moustache, but his fury at hearing a word said against it had produced a conspiracy of silence among his staffers.

'The military applications, you see,' Mosley was reflecting again. 'They don't just include the obvious boost to resources and the potential for superweaponry. No, perhaps of more value are the intelligence gathering applications. How does one intercept a spy who's a quarter centimetre tall, Smythe?'

'With great difficulty, sir.'

'Indeed, indeed.' He plucked out his olive-stuffed-olive and chewed it up without pausing.

'And how does one locate a kidnapped man, when they could

be hidden in a rainforest the size of a shoebox or… or, playing marbles with the sun?'

'Quite, sir.'

'We're going to have to think about borders too, Smythe.'

Mosley wagged his finger, sinking his second martini.

'Write that one down: "borders". Now, what do you think the old smoking policy is here, eh?'

He took out a cigar and lit it. Noticing someone else smoking, dignitaries from four other nations took out their pipes, cigars and, in the French defence minister's case, galoises, and the terrace filled with smoke.

'Don't misunderstand me here, Smythe.'

Mosley gazed around, surreptitious, then tapped his nose; 'but the one who cracks this size tool business; he's going to be the one with the real power. And by he, Smythe,' he pulled at his staffer's robes, 'I mean me. Got that?'

The staffer nodded. It was time for the meal, and after that, to start the real bidding.

*

No-one knew who purchased the first size tool. Journalists speculated, but the change was not immediately apparent. When evidence did start to go public, the great advantage promised to the first purchaser did not seem to have materialised. The Russians, it was discovered, were rolling hundred-foot-high tanks around on the Steppe. The vibrations from their engines were felt from Ulaanbaatar to the Ukraine. It was as if they'd turned the whole of Russia into their personal drag strip.

So the Russians had the size tool? Not exactly. Or, at least, not exclusively. Two-inch-tall Mossad agents were found living in the desk of the British Prime Minister, raising questions about her legitimacy to govern. Tiny Pakistanis too had been found in Indian manufacturing facilities, carrying away blueprints for high tech machinery like a line of ants. The Chinese, for their part, suddenly boasted of a perfect human rights record. It was suspected that they had shrunk all their dissidents and sweatshop labourers down to microscopic sizes. No country, it seemed, was without some access to size tool technology.

It was only a matter of time before the size tool went commercial. Outpaced by the tiny Chinese workshops, the American President announced a third industrial revolution and, with the collaboration of Silicon Valley, transformed manufacturing plants across America. Size tool technology was incorporated into assembly lines to make products quicker and cheaper than ever before. The rest of the world was fast on their heels.

The Lund Corporation remained silent throughout this process. There were no more summits or announcements. There were no interviews with Zane Lund. No tours of their resorts. Lund Acres was swamped by protesters. Any celebrities spotted nearby were publicly shamed. It closed its doors within the year. The Economist speculated as to whether the Lund Corporation had moved out of size tool production altogether, focusing instead on their swelling financial portfolio. But this was not the case.

By 2033 the world had known of the size tool for five years. It had grown complacent about it. Only governments and megacorporations, after all, had access to these rare devices. Things were cheaper now, people had more stuff, but had life really changed? It was at this point that the Lund Corporation released the Size Tool Pro. No longer did you have to step into a sealed re-scalable environment to use the size tool. The Size Tool Pro instead took the form of a ray. Simply point the size tool at what you want to grow or shrink, highlight it in the reticule, select the size tool, drag and click; and there you have it. The uridium microengine could be held in a container the size of a backpack, fashionably sleek in stark white with neon turquoise lettering. It went on sale for $289.99.

A second set of mass protests met the release of the Size

Tool Pro, but these were a much smaller, hard core of radicals. In something of a PR disaster for the Lund Corporation, the first widely publicised demonstration of the Size Tool Pro took place when a group of young, drunken tech-bros charged into a group of protesters, indiscriminately shrinking them. They wore ghostbusters parody outfits that read 'Commie-Busters' across the back and carried logos of a big red cross over a stereotypical female protester's face. The Commie-Busters incident made headlines across the world and, when everyone realised there was currently no law against shrinking people out of existence, the protests quadrupled in size. Running battles could be seen in the streets of major cities. Students and activists of different political stripes were shrinking each other everywhere you went.

Yet the economy was booming. Individual items may have lost nearly all of their value but as every person with a size tool could now turn their flat into a mansion, or even into a city full of mansions, sales of particular items skyrocketed. Unexpected shifts in value affected every commodity. Yachts, for example, were sold in bulk. Being a difficult thing to resize without damaging their engines or interiors, people bought one for every size at which they chose to live. Toilet paper went the other way. One sheet, constantly inflated, would last a lifetime; so now there were showrooms devoted to selling individual sheets of extremely luxurious paper for huge amounts. A quality sheet of toilet paper could set you back the equivalent of 15,000 yachts. It was a time of change. A creative entrepreneur could make a fortune overnight. Many of the established firms that had dominated the market only months earlier went bankrupt.

Amazon were one such company that seemed to be sinking in the new post-size tool environment. Their next day delivery system was widely considered to be punishingly slow. A thing of the past. Especially now that your average local corner shop held over a billion separate items in stock. If it wasn't for their grip on American media, of which they still controlled 67%, the company might have been done for. Instead, March 2039 saw the launch of Amazon Rail.

Established in collaboration with the Lund Corporation, Amazon Rail comprised of a fibre optic cable network running parallel to the internet. The Lund Corporation locked off a specific size-setting on its size tools, implementing the restriction in a downloadable patch. Users now had to pay to unlock that size-setting and shrink themselves to the required size to use Amazon Rail. Anyone with an internet connection could simply attach an adaptor to their phone line and they were now an Amazon Rail station. As a result, many cities emptied. People who worked as toilet paper salesmen in Liverpool could commute in from a remote Tibetan monastery every morning. The head monk of that remote Tibetan monastery could equally choose to live in Liverpool, although he preferred not to.

Society changed. People expected everything, all the time. A bad coffee or a five-minute wait for a delivery would send people into fits of hysterical screaming. Each of these was captured on camera, as was everything else. Privacy, as Zane Lund had predicted, was becoming redundant, and not because of governments, but because people couldn't stop filming each other. Malicious shrinkings were on the increase. People were filled with puritanical hatred when they encountered anything that wasn't to their liking. Any time anything was denied to them, or when they saw someone misbehaving, they were filled with an impotent, self-righteous rage. Part of this was real, sincere frustration, and part of it was a performance conducted to direct attention away from themselves. Someone else being targeted meant that the cameras momentarily turned away from you, or so people seemed to hope.

The possibility that at any time one could be surrounded by unseen people with unseen cameras produced a double-effect. The ugliness of the hatred and rage, yes, was very palpable. But, equally, there was a movement towards strict homogenisation. The Size Tool Mini was released in May 2034, and with it came the potential to select individual body parts to resize and sculpt. Some people rushed into full-body transformations. These were mercilessly punished. Some were merely humiliated, while others were contorted into strange shapes by laughing mobs before finally being shrunk into oblivion. Despite these riots, however, everyone slowly began to morph towards a set of standardised appearances. A lip plumping here, a nose reduction there. It all added up. Older people began to struggle telling their grandchildren apart.

Despite the changes, the wealth gap between rich and poor continued to grow.

'If anything,' the head of a prominent financial organisation stated, 'it's more unbridgeable than ever.'

It was with this in mind that the World Bank stopped its measurements. Academic reports were produced arguing that the measurement of wealth was itself an oppressive construction. Affixing values to things, they argued, was not only hopelessly reductive in the wake of the size tool, but it had always been reductive. It was only now, the academics believed, that progressives were finally waking up to this fact. From 2037 onwards there was no more measurement of human wealth, and, by 2038, asking about someone's income or capital holdings was registered as a hate crime.

By 2039 the governments of the world had finally reached agreement. For thirteen years they had trialled a variety of legislational approaches and none of them had worked. China had attempted to ban non-Party members from using the size tool. They had to back down when China became, as a direct result of this policy, the world capital of size tool crime.

Other countries had attempted to regulate areas of usage, types of usage, or else set parameters on usage within commercial or manufacturing environments. America proudly boasted of its unregulated size tool sector, although the shrinking of the White House by terrorists made many question this. Even die-hard constitutionalists began to wonder whether the size tool was really a matter for the second amendment. A statue of the lost President was erected where the White House had once stood. The newly incorporated military arm, the Size Force, did a flyby. The statue was pulled down by rioters a week later.

*

The First International Conference on Proportional Governance met in April 2035. For two whole months it thrashed out the details of the world's first ever universal law. All nations would comply with it, and all would be involved in the policing of it. The wording of the law would be identical across all nations, and each head of state would sign the original document and stamp it with their official seal. The document was then photocopied; each nation placing a version on public display in their central legislature. The original would be kept alongside the original patent for the size tool. That is to say, it would hang on the wall in Zane Lund's office.

'Where confusion and disorder have been all too paramount,' the elderly Prime Minister, Sir Tallow-Wansworth Mosley, mumbled through his grey toothbrush moustache, 'we shall now bring order, and civilisation. Our new technologies have, in many ways, been a trial of humanity's utopian potential. We were given, as my dear friend Zane Lund once said, an entirely new world, and yet...'

He began to shake his head. It was this performance of dismay and regret that had drawn the public to Mosley. He was the one man who had seemed to understand the size tool all along.

'Humanity, you see... humanity is a greedy and a jealous creature. It cannot help itself and it cannot help others. It can only help itself to others' possessions. Humanity, it was said, would earn its Eden. Well we were given an Eden, and we went straight for the bally apple. We scoffed down the fruit of knowledge, spat out the pips, and grew a bally orchard with 'em!'

The crowd of journalists grouped around Prime Minister Mosley were silent. He'd just stepped off a plane from the conference. The plane itself was an affectation. It had been four years since Amazon Rail had put every commercial airline out business.

'While I am in some ways sorry, I am in other ways very pleased. For today, I can announce that we have brought an end to the madness. Humanity may one day reach divinity, but for now it must regain its humility. The third industrial revolution, driven by the revolution in scalage technology, has reached maturity and, in tandem with it, we, as mature representatives of the world's governments, have reached an understanding. We can, for the first time, celebrate the inauguration of a universal law.'

The line was delivered as if to applause. Mosley held his breath. He let it sink in. The journalists, still, were silent. Swallowing and lifting his head, the old man continued. A steely glint now showed in his eye.

'The contents of this law are as follows: firstly, that size tools not produced by the universally recognised charter-partner, the Lund Corporation, will be from here-on considered contraband.

'Secondly, that size tool usage shall be limited to four set sizes, consistent with four regulated speeds, or wavelengths. The smallest of these, Travel Size, shall be limited to Amazon Rail transit only. The medium permitted range, Family Size, will comprise of a ratio of one inch to every one foot of the largest permitted range, Man Size. The expectation is that humans will return to Man Size for everyday business (this being the size to which people and objects were accustomed prior to the size tool), while habitation, or home life, will take place at Family Size, thus allowing for the more extravagant lifestyles to which we are all now accustomed.

'The fourth and final permitted size, Super Size, is permitted for military use only. Any infringement of this law by nations will result in the immediate shrinking of their leadership and an international embargo. Any infringement by an individual will result in life imprisonment. As is clear for all to see, we are not messing around.'

The excessive nature of these punishments had been on the insistence of the more brutal nations. They had shocked the Prime Minister on first hearing. However, after a thorough debate involving all parties, the more liberal nations were won around to the draconian position. Without extreme action, it was decided, there would be no solution to this ever-deepening state of crisis.

Still, as the Prime Minister walked away from the cameras, flanked by two blue-robed guardians, he couldn't help but feel that things were moving faster than even he had predicted.

*

'Bullshit!' Sammy roared across the bar.

It was 11am and the landlord had agreed to put the news on, but now he turned it off. The small and furious Arabic woman was already drunk. She sucked back her bottle of beer and spoke loudly, as if to the whole room.

'I tell yer, I told yer! Didn' I tell yer? I told yer!'

'Can you keep it down, miss? People are trying to eat breakfast here.'

'Yeah, yeah, whatever,' she said. But she complied.

Sammy hadn't included the audio recording in her final article. She thought this would give her an 'in' with Lund but, as it turned out, it just gave Bantz an excuse to run the story without a byline. When Zane Lund immediately went back into seclusion, Sammy was left without any credit. She had been cut out of the very story that she had almost died to break. Since then, she'd watched from afar. Mostly drunk.

'I knew all this'd happen,' she whispered to herself, slunk over a stool at the Sand Bar. She burped. 'I told yer, it's all always gonna be going to shit, right!?'

And with that she yawned, folded her arms, and fell backwards off her chair.

2

No job. No friends. Not even a cat. Life was pretty dire for Sammy Habib in the year of 2035. She'd been renting a 'studio apartment' in the city centre. A place so small you didn't have to get out of bed to cook breakfast. She was still paying a sky high rent even though now, after Amazon Rail, city apartments were pretty much worthless.

After Bantz took her name off the size tool article, she'd kicked off. She'd slashed Marley's tires and threatened his family. She wasn't going to get return work anytime soon. Bantz soon overtook its competitors to become the biggest news-related content provider in the country. Sammy had picked a bad company to be blacklisted from. She sent articles off to MumsNet and GossipWyr but nothing was taken. Every editor in the game was looking for their moment to jump ship to Bantz. They weren't going to throw that away for a few Sammy Habib articles on post-size parenting or Top 10 Celebrity Microsurgeries. Sammy was untouchable.

It was a rapid tumble down the internet rabbit hole for Sammy. The lower your Klout score, the stranger things got. First she took proofing jobs, which she was always terrible at, and then writing copy. Often bizarre copy. She would spend lonely, drunken evenings writing the blurbs to fetish porn videos. The morning might bring a series of paid-for reviews on movie sites. She never bothered watching the movie in question, just gave the damn 5 stars they'd paid for. There would be fake personas to keep alive in the afternoon. As the sun finally came in through her curtainless window, she found her job was easier to do with a bottle of wine beside her.

'Siri?' Sammy asked one afternoon. The now-ancient robot had been left behind by a previous tenant. Sammy had kept her on as a type of prehistoric pet. Like the Flintstones, she thought.

'Yes, Say-me.' Siri never could master her name.

'Siri, how many other people are living like I am now?'

'I'm sorry.' The voice did not sound sorry. 'I do not understand the question.'

'Siri!' Sammy rolled over under the covers, shouting up through the fabric. 'What are the current unemployment figures for the UK?'

'Calculating...'

Sammy enjoyed it when Siri calculated. Once AI became immediately responsive to human demands it was easy to forget that their thoughts were fundamentally different from our own. Back in the good old days, Sammy smiled, it was easy to tell the machines from the people. The machines, for a start, were dumber. Maybe, she wondered, this is how we now seem to machines? Under her breath she whispered: 'cal-kew-lay-ting...'

PING! 'Current unemployment rate of UK equals zero-point-four percent. Has this answered your question?'

'What?' Sammy scratched her head. 'No, Siri, it doesn't really-'

'I'm sorry, I do not under-'

'Siri! How many people are on zero hours contracts?'

'Calculating...'

'In the UK, Siri. Not everywhere. Just in the UK.'

'Calculating...'

That must be what it is, right? Sammy pondered to herself. A lot of companies now required all applicants to sign a zero hours contract before they'd offer them an interview. It was a scheme pushed by Prime Minister Mosley's predecessor who was elected to end unemployment. Of course, you couldn't get the dole if you were on zero hours.

'WARNING!'

Sammy clapped her hands over her ears as Siri's soothing female voice was replaced by a harsh klaxon and the sound of a distorted male bellow.

'WARNING! USER - Kayleigh Minnows – YOU HAVE BEEN IDENTIFIED AS A HATE CRIMINAL. YOUR STATEMENT HAS BEEN FORWARDED TO LOCAL LAW ENFORCEMENT. REMAIN WHERE YOU ARE. OFFICERS ARE ON THEIR WAY. ATTEMPT TO ABSCOND WILL RESULT IN A CHARGE OF PERVERTING THE COURSE OF JUSTICE!'

'Alright! Alright! Calm down.'

Sammy threw the covers back over her head and dragged herself over to the device. It was a routine operation for her. She was always doing accidental hate crimes. Now they'd repealed the laws protecting women and minorities and replaced them with laws protecting millionaires it was hard not to. That's why she'd left Siri programmed to her old owner.

Every time Kayleigh's babyish voice came through the speakers Sammy had a twinge of conscience. Poor Kayleigh, she must have a police record as long as your arm. With any luck she'd be dead by now.

Sammy plugged in her phone – now there was a retro experience – and used CacheBlastr to scramble Siri's brain. Poor robot. She'd be back online tomorrow. Sammy patted her on her little white head. Night night, Siri.

So unemployment is impossibly low, Sammy reflected. She lowered herself back into her snot-and-wine-stained bed and wondered about the faceless people in low-to-no paying work. All of them piled up on top of each other, with her in the middle of them.

'Well.' Sammy slugged another mouthful of a red wine called Red Wine. 'I guess this is utopia. What a wonderful fucking surprise.'

*

The problem with being poor is that nobody believes that you exist. Sammy had been stuck for years, wandering around a variety of crumbling city centre apartments, making no impression on anyone. The people she met were angry and bitter. They stank. They had made the same terrible choices as everyone else, only they didn't have the means or the wherewithal to hide them. Rich people, by which Sammy tended to mean anyone with a full-time job, probably drank more and lived more unhealthily than your average unemployed. The difference is a comfy bed, a hot shower, toothpaste and smelly stuff. A loving hubby to cook a big, greasy sympathy breakfast. Poor people, by which Sammy tended to mean herself, just had to wallow in it.

Casualization had followed on from the size tool like a medieval dancing plague. Every time there was a technological breakthrough, some communist would declare it to be the end of work, and all the bosses rushed out to see which workers they could replace with casuals. With the size tool it was the professionals. Doctors, architects, lawyers and lecturers joined the cooks, cleaners and clerks in the no-contracted-hours brigade.

'Many would consider it a retrograde step,' Prime Minister Mosley said in Parliament, 'but the size tool is the future. Increased labour fluidity is the price that must be paid for modernisation.'

The exact relationship between firing doctors and the size tool was never really explained. Casualization just somehow felt right. Leaving your office on Friday and expecting the job to still be there on Monday morning was, many felt, positively Victorian. After all, with the size tool, there was no guarantee that the office itself would be still there, never mind your desk. If the fabric of the material world wasn't secure, why should you be?

Sammy had written a series of articles on these subjects. All were rejected. The only one that got any traction was a video following three homeless architectural technicians around the abandoned hotel where they lived. She'd called it Homeless Cribs, added ironic hip hop music and funny edits, then sold it to a YouTuber.

Bantz reposted it as "**This Woman Followed Homeless People Back to their MANSION?!?! [UNBELIEVABLE] [MUST CLICK]**". It got a few hundred million hits, proving Sammy still had it, even if those hits went to Bantz and not the YouTuber. Obviously, Sammy got no money for them.

*

The problem was that it was impossible for most people to believe that people like Sammy existed. The idea that some people did not have their own size tools, or even access to a size tool, was astounding. Almost everybody used the size tool at all times. It was integrated into every element of their waking, and sleeping, lives.

Sammy's apartment overlooked a restaurant. She could watch the rich people eating outside on sunny days. These people, she realised, might live and work anywhere on the planet. They could be lunching in Manchester today, had sushi in Tokyo yesterday, and be going for tapas in Buenos Aires tomorrow. This is how eating out worked now. And yet, as she glugged her wine above them, she noticed how none of them ever looked up. They simply weren't interested. They could have been anywhere. It made no difference. It made Sammy sick.

*

She was at a low point one night when she made the decision to leave. She had polished off a third of a whisky bottle; a heroic amount for someone not quite five-and-a-half feet tall. As the alcohol clotted in her brain she lay on the floor, flicking through her contacts list and deleting anyone she decided was a wanker.

'Marley Arrowsmith,' editor at Bantz, 'definite wanker. DELETED!'

'Bob Aston,' paparazzo, 'yeah, pretty much a wanker. DELETED!'

'Charlotte Austin,' her inside source at a celebrity fashion palace. 'Oh, big old wanker. GONE!'

She enjoyed yelling as she deleted each one. With each deletion she was closing another door on her career. The impregnable, unstoppable Sammy Habib was finally losing the game. The only person who could take her out was herself. Each contact, BANG, like cutting off a finger. Just one less finger to worry about...

'Sally Barch,' military attaché, exclusive leaker of government secrets, prime contact, 'defo a wanker. DELETED!'

'John Barton...'

The name sent blood rushing through her face. Suddenly she could feel the alcohol in her. It was making her lightheaded. The pit of her stomach seemed to drop away. She sat up and tried to blink it out for a moment.

'John Barton...' she whispered to herself. 'Poor John.'

She thought about how much she'd hurt him. About how she'd run back to the city because that town - what was it? Avon Murray - had seemed so tiny. Now... well, now everywhere seemed tiny. You couldn't help but feel tiny, whether you were microscopic in size or not. The countryside...

She rubbed her face and remembered his wobbly horse and lying on the grass by the river as he moved on top of her. She remembered his kisses. She remembered the bonsai tree they had found, planted by the riverside – oh, shit! That was Zane, wasn't it! – never mind. She lay there remembering.

'U up?' She sent the message while she was remembering. She couldn't help herself.

'Who's this?' Two words blinked back on her screen.

Oh, so he'd deleted her, had he? Charming! She rolled over and held her tummy. She rubbed herself where she'd once lost all her guts. How strange that all that bleeding and dying would be one of her fondest memories. She slugged back another shot of whisky and realised she'd gone through ten phones since she was last with John.

Yes! He'd simply not got her new number. Hope returns!

'Smmey' she sent.

'Samy*' she sent again.

'Sammy*' she sent again.

'Oh,' he sent back.

She waited for something else. She watched as a minute ticked by, then two. She dragged herself over to her mattress and lay with her back against it, propping herself up. He wasn't replying, was he?

She opened up the keyboard and took four attempts to write.

'Did you mean Oh or Ho? Haha! I don't miss you. What you doin?'

'You drunk?'

'Maybs. Who askin?'

Radio silence again. She was starting to remember his parsimonious attitude to language. A man of few words. She'd always thought he was a bit stupid for never talking, but now it sort of appealed. Strong silent type, or something.

'Whachu doin?' she sent again.

'It's 2am. I'm in bed.' He sent.

'Nice ;)' she sent again. Then she got embarrassed.

Panicking, she threw the phone over to the corner. She had a cheap charge hub over there. Her phone would charge wherever it skidded to a halt. A modern hub would easily cover the whole building. When had she got so far behind on her tech?

She rolled herself onto her mattress and felt her tired muscles sinking into it. She had reached some kind of limit. As of tomorrow, she promised herself, she was out of the city. She was going back to the last place she'd felt at home. John

Barton would welcome her back and they'd crack jokes like the old times. She had made her mind up; she was going to be a country girl. Avon Murray beckoned. She'd leave first thing.

*

Sammy got out of bed at three in the afternoon. Packing her stuff, she realised, was going to be quite a job. Measured by weight or quantity of items, she didn't own much; but measured by square footage, she had amassed a vast sedentary sprawl. The pounding headache and vomit-induced hunger didn't help either. She decided to leave tomorrow instead and ordered a McDonalds online. She would have killed for a curry, but without an Amazon Rail line, she could only order from companies with the old-fashioned drone delivery still in operation. McDonalds had kept the drones going, as had KFC, meaning that many old people and those chronically zero-houred now lived purely on a diet of airborne fast food.

*

The next day Sammy left her flat, her worldly goods slung in a pack on her back. She felt the weight on her shoulders. It felt good, like something meaningful was being carried there. Not just everything she owned but, perhaps, her destiny too.

She carried her clothes, electronics and destiny down to the bus station. It was here that she discovered that public transport had ended. The announcement had clearly been lost in some fevered news day. She had never noticed. As the vast majority now travelled by Amazon Rail, the streets were deserted. Most had been pedestrianised, which was lucky as the new habit of daily international travel brought pedestrians into the city in huge waves. As Sammy walked the streets at 10am, Manchester was entirely uninhabited, but by 12 she would be struggling to move. For some reason she had presumed that buses would still be running. But no. It would be like waiting for the next horse drawn carriage or the next steamboat to arrive. As Sammy told herself over and over like a mantra; they refuse to believe people without a size tool existed. She'd have to find another way.

She meandered down through canal street, itself transformed into a strange hybrid of different sized clubs and cafes, warrens and tunnels. A Perspex disco hung above the main road. Tiny figures were still partying away in there. They were six-inches-tall; regulation Family Size. She was on her way to the railway station, trying to find a timetable online as she walked. The National Rail Enquiries site had been shut down, as had the TrainLine. In fact, all of the ticket booking sites seemed to be inoperable. Some had shut down officially, others were simply abandoned. It didn't look promising.

As she arrived at the station her spirits lifted. Where once there was a tired looking 1980s relic, Manchester Piccadilly was now a gleaming bowl-shaped building in the popular cyber-nouveau style. Sammy even saw figures walking around inside. Some alone, some in groups. It was inhabited at least, which was more than the bus station was.

But, getting closer, she realised that once again she was to be let down. Above the wide glass entrance was a sign. It read: Piccadilly Station. Stepping in through the doors Sammy was hit with the warm aroma and gentle music of an air conditioned shopping centre. Whatever the station in the title referred to, it didn't appear to be a train station anymore. The bag suddenly felt a lot heavier on Sammy's shoulders. Her place in the world was uncertain again. Her sense of purpose leaked out of her, the way it had at the end of her last adventure. Perhaps she'd never be confident in her travels again?

If she could just get to Avon Murray, she told herself. If she could just get out to the countryside, then she could give up. At least then she'd be giving up in nature. Giving up like cows and sheep and things give up, happily plodding about in their square fields.

Sammy walked out to the central square. In her head she imagined herself wandering through a wheat field, rolling in mud and chewing on grass. John Barton stepped off a tractor and patted her on the head. She sat down, daydreaming, on one of the homeless-proofed benches scattered around the square. Everything looked out onto a single railway line. The rails were burnished to a gleaming golden colour and Sammy doubted any trains would actually use it. There was no ticket office. She expected that the track was just a kind of sculptural feature now; a piece of defunct technology made into a charming centrepiece.

She tried lying down on the bench but the strategically placed handrails hurt her. She tried dozing while sitting up instead. Nope, the rubber of the chair seemed designed to push the back forward. Only the physically proactive could sit. She had once been proactive, she reflected. Perhaps not physically but certainly in spirit.

She gazed blankly around at the shops. Without a set destination, she glazed over and watched the world happening before her. The fourth floor seemed to be entirely made up of cosmetic microsurgeons and micro-muscle-massage specialists. You needed a licence to practice these things nowadays as the work involved non-regulation sizes. The people who walked in and out of them looked like standardised templates. Though I guess we all do, Sammy thought, even herself to an extent. She patted her still-flat tummy. The rest of the floors were clothes and food, mostly, with a solitary game shop selling VR experiences.

In some places, the new flexibility of size tool production had inspired a DIY, artisan, homemade backlash. This was not one of those places.

*

Sammy sat in the station for over an hour. She had managed to have a small nap while sitting bolt upright, followed by both a good cry and a good laugh. She was thinking of leaving. It was then that she heard a whistle.

'Ladies and gentlemen, xim and xir,' a fey voice announced over some hidden speaker system. 'The A-Train is now entering the station. For those interested there will be a short demonstration followed by the chance to take a trip in this marvellous old device.'

'The A-train?' Sammy pepped up.

Sliding into the station was a beautiful old engine. It huffed huge clouds of steam into the air, its whistle roaring.

'What a beaut, eh?' A man was pointing the engine out to his son.

Sammy looked around and, as if from nowhere, saw crowds of parents and children rushing out to greet the train.

'Excuse me!' Sammy walked over to a man with a pork pie hat who looked like he was involved. 'Can you tell me what all this is about? What's the A-Train?'

'Well, ma'am, this is one of the last six engines left on the tracks. The A-Train travels the whole length of the North. Come from Newcastle, she has, past York and Leeds, and she'll soon be on her way out to Llandudno, with a few stops along the way. Now the B-Train, she goes-'

'Which stops on the way?' Sammy butted in.

'Pardon?' he was taken aback. Train enthusiasts described the six final engines in the way a worshipper recites the Lord's Prayer. To interrupt it bordered on blasphemy.

'You said the A-Train stops at other stations before Llandudno?'

'Yes.' He raised an eyebrow.

Sammy smiled as she felt her cunning come back to her.

'Can you list them?'

'List them?'

'Yeah,' she winked, 'name all the stations. No checking your phone!'

'Of course I can name them!' the man laughed nervously, 'there's Stockport, Strines, Macclesfield, Chester...'

Sammy walked away as he plucked the names off on his fingertips. Strines. That was all she needed. She remembered the name from the first time she had been to Avon Murray. She remembered stepping off a far less impressive train, then limping the – how many? Ten, twenty, thirty? – miles all the way into town. That long walk had made a deep impression on her, as had the man who had rescued her when she fell bleeding into the pub.

Yes, she realised. This was the way to return to him. She would come back to John Barton, carried along on a bright blue steam engine. She would cut through the countryside on a romantic black-and-white cloud. Yes, he'd have to take her back then.

As the train pulled to a standstill she jumped on board. Around her, Sammy could hear thirty or forty dads explaining to their children how trains used to work. They were all mobbing the carriages, desperate to climb in.

Sensing her moment, Sammy rushed into the cabin and hid herself. As she heard the driver coming, she crawled back into the tender. She sat in the dark atop a pile of coal. Through a crack in the old iron she could just about see the outside. That would be enough for her to identify Strines. Safely stowed away, she sat, waiting for the engine to move.

3

Staring out from the gap in the tender, Sammy saw a very different landscape go by than the one she had seen all those years ago. The rolling farmland, the manicured forests, the sullen redbrick farmhouses; all of it was replaced with a tangled wildness. Trees grew up everywhere, battling for light, while beneath them vast fields of brambles and nettles dominated. The occasional mass of bushes could be seen, growing up in huge overflowing mounds.

'Looks like shit out there,' Sammy sighed.

As the size tool was transforming the manufacturing industries, the giants of agriculture were also revolutionising their businesses. In the third industrial revolution, fortune favoured the bold. In farming, the boldest was Monsanto Labs. Already pioneers of genetically modified crops, the scientists of Monsanto were quite comfortable breaking taboos. In 2031 they broke the biggest taboo of them all. They created the landless farm.

A landless farm comprised of a scaling set of platforms. Giant grains and vegetables were fed to tiny livestock, and giant livestock were turned into tiny meat products. These were, in their turn, made giant. Done correctly, an acreage of landless farm could produce ten thousand times the tonnage that a single acre could before the size tool. There was no way for traditional farmers to compete. After a struggle with the National Farmer's Union, Monsanto had its invention was ruled legal by the courts. To prevent monopoly, however, they were not allowed to patent the idea. Landless farms sprung up across the country, driving landowning farmers out of business.

At the same time, Amazon Rail's analytics division released a report showing that rural tourists only ever visited a series of, what they called, "central leisure hubs". In Britain these included the Scottish Highlands, the Welsh coast, the Lake District, Sherwood Forest and the Norfolk Broads. These locations, Amazon reported, drew 98% of rural tourists and yet only received 14% of the country's expenditure on forestry and maintenance. Flooded with tourists from around the world, these areas needed access to vastly expanded resources if they were to survive as areas of outstanding natural beauty. Campaigners suggested raising taxes or charging for entry into these regions, but both plans proved impractical and unpopular. With a heavy heart, the government finally bowed to the pressure and transferred all forestry and wildlife provision over to the leisure hubs. The forests of Britain would be left unmanaged. Fields would return to the wild.

Sammy watched mile upon mile of wilderness flying past. Carefully managed for centuries, the landscape didn't know what to do with its freedom. What looked like a tangled mess to her, was in fact a brutal war for survival. Plants were fighting it out with stinger and thorn in a ruthless battle for domination. The countryside, in other words, was uninhabitable.

*

'The train is now pulling into Strines station.'

Sammy heard the voice echo through her iron hiding place.

'Strines is your next stop.'

She waited for the train to draw up. As it slowed to a walking pace, she dived out of the tender and into the cabin. The driver and fireman shielded their eyes as she sent coal dust everywhere. Before the dust had time to settle, Sammy was already vaulting the turnstile and sprinting along the road to Avon Murray, her backpack flapping behind her.

*

John Barton had just sat down to watch Masterchef. He held a bowl of hotpot on his knee, a dollop of piccalilli glowing on the side. He liked to watch cooking shows and pretend that he too was eating gourmet food. He found that enjoying food was less about the ingredients or preparation and more about taking the time to concentrate on what it actually tasted like. Most evenings he was too hungry to do anything but wolf it all down.

BZZZt. He had a message. It was from Sammy. He ignored it and ate a carrot.

BZZZt. Another one. He continued to ignore it. But now he couldn't pay attention to his programme. Nor the food he was eating.

BZZZt.

'Fine!' He picked up the phone and initiated the ocular scanner. Verified, it displayed her words:

First message: 'Your doorbell's broke.'

Second message: 'That means I'm at your door, genius.'

Third message: 'You coming or what?'

'Wonderful,' John groaned. He walked to the door, steadied himself, closed his eyes and sighed.

'Let's just see,' he told himself. 'Let's just hear her out.'

'You took your sweet time.'

Sammy pushed through the door and stomped up his stairs.

'Hi Sammy...' He said to the doormat.

'New place?'

She had already settled herself down onto his sofa.

'Yes, Sammy.' He stood in the doorway. 'It is.'

'So...' she shrugged. 'Tell me why you've got a new place, maybe? I liked the old one.'

'The old one where you convinced me to steal the farmer's shotgun? Where we robbed a man who was both my landlord and my boss?'

'Yes, smartarse. That one.'

'That one is now part of the forest,' he sighed.

She was slapping the sofa, indicating he should sit. He looked around for any other chair, but knew he didn't have any. He went and sat next to her.

'That's very poetic,' she said, her eyes narrowing. 'Part of the forest... You remember when we got lost in the forest, John?'

The sofa was small and he was aware of the heat of her body pushing against him. He was aware of something else too.

'Sammy, I don't mean to be rude, but you smell quite terrible.'

She looked briefly offended, before lifting her shirt to sniff under it.

'You might have a point there, John. After all, I've been walking all day to get here.'

'You have?'

'And I hid in a pile of coal, and cut through a mass of brambles, and was chased by an angry pig, and then, after all that, I had to rummage through your overgrown old shack looking for some kind of forwarding address.'

'You went through the forest?' John said, his eyes widening.

'Sure,' Sammy was still sniffing at her armpits. 'It's not much of a forest though. More like a jungle. Do I really stink?'

'Aye,' John replied, softly. 'But you've a right to if you've been out in the forest. Folk round here don't go out there anymore. I certainly don't.'

He felt it again, that attraction to her madness, her wildness. Even now, when the rest of Avon Murray was too afraid to leave town, she was out there chasing... well, chasing him.

'Can I run you a bath, maybe? Do you a smoothy?'

Sammy had given up sniffing at herself. She knew the day had not been kind to her. She made the concession of taking her boots off and put her feet up on the table.

'I can eat food now, John. Microsurgeries and that, remember? I could do with a bath though. Nice place you've got here. Got a bath and everything, yeah?'

'Yep,' John Barton nodded. He went to run the bath. 'After the farm closed I had to move closer to the pit anyway.'

The hot water ran loud and echoing. Steam filled the evening air and frosted the window.

'I'm a miner now, y'know?'

'A miner?' She shouted from the next room.

'Aye!' he shouted back.

He checked the water with his hands, sloshing it around.

'There are only two types of jobs left in Avon Murray at this point. Either you're a warden, keeping the forest from eating up the whole town, or you're a miner. All the seams we thought were used up in the 1970s actually have tons of tiny bits and bobs left in them. It wasn't economically viable to dig them out at normal size – sorry, Man Size – but now we can resize them it's a different matter. Mind you, those tiny rocks don't feel so small when we're digging them out.'

Sammy appeared at the door. She was naked. John Barton stared up at her, his face flushing. Through the warm steam she looked like a smelly apparition. She stared at him smugly as he gazed at her body. She nodded at the bath.

'Is that thing ready yet?'

'It's…'

John turned to find the water was nearly overflowing. He fumbled to shut off the taps.

'I guess so,' Sammy smiled.

She sidled over to the bath, swaying her hips in a sensual way. It emphasised the bruising on her legs, the black marks of the coal. As John watched she held out a leg and dipped it into the water.

'Argh!' she pulled it back out. 'Bloody hell, John Barton! Are you trying to boil me or alive something?'

He waddled over on all fours and put his head between her legs.

'I know your plan, John Barton.'

Sammy sighed as she felt her head filling with the steam. 'You're planning on making me into a hot pot, aren't you? You're going to boil me into a hotpot you nasty little slut…'

*

An hour later they lay on the bed together, scrupulously clean. The bed was a sodden. As they lay there, exhausted, steam rose from their bodies into the still night. After years of crushing defeat, Sammy finally felt happy again. It was like it used to be, she felt, as if she'd managed to get it all back. John Barton had even kept his endowment the same, at its rather unimpressive size. Considering the ubiquity of size tool genital enhancements, Sammy found his commitment to his original size admirable. John Barton's quiet contentment was what she wanted now. She wanted his smallness of vision, his narrow perspective. The world was too big now, even for her.

'So, what brought you back here?' John mumbled, his lips still post-coitally numb.

Sammy sighed. 'Can I just say you?'

'You can, but it would be very hard to believe.'

She chuckled and rolled over, blinking her eyes at him and putting on a breathy Marilyn Monroe voice. 'But I love you, John!' She fluttered her eyelashes, 'Boop oop de doop!' and burst out laughing.

'Laugh it up,' he leaned across and spanked her. 'But seriously, you've got to be tracking down some international espionage ring or something, right? Some huge scandal waiting to be broken? You're Sammy-fucking-Habib after all.'

'I was, John,' she sighed. 'I was. Not so much anymore.'

'No?'

'Nope,' she sat up. 'That stuff's all over now. No editor will touch me. All my sources have dried up or found other journos to be friends with. The best I can manage these days is sneaking military secrets into Yelp reviews.'

'But what happened? I thought after you left here you went off and wrote about the size tool? Shouldn't you be famous or something?'

'By right, John Barton, yes I should. But this world doesn't respect rights much. Certainly not if you're freelance… and I guess I'm not even that anymore. I'm lower than that, if such a thing's possible.'

She rubbed her eyes and changed tack.

'Or I was, anyway. I'm out here now, John. I want the quiet life. I want to be with you and stuff.'

'-and stuff?'

'Stuff, yeah.'

'Well it's all very sudden, Sammy. You rush out of my life and you rush back in. Who's to say I'm happy, anyway? It's a strange world that can take for granted a man's happiness when he works down a tiny pit all day.'

He went quiet, looking at her. He didn't want to make himself angry.

'What happened to Zane Lund, anyway? Weren't you and him best mates after you broke into his resort?'

'I don't know what happened to Zane Lund, John.' Sammy sighed. 'I don't think you're getting it. They cut me out. The Bantz lot, Lund, they all cut me out. They can fuck 'emselves now, for all I care.'

'So you've not been following anything?' John sat up now, his eyebrows furrowed. 'Not even reading the news?'

'News is all lies, John.'

She burped as if she were burping the whole corrupt system out of her.

'Not even worth opening the app.'

'Well, Sammy,' he stood up and pulled on some boxers, 'I think that's shameful, that is. A shameful attitude to have.'

He stomped from the bedroom.

The flat was small. Sammy could hear him angrily filling the kettle only a few feet away. She pulled on a pair of his boxers and a t-shirt before stumbling out after him. Her legs protested the climb off the bed.

'What are you getting so angry about, John?'

She rounded the corner to find that he couldn't be too angry; he'd got two mugs out after all. His face was still knotted up.

'I just thought you were better than that, Sammy. Better than all this pessimistic, giving up rubbish. And to come here now and sell me a line about settling down and being happy with your lot? That, I could do without. I hear that from every bloody woman in Avon Murray; settle down, settle down. I mean, maybe it's my fault for having expectations, but I thought you were different from that, Sammy.'

'I am. I mean…' she gathered herself, 'what's that got to do with you anyway, John Barton? You want me to be some kind of symbol, eh? Am I your *#FeministIcon*, John Barton, eh?' She pronounced the hashtag. 'Because you sound stupid, going on like that.'

'Okay, so maybe it's not you then. Maybe it is just me. Maybe I was putting some faith in the idea that, somewhere out there, there was someone keeping track of all the evil that's going on. I thought that was you, but obviously I was wrong. Maybe it's not anyone! Maybe all this stuff that's happened has just… happened. No explanation necessary!'

'There is no explanation, John. There never was. It was just moving words around, don't you get it? Something happens here, something happens there. We tell stories with it. They tell stories. The world won't fit in a newspaper, John. Goddamn it! We have 24 hours of interactive news now and we're still getting nowhere close to the truth. If anything, we're further away than ever!'

'So you were lying all that time then, is that what you're saying?'

'I'm not saying that, John.'

'Okay, so you're saying that there's no truth at all then? That it's all just stories?'

'I'm not saying that either.'

'Then what the hell are you saying, Sammy? Because you left me once over your principles and now you're back - I still don't really know why - and now your principles are totally different!'

He dropped a teabag into each cup and added two sugars for Sammy.

'Just tell me who you are, Sammy, eh? Let's just start with that.'

'I'm Sammy Habib.' She met his eye. 'And I take two sugars in my tea.'

John Barton sighed.

'And that's it, is it?'

'That's about as much as I can manage at this point in time, John. Yes.'

He poured in the milk and passed her the tea. She blew on it. He blew on his.

'So...' He spoke softer now. Whatever was bothering him seemed to have passed. He was calm as he nodded to her backpack.

'You got all your spy stuff in there?'

She took a sip. 'Spy stuff?'

'You know, all your gear for getting into secret government databases?'

'I guess that stuff's all still in there, yeah. Why, John? You planning on doing some investigating?'

'Well, someone around here has to.'

He smiled and walked over to the bag. After setting down his tea he unzipped it and let the contents spill all over the floor.

'Hey! Some of that stuff was folded!'

'Yeah, I bet it was.'

Setting all the pieces out on the table, John started plugging plugs into sockets, trying to piece something together. Sammy sipped and watched him make a mess of it. She waited for him to turn to her and ask. 'Alright, Sammy. Can you help me?'

'What's the magic word?'

'Please?'

She set down her tea and fixed the mess he'd made. It involved unplugging everything he'd plugged in wrong, which was all of the things that he'd plugged in, and then reattaching them all. Sammy held her hand out.

'Pass me your phone.'

He took it out of his pocket and she placed it at the centre of the network. His phone became the head of an octopus.

'There,' she said, 'now you've got full control of the spy stuff. Enjoy.'

She walked away, scratching at her tummy.

'You don't want to know what I'm going to do with it?'

'Not particularly.'

'You have changed Sammy.'

She paused in the doorway. 'Just don't bookmark any porn on there. I've already got my collection just how I like it. I don't want your weird sheep fetish vids getting in there and messing up the system.'

'Not a problem, boss.' John saluted as she walked into the bedroom.

*

Half an hour later Sammy still hadn't emerged from the bedroom. Though it wasn't for lack of curiosity. After hitting thirty there were certain things which a body - even a body like Sammy's, tuned up from microsurgery and manic energy - could no longer overcome. A day of confinement, bruising and heavy physical exercise followed by a hot bath and a good shag was one of these things. The moment she'd stepped into the bedroom it was lights out.

Not that John Barton noticed. Five minutes into searching Sammy's spy networks, his blood was pumping with secrets.

There was something he'd been longing to tell Sammy ever since the farm closed. He'd written it in an email a few times but never felt confident enough to hit send. She, he hoped, would already know. The mine he worked for was owned by the Lund Corporation. All the micromines in the North were. He was never sure why, but it gave him a bad feeling. Lund were infamous for limiting their operations purely to the size tool, media and finance. Why would they get into mining?

Most manufacturers had simplified supply; simply holding one boulder of each necessary material, cutting parts off and expanding it when necessary. For most products, those to be used at regulation sizes, this procedure was fine. For precision work, however, meaning anything smaller than Travel Size, the process of continual expansion resulted in atom destabilisation. Microscopic bodies could experience mutations similar to those caused by unrefined uridium. Something to do with wavelengths, John reckoned; they'd never gone very deep into it at work. All he knew, and was certain of, was that the material he was mining was destined for use at non-regulation sizes.

'In that case,' John found himself wondering, 'why do they need so much of it?'

John Barton was on the hunt to find out. He was searching the World Bank's Piketty databases. They listed every piece of property owned in each nation, as well as stock holdings and any liquid assets held in banks, even those in tax havens. Through these, John Barton traced the ownership of the Avon Murray mine back to a Lund Corporation holding company in Somalia. The holding company owned no property in Somalia and appeared to be using it simply as a geographical pin from which to conduct operations without government oversight. Still, the Piketty databases had managed to trace the lines of its influence and, opening the master documents for Canada, France, Russia, Zimbabwe, New Zealand and the Congo, John pieced together a network of mineral mines that spanned the globe and took in vast quantities of unscaleable metals, alongside coal and uridium.

The uridium mines were only found in the Congo. The other mines mined fairly common materials and could be moved at short notice. Only the Congo mines were immovable.

For John Barton that meant one thing: if he wanted to find out what was going on with the Lund Corporation, he'd have to go to the Congo.

He looked up at the closed bedroom door. Sammy had not emerged. In fact, now he listened, he could hear her snoring.

So, he sighed, she really has changed. The one woman he had trusted to solve this mystery for him, the person he'd spent all of these years waiting for, his thumb hovering over the send message button; here she was, next door, asleep, and as cynical about the world as the rest of them. He swallowed. He looked back to the address on screen. He hit the screencap function on his phone. That's where he'd have to go. That's where he'd find his answers. Maybe that's where he'd find the woman he loved again, too. Because the girl in his bed, it was like he didn't even know her.

*

The next morning, Sammy Habib woke up on top of the covers. She had collapsed last night in boxers and a t-shirt, and hadn't moved for a whole eight hours. The light was still on and now, as she sat up and rubbed her eyes, she could hear birds singing.

'John?' she mumbled. 'John?!'

She realised he hadn't come to bed. The covers were unruffled. Had he slept on the couch?

'John?' She climbed out of bed and stumbled to the living room. Her legs were black with bruising. She couldn't find him anywhere. She staggered along, calling out to him. 'John?'

The mugs were still out where they'd left them. Her backpack was still there and, next to it, a mound of her clothes. What was missing, she noted, were her electronics. What had John called it? 'Spy stuff?'

As she approached the table she saw a note. Her heart began racing. What had he been angry about last night? Had he left her? She picked up the paper with a trembling hand.

She opened the letter and read.

Off to the Congo. Catch me if you can ;)

Underneath he'd signed it – 'John' – which she found sweet.

Jesus, John. I've heard of playing hard to get, but this is ridiculous.

Just then the door smashed off its hinges. Sammy jumped back as a figure marched up the stairs, followed by blue robed guardians. The guardians carried guns. The figure wore wings.

'Samra Habib?' Captain Pixie Adisa barked at the cowering Sammy. 'Of course I should find you here!'

'W-what is this?' Sammy was very aware of being in her pants. 'Why are you here?'

'I had heard that you were washed up, Sammy, but I didn't realise you'd got sloppy as well. The phone you used for your little hacking mission last night was not even encrypted. You are lucky that we got here first. The police of seven different nations spent all night arguing who would come for you. Interpol are on their way as we speak.'

'But, I… I was asleep all last night.' She stared up at the Captain, dazed. 'Please, Pixie, I don't want any trouble, I really don't. I've given up the life. I'm stood here in my boyfriend's undies for god's sake! I'm not a danger to anyone.'

'If that is so,' the Captain answered, 'then you can consider this a rescue service. Come, we will provide robes for you at the compound.'

With that, the guardians closed in. Sammy felt herself pinned by two strong arms and led out to a waiting vehicle. It had a strange design, sort of like a submersible, patterned with the white and blue colour scheme of the Lund Corporation. Sammy found herself strapped into a seat. The Captain strapped herself in opposite. They faced each other.

I should ask what's going on, Sammy thought. But somehow her motormouth had fallen silent. Instead, she just sat there, quietly, her hands folded in her lap. Then, suddenly, she heard a whooshing and felt her stomach turn. They launched into the sky. The ship shrank smaller and smaller until it was clear that they were no longer visible to the naked eye.

4

As they arrived at Lund Acres, Sammy noticed a change.

'Where are all the celebrities?'

'Oh, them?' Pixie recalled. 'They left after you told your little story. The resort was relocated and, soon after, they all had size tools of their own. They run their own resorts now.'

'So what is this place now?' Sammy asked.

'Training.'

Sammy seemed to be the only one in white robes. The rest of Lund Acres was a mass of blue. Squadrons of guardians jogged along the streets or marched in step between the Grecian buildings. The buildings no longer housed cafes but weapons caches and barracks. In the background there was the sound of shooting drills and, even further away, mortar practice.

'Are you building an army?' Sammy asked, wide eyed. They stepped to the side of the road and let an armoured car pass.

'It is military training,' Pixie answered impatiently, 'but not for war. Our guardians must be ready to face any challenge, and should excel in every field. Foremost among these skills is martial discipline, but that is only for the present. You will note that we also have a considerable library here, as well as a science park for practical demonstrations and experimentation. The use of these facilities is not optional.'

'It seems like you're making supersoldiers to me.' Sammy shrugged, 'but what do I know, right? I mean, they're called guardians after all. That's not sinister.'

'Your flippancy does not impress me, Samra Habib.'

'I'm very sorry to hear that, Pixie.'

Sammy smiled wryly. 'Can I call you that, by the way?'

'It is my name,' Pixie replied, 'and you are neither my superior nor inferior, so it would suit you better than calling me Captain.'

Sammy yawned and stretched as they crossed a parade ground. Guardians were hitting each other with sticks.

'Awwww!' Sammy chuckled, 'Are we friends now, Pixie?'

'You are not my friend,' Pixie answered coldly, 'but as I just saved you from Interpol, perhaps you should consider me to be your friend. Perhaps I am your best friend.'

'Besties!' Sammy clapped her hands together.

Without warning, Pixie turned and wrapped Sammy in a huge seven-foot-tall hug. For a second all Sammy could feel was the Captain's rock hard abs pushed against her. There was a faint scent of spice and the sensation of arms tightening around her lower back. Sammy's face was pushed into Pixie's breastplate. She wheezed onto it as she felt Pixie's huge wings open and launch them into the sky.

'Holy Jesus!' Sammy mouthed.

The rush of the wind alone told her they were high up. It had an alpine crispness to it which told her that, were Pixie to let go, there would be plenty of time for Sammy to take in the sights before she hit the ground.

Instead, within only a few seconds, they had landed on a branch of Lund Tower. Sammy blinked. Her arms and legs were still wrapped around Pixie. Peeling herself off her, Sammy realised she was in Zane Lund's office.

'Don't suppose there's a toilet up here, is there Pixie?'

'In the back,' she pointed, her wings folding back in, 'to the left.'

*

As Sammy walked out of the bathroom, Pixie was reclining on one of Zane Lund's animal skin settees. She seemed comfortable, although her body was contorted to make space for her wings. 'You know about the Congo operation, Samra?'

'The Congo operation?' Sammy decided not to play it smart this time. 'All I know is, that's where John Barton's gone'

'And who is John Barton?'

'He's…' Sammy sought after the right word. What was John to her? She felt a warmth inside as she thought of him. Putting her hand to her chest she continued. 'He's my lover.'

Pixie pulled a face, as did Sammy.

'I'm sorry. That sounded better in my head.'

Pixie let the awkwardness settle for a moment before continuing.

'Well, Samra, if your lover truly is heading into the Congo then he is making a terrible mistake. I have seen the situation in Congo myself, and it is not a place for naïve white men. Journalist or not.'

'Oh, he's not a journalist,' Sammy said, sinking herself into a plush leather chair. 'And how do you know he's white?'

'Your lover?' Pixie smiled a rare smile. 'Let's just say that I have known women like you, Ms Samra Habib, and you all have a type.'

'You know, Pixie, something tells me that in another life you were a real catty bitch!'

Pixie laughed. She had a deep and booming laugh. Sammy liked it. She rearranged herself on her chair and looked around the sparse room. 'Now, what say you and I get some mimosas in here, Pixie, and we have a chat about the Congo, yes?'

Pixie clicked her fingers and a guardian walked in carrying two drinks.

'The situation that your lover finds himself in is a perilous one,' Pixie said, pausing to sip her mimosa. 'You are aware of uridium, Ms Habib?'

'Sammy, please, call me Sammy...' the Ms stuff was getting annoying, 'and yes, of course I know uridium. It's what the size tool runs on.'

'Not 'runs on' as such, but you are essentially correct.'

Sammy rolled her eyes. Pixie decided against giving her a science lesson.

'Uridium is the principle compound involved in the operation of the size tool. To our current knowledge it exists in only one area of the world. Deep within the Congo. This scarcity is curious. We are currently working on the presumption that it came from a meteorite. One that crashed over seventy million years ago.'

Pixie frowned as she noticed Sammy's attention wandering.

'Now, Sammy, imagine that there is only a tiny amount of an extremely useful substance to be found on the Earth.'

'I'm imagining.'

'Now, imagine that small amount is in an area far from government control, in a country where the government itself is inefficient and corrupt.'

'Yes, I can imagine that.'

'Now, Sammy, search your imagination. Exactly how many different organisations would be willing to take up arms in pursuit of that small, small amount of substance?'

'I'd say,' Sammy sipped at her drink, 'probably all of them. All of the organisations. Armies. Gangs. Terrorists. The Girl Guides. Walmart.'

'You joke, Sammy, but you would not be far wrong.'

Pixie drained the last of drink and set it down before continuing.

'I have seen tanks driven by thirteen-year-old boys carrying the most expensive rifles money could buy. I slaughtered them, and among the wreckage I found documents showing they had been sponsored by a major fast food corporation.'

'Fucking hell.' Sammy too necked her drink. 'McGenocide.'

'It was not that corporation,' Pixie clarified, 'nor is it a genocide.'

'Well, whatever it is – wacky races with ultraviolence – I'm no wiser as to why John Barton-'

'Your lover,' Pixie smiled again. Sammy ignored her.

'-why he'd feel a sudden urge to get up and head into the middle of it. What was it that he found in those databases that he was searching? The ones that brought the police down on him?'

'Sammy, the Lund Corporation controls that uridium. I can tell you what he found: the full extent of our mining operations. What I cannot tell you is what conclusions he drew from that information. And what I definitely cannot tell you is why he was even looking for that information in the first place.'

She clicked her fingers and another guardian sidled in, this time she carried espresso martinis.

'What I am hoping, Sammy, is that you can explain to me why he went looking. Then, if you are honest with me, we might be able to work out what he went looking for.'

Sammy supped on her espresso martini and wondered if she was being loosened up. Pixie seemed genuine but then, why would she suddenly come on all chummy? Why was she giving her a guided tour of their secret training facility? It didn't add up. Something was rotten.

Not the martini though. That was gorgeous.

'First, Pixie, I want to know why you want to know. I mean, who is Pixie in all this?'

Sammy lounged back like she was David Frost.

'I am an operative of the Lund Corporation and I am tasked with protecting their assets.'

'Their assets?' Sammy smiled. 'So it's fair to say that their interests are not automatically your own interests?'

'This is not a question of my allegiances, Sammy, and you will not get through to me that way. The reason you are here and not being worked over by Interpol interrogators is because I need to ascertain why you, or your boyfriend, or whoever it was, went searching after our secret business.'

Sammy stirred the dark liquid around with her finger. She picked out a coffee bean and crunched on it.

'You've already decided it's not me, haven't you?'

'Not necessarily...'

'Yes, you have.'

Sammy grinned and sucked down some more martini.

'Because you know that I wouldn't fuck up so bad as to go in unencrypted. That's rule number one in my game, Pixie; always use protection. You know something's up and now I've told you. It was John Barton, my lover, using my kit.'

She swallowed the last of the martini. It was intended as a dramatic pause but she'd underestimated how much liquid was left in the glass. As she dabbed at her now-stained white robes, she continued.

'Now, from my perspective, I have a case of the runaway boyfriends, and as I was kind of counting on him hanging around for a bit and being in love with me and shit, I could do without him being cut to pieces by toddlers wielding sponsored machetes.'

'So you want to go after him?'

'As do you,' Sammy smiled. Martini was still dark around the corners of her mouth.

'But you cannot offer us any more information about what he is intending to do?'

'Well,' Sammy pondered, 'if he's anything like me - and I'm guessing this whole stunt is because he wants to be like me - then he has probably identified some rudimentary correlation of facts and is now charging at it headlong and with barely any consideration for the consequences.'

Pixie finished her own martini and rose from the sofa. As she straightened up, her feathers seemed to bristle on her wings.

'You know, Sammy, you are the only person whose initiative Zane Lund respects. He was most surprised when you disappeared after you broke the size tool story. He has always suspected that you were somewhere out there, in the shadows, following his every move.'

She walked over to a full length mirror hanging free of the wall.

'No-one else had the vision to even comprehend his work before you came along. I believe that he considers you a nemesis. I believe he fears you, as the one person who is always ahead of him.'

Sammy thought back to those long, painful weeks writing puff pieces for small change and was thankful that Zane Lund didn't read Mumznet. Pixie turned and flexed her wings. Her face was rigid with focus.

'Now you tell me that you have made all of your discoveries by chance? That you are forever rushing into situations blindly, caring little as to whether or not you are killed as a result? Well, Sammy, if this is truly what it takes to outwit a man like Zane Lund, then we must stop talking now and act!'

She walked over to Sammy who was still lounging. The tall woman offered the short one her hand.

'Will you come to the Congo with me? Will you come and find your lover?'

Sammy took the offered hand and pulled herself up.

'I will. And you, Pixie? Will you find whatever it is that you're looking for?'

'I have been ordered by Zane Lund to track down the person responsible for the breach. I am merely following his orders.'

Was that the threat of a grin that Sammy saw moving across the Captain's face?

'Now, Sammy, we must fit you with armour if you are to travel to Brazzaville.'

*

From a rooftop tent, they stepped out into the African sun. The Lund Corporation had a private wavelength, set aside from the civilian Amazon Rail lines, through which they could travel in total secrecy. The Brazzaville line took them to the top of a six story concrete tower block. The sun beat down on their skin and Sammy was already regretting her kevlar breastplate.

From the rooftop you could see out over the gleaming white rooftops of Brazzaville. A spike of tall towers in the centre indicated the corporate zone. High up in these gleaming spires, deals were made that kept the city flowing. What was currently flowing, more than anything else, was the trade in guns and in people willing to use them. Sammy noted the UN armoured vehicles patrolling the streets. Blue helmets moved assertively through crowds of shoppers. Some of the shoppers wore camouflage themselves.

'Have you been to Africa before, Sammy?'

Pixie was moving her fingers through the air, operating her suit's holographic UI; a series of glowing buttons that only the wearer could see.

'I can't say I have,' Sammy said.

She shielded her eyes from the light bouncing off the guardian's guns. They had brought a squad of fifteen with them and another squad had met them on the roof.

'In that case, all you men are dismissed.'

They weren't all men, but Pixie clearly used the term to address female guardians too.

'The café down the road does the best mwambe chicken in the country. We will have lunch before making for the river. A message has already come through. John Barton was seen travelling upriver yesterday. He will be heading for the mines. We will be travelling to the interior by boat, and will be eating cossa cossa shrimp for the next three or four days. So come, we will eat some real food before then.'

'You're talking my language,' Sammy said, following Pixie down into the stairwell. 'I've been gagging for some grub since those mid-morning martinis. You know, Pixie, the more time I spend around you, the more I like you.'

*

The boat set off from a shaded dock in the suburbs. On the orders of the UN, Amazon Rail had cut all lines heading east out of Brazzaville. If they wanted to get to the interior, they had to travel the old fashioned way. Their boat was of a decent size. It was large enough to carry the crew plus thirty soldiers. Pixie, being a Captain, claimed the captain's quarters. Sammy suspected she needed the big bed so she could sleep in her wings.

Sammy was bunking with a woman on nightwatch duty. They would go tagteam on a single hammock; the guardian in there by day, Sammy in there by night.

Sammy would spend most of her time up on deck, however. Partly to watch the jungle go by and partly to steady her stomach. The meals were indeed dominated by prawn, which the cook only seemed to know one recipe for. Whatever spices he was using did something mean to Sammy's guts. Once again, the white robes seemed a curse. At least she wasn't the only one wearing them now. The crew wore white to distinguish them from the guardians. This occasionally meant that sailors would yell aggressively at Sammy, thinking she was a crew member slacking off, but she'd become adept at ignoring them.

As they moved further into the interior, they began to encounter wreckage.

At first, it was burned out troop transports and armoured vehicles. Some of them were still smoking from recent air strikes. Later there were bodies. Around a bend they found a multitude bobbing in the river, maybe sixty or seventy. The crew leaned over the front with barge poles, poking them away from the boat, away from the propeller.

Another ten miles and there was scorched earth. A village and its surrounding jungle had been burned to the ground. Not all of the charred skeletons seemed fully grown.

'Is it going to get worse than this?' Sammy asked, gazing out over the destruction.

Pixie turned away, marking off their progress on a series of holographic maps and charts.

'This is usual,' she closed the charts and turned to Sammy. 'But we must be prepared for the unusual too.'

'I don't even have a gun.'

'I cannot give you a gun, Sammy.' Pixie lifted her pistol from its holster. 'I give you this and you are a combatant. Until then, you are still a reporter. Geneva Convention, you know?'

'I wouldn't have thought the Geneva Conventions counted for much out here.'

Sammy eyed the charred corpses again. She hoped they died before they burned. Sammy had a fear of fire. Although, admittedly, fire is a reasonable thing to be afraid of.

'You would be surprised, Sammy!' Pixie waved to her. 'Now, come. Come.'

They walked over to a stack of crates which sat at the nose of the boat. Sammy had presumed they were supplies of some sort or another. Pixie clicked her fingers, whistled and twirled her finger around in the direction of the boxes. From nowhere, three guardians leapt up, unclipping hidden straps and pulling back hatches.

The facade was quickly packed away and Sammy was left staring at a huge cannon. Its barrel was as long as she was tall, and it seemed to be powered by orb-like containers, each glowing a sickly neon blue.

'This is not a gun, Sammy,' Pixie chuckled, 'at least, not according to the UN. It is a military grade size tool. An expansion of the Size Tool Pro which, as you may remember, fired only five or six feet.'

'I never had one,' Sammy shrugged. 'I saw them on the news, though.'

'Well, now you are looking at a size tool capable of resizing objects over 3000 yards away. All without any ray diffusion.'

She lay a hand on it as if to pet it.

'Anything you point this ray at, no matter how far away, it will shrink out of existence in the blink of an eye. It is top secret. Only available to Lund Corps guardians.'

She swung the cannon around, its grip facing Sammy; 'and now you.'

'I don't know,'

Sammy hesitated, yet she felt her hands moving out and taking hold of the grips. 'Shouldn't I start with a normal sized gun before using this?'

'It is not a gun, Sammy, I told you. It's easier to use than a gun, for a start.' She indicated the viewfinder. 'Look through here.'

Sammy looked through the viewfinder and felt the world shrink around her. A light suction pulled her eye-sockets tight to the viewport. Quietly whirring, it calibrated itself to her vision. She felt foam appendages reaching out and pulling her face in to the cannon. Suddenly, she could see everything. The thick foliage of the surrounding jungle was replaced with a transparent mesh. On it were infrared animals, shining bright and clear in the light of the scope. She moved the reticule over one and it gave her a readout. A monkey, apparently. Then a tiny parrot with her chicks. Sammy found she wanted to see further and the cannon responded to her thinking, pulling back to a wider field of view. She could see acres and acres of translucent forest.

Out there she saw crouched figures cradling guns. The reticule confirmed they were soldiers.

'There's men out there,' Sammy whispered.

'There are men all over this part of the country,' Pixie replied. 'Most of them stay away from the river, but it is wise to keep our eyes peeled. Look ahead of us.'

Sammy moved the cannon around to face the river ahead. Her eyes were still fixed to the viewfinder. Up the river, perhaps a few miles, she could see a conflict. Bright yellow sparks caught her eye and the cannon zoomed in for her. She saw men, crouched, shooting. An armoured car was hammering a building with a powerful machine gun. Then, stepping up to face them all, she saw a huge infrared silhouette.

'Is that a giant?'

'That,' Pixie answered, gently pulling Sammy away from the cannon, 'is a UN peacekeeper. The blue hats. Sadly we have not yet perfected a full-colour version of the cannon's HUD, otherwise it would have been plain to see.'

'But, but...' Sammy felt stupid but also astounded. 'He was the size of a house!'

'The size tool, Sammy!' Pixie shook her head. 'How have you never seen such things before?'

'I guess no one wanted to be huge where I lived!' She crossed her arms. 'Anyway, shouldn't that be against the law? That's not a regulation size. Those are supposed to be government troops.'

'UN troops, not government. But you are right, they still must obey the regulations.'

Pixie powered down the cannon and placed it in resting position.

'That is Super Size, Sammy. The fourth of the regulation sizes. Military application only. You will not have seen it, I suspect, as you have not been in a warzone since the size tool became popular.'

'You've got me there, Captain.'

'Well, Sammy, now you're in one.'

She held up her arms and her wings spread out behind her in parallel.

'Welcome to the warzone!'

'Jesus,' Sammy walked past her and made for her cabin. 'You just keep us all alive until we find John Barton. I'm going for a lie down. I'm getting too old for this shit, and I've only just turned thirty.'

5

They were four days on the river. The heat never got any easier to bear. If anything, it intensified as the boat wended its way down the long and winding waterways. On the second morning they had to hide under trees as a patrol of gigantic UN troops swept past. The third morning saw them idly strafed by a jet fighter. Thankfully no one was hurt. Other than that, the journey had been tense but uneventful.

Sammy found herself wondering about John Barton. Had he felt this same mix of tension and urgency? Had he seen the giant soldiers? Had he the sense to avoid them or...

She found she couldn't finish the thought. She didn't want to think of him anywhere but Avon Murray, fixing some stupid gate and feeding her blended-up pies. She refused to think of him as a corpse.

The boat pulled to the side of the river. Pixie approached. Something was happening.

'Sammy!' Pixie took her by the shoulders and guided her inside. 'You must stay below deck now. We are passing the first of the mines.'

'The uridium mines?' Sammy stopped, confused. Isn't this what they were heading for?

'It is a uridium mine, Sammy,' Pixie explained, 'but I doubt that John Barton stopped here. Most traders continue along the river. There is a trading post not two hours from here. This mine, a lowland mine, is small, close-knit. If he wanted to get into a mine, he would not get into this one.'

Sammy paused and thought.

'But there's no reason why we can't go in, right? I mean, it's a Lund Corporation mine, isn't it?'

'It is, and there is no reason why me and my men cannot investigate.' Pixie gestured down the stairs. 'You, as a guest, however; this would be harder to explain. It would be easier if you stayed below decks.'

Sammy couldn't help but feel she was being played. There was a lingering sense of ambush in it. She'd trusted Pixie this far, but how much further would she go?

'Okay,' Sammy finally nodded, 'I'll stay down here and have a cup of tea. If you're not back by the time it's done then I'll be leaving without you.'

'That's fair, Sammy,' Pixie shut the door on her. 'It shall be the work of moments.'

*

Sammy went down into the mess, positioning herself by a porthole. They had started to move again already. They had shipped to hide the guns and fly the Lund Corporation flag. Pixie wanted a warm welcome.

The jungle tangle passed by at the creaking pace she'd come to find familiar. Nothing moved fast on the river. As they rounded a corner the sounds of industry became clearer. There were even some muffled blasts. Uridium was a soft element, but to detach it from the surrounding stone took dynamite.

The percussive booms were visible in the water. The surface trembled with each shockwave.

Sammy watched the jungle peel back. The muddy riverbank now bore an array of corrugated iron huts and slimy pits. Moving drunkenly among it all were black bodies. They were skinny, some even showing the swollen bellies and ankles of starvation diets. Sammy couldn't tell whether their defeated staggering was a result of overwork, underfeeding, or maybe the effects of constant blast percussion on their inner ears. The only protection she could see them wearing were the occasional pair of goggles and gloves. The guardians who stood watch over them wore full breathing apparatuses and steel helmets.

'It's like hell, isn't it?' Sammy said, as if to no one.

Hearing her, the cook emerged from the kitchens and walked over to the porthole. Sammy looked up at the cook's big, sweating face as it frowned. He spoke in a French accent.

'This is not hell. In hell they have more taste. This is just human cruelty… human stupidity.'

And with that he walked back to the kitchen. It was prawns for lunch again.

Still, Sammy couldn't tear herself away from the window. It was hard to believe that human suffering could be so abject when, for so many on the planet, life had become a dreamland. The fact that one of those things was a direct cause of the other… that the team of miners now staggering from the mine with bleeding ears did so in order to make the size tool possible… it awoke something in her. It was something she'd not felt in a long time. It was what she'd felt when, as a teenager, she'd discovered a sexual abuse ring operating in her town, preying on her school friends. It was the event that first made her name. Like then, she had two options: become a Christian and forgive them, or else become a journalist and fuck them up.

'Say cheese,' said Sammy, as she lifted her high res cameraphone to the porthole. 'It's time for your close up.'

As the boat pulled in to a makeshift pier, Sammy saw ropes flung from the deck above. The gangway lowered. A team of guardians ran down from the mine complex to salute the disembarking Pixie. Pixie did not salute back. She simply stepped on to the pier and nodded to the most prominent guardian. Snapping his heels, the blue-robed figure turned and ran back to a squat building that Sammy had not yet noticed.

Sammy zoomed in on her camera.

From out of the building came a sagging, official looking man, rotund and wearing a colonial-style suit and hat. He gestured to Pixie that she should come over to him but, finding her fixed in place, he groaned and manoeuvred his sweating mass towards her. There was plenty of time for Sammy to find his best angle.

The sweating man spoke some brief words to Pixie. She shook his hand and then climbed the gangway back up to the boat. The ropes were pulled up and three long bargepoles splashed down into the water, pushing them off. They were back on the river.

Sammy waited roughly five minutes before coming back up on deck.

'So, what was all that about?'

'Sammy!' Pixie turned. 'We have barely pulled out. Can you please wait below decks until we are out of sight?'

'What are they going to do?' Sammy grinned. 'I'm here now, anyway. Tell me what's going on. Who was the fat guy? Why was he dressed like Sgt. Pepper? Has John Barton been here?'

'One question at a time.'

Pixie pulled out a chair for Sammy and sat down herself, her legs spread wide and hands on her hips.

'That man is what's known as a commissioner. All of the Lund Corporation mines have one. They are agents of Her Majesty's Diplomatic Service, remnants of the old Colonials. They believe they are in charge, but we keep them only to guarantee diplomatic neutrality.'

'Of course, very important in a warzone.'

'The warzone is unofficial. The presence of commissioners keeps it from becoming official.'

'Cracking!' Sammy span a map round, searching for their current location. 'And John Barton?'

'The commissioner said that nobody had stepped onto the bank for eight days. The trader ships were all making for the post, as I told you they would be.'

Pixie passed another map to Sammy, tapping a point marked with a tiny pickaxe.

'If John Barton has made it this far, he will have carried on into the interior.'

'I see.'

Sammy ran her finger along the river to where the trading post was marked.

'But if there are British government agents here, we should be alright, right? John's a British citizen.'

Pixie leaned back in her chair. Sammy noticed her check that no one was listening. The guardians were all far off and busy working. Pixie leaned forward and spoke quietly.

'It is the presence of government forces that worries me most. Before I joined Lund, I was a mercenary, and let me tell you, Sammy; governments were the worst. They were the cruellest, the most deceptive, and the most dogmatic of all the clients I worked for. Governments believe they are always right, no matter what they do. When I first met Zane Lund he agreed with me that the world would be better off without them. Now, they are everywhere. He thinks he is using them only as security, to avoid red tape. But I'm telling you, Sammy; they are using him.'

It was Sammy's turn to lean back and look circumspect. She folded her arms and replied.

'I'm beginning to see why you want me here, Pixie. You might come across as a cynical gun-for-hire, but you're just another bloody do-gooder.'

The Captain scratched at her upper lip.

'Not a do-gooder, Sammy. Just a woman in search of, how would you English phrase it? Fair play.'

*

Two and a half hours later they were pulling in to the trading post. The place had six or seven different names depending upon which of the local languages you spoke, but the English signs simply read: Trading Post. It was the only one for two hundred miles so no one was likely to get it confused. The guardians had just finished their shrimp as the boat tied up. Pixie had warned Sammy to eat before disembarking. The food in these places was riddled with parasites.

'It is as if they add them to enhance the flavour.'

As they stepped off the boat and began striding through the cramped and crowded streets, Sammy couldn't help but feel conspicuous. Their sparkling blue and white robes were dazzling compared to the stained t-shirts and shorts favoured by the traders. Some of the Arab merchants wore off-white headdresses but nothing quite so outlandish as the guardians.

'Where are we headed?' Sammy asked, struggling to keep up with the long strides of the Captain.

'I have an idea,' Pixie replied. 'But I do not know if they will meet us.'

Sammy bounced off an old woman who began yelling. They really were walking very fast.

'If who will meet with us? Is it someone who'll know John Barton?'

'If your lover has come through here they will know of him. If he has any of his wits about him then he will have spoken to them.'

'It's a long shot then.'

Sammy tried walking directly behind Pixie. The Captain had a way of cutting through crowds as if they weren't there, which was impressive for a seven-foot warrior with wings.

'You don't have to keep calling him my lover. When I said that I was just joking.'

Pixie laughed a rare laugh.

'Don't worry, lovergirl! We shall find your lover soon!'

They turned a corner and moved down another bustling street, then out into a square. Across the square was a building with a red and black flag. Sammy moved close in behind her, aware of the desperate push of bodies all around. Behind them, ten guardians followed. It might have been this that gave them away.

On the roof of the red and black banner-draped building, a sleepy guard perked up. He was shirtless but wore a red armband on his upper arm. He began banging on the corrugated iron roof and yelling into a walkie talkie.

'They have seen us.'

Pixie lifted her hand and made a series of elaborate pointing and circling gestures. The guardians fanned out into the crowds. They moved fast and kept low to the ground. Pixie continued walking; tall, unhurried. Sammy followed behind.

'Wait! Are we attacking them?'

'It is not an attack,' Pixie clarified, 'it is a tactical approach.'

Figures wearing red and black bandanas over their faces rushed out of the building's doors. Some disappeared effortlessly into the crowds. Others weren't so agile and Sammy could see the guardians moving to intercept them through the huddle.

'Who are they?' Sammy asked.

She soon found out.

As if from nowhere, a young man tripped and fell into Pixie's outstretched arm. She wrapped his t-shirt around her fist and lifted him into the air with it.

'What are you running from?' She barked at him. 'Where is your leader?'

The man scrabbled at her hand, trying to grab it. His legs kicked pathetically in the air. Pixie gave him a second to reply. Hearing nothing useful, she dropped him onto her knee. He doubled up and rolled along the ground. Pixie kept walking.

Somewhere out in the crowd there was a scream. The guardians weren't messing around, Sammy realised. She felt lucky to be on their side. Well, at least for the moment.

Am I on their side? She couldn't really remember.

The panic and violence had spread out into the crowd. There was a lot of rushing around in the square, and the sound of fistfights.

The mass of people who had only a moment ago been busy buying and selling were now starting to riot. Whatever Pixie's plan was, Sammy realised, they would have to see it through fast. The police would soon be on their way and here. In the warzone, in bandit country, Sammy doubted they could talk their way out.

As they reached the front door, a guardian emerged and saluted Pixie. Sammy realised he had flanked the building. Pixie nodded and he spoke.

'The chairman is secure, ma'am. He's in his office. Didn't even try running.'

'Very good,' she nodded and the soldier stepped aside. As they entered the door Sammy noted the sign: The Congolese Miner's Union.

The office was a mess of revolutionary flags, piles of paperwork and three worn-out, off-white PCs. The posters on the walls read things like "Solidarity with the MicroCity" and "Boycott Lund". Sammy noticed a Colonel Gaddafi bust sitting on a filing cabinet, flanked by Lenin and Marx. She followed Pixie through to the back office. Two guardians stood guard outside.

From behind his desk, a man in a scratty suit rose to his feet.

'Captain Adisa!' He smiled grimly. 'I am honoured that it is you they sent. I was expecting only the usual goons. They must think highly of me over at head office. It is most appreciated. You notice that I did not run?'

'I did notice that, Banza, and I admire your heroism.'

Pixie stood at least a foot taller than the man. Sammy presumed he was chair of the miner's union.

'As much as I would like to, Banza, I am not here to kill you. At least not today.'

The chair raised his finger to his lips, adopting a comically exaggerated pose.

'Oh? You are not? Why, how generous of you, Captain. This is certainly a rare treat! A gala day!'

He walked over to his cabinet and lifted out a bottle of rum.

'Now, if you aren't here to slaughter me, as your goons have done to, oh, soooo many of my predecessors, then perhaps you have merely come over for a friendly drink?'

He poured two glasses of rum, sinking his own in a mouthful.

'You have a sense of humour, Banza. This is good. You Trotskyists and funnier than the Stalinists.'

Pixie picked up the rum and passed it to Sammy who was cowering awkwardly behind her.

'Oh, Comrade Trotsky was a noted wit, Captain Adisa. You really must read him someday. Perhaps then you will deign to share a drink with me instead of handing it to your tiny friend here.'

'I'm taller than you,' Sammy muttered.

'No, you are not.'

'This is Samra Habib,' Pixie announced. 'A world famous journalist.'

'A journalist?' She saw his eyes widen, curious.

'Yes, and she has lost her lover.'

'Her lover?' His eyes widened further, as did his grin.

'Yes, he goes by the name of John Barton. He is a white man.'

'A white m-'

'Yes, Banza, we all appreciate your repetitions. Now don't make me kill you, and tell me whether or not you are aware of anyone heading upriver who answers to the name of John Barton.'

'Well,' Banza chuckled, pouring himself another rum with one hand and lifting it to his lips with the other. 'What an interesting situation we find ourselves in. You see, there was a certain John Barton who came by here only yesterday. He was pursuing certain information and some friendly directions, with which I was happy to assist him. Now, I am not a gambling man, Captain, but what do you suppose the odds are on this being the same man?'

'Where did you send him, Banza?'

'I did not send him anywhere, Captain! He went of his own free will.'

The union chair sat back down and fanned lazily at his face. He was sweating buckets, Sammy noted, but then so was everyone else.

'Now, what troubles me, Captain, is that I have been a member of this union for nearly six years now and never has a western journalist taken the time to come and visit us. Frankly, I had presumed that nobody cared. Now, I am faced with two journalists arriving in just as many days... and world famous ones, no less.'

He leaned forward, staring this time at Sammy.

'And one of them is accompanied by the chief murderer among the Lund Corporations many, many death squads.'

Pixie turned and shut the office door, leaving the two guardians outside. As she tuned back she gestured to Sammy to take a chair. Pixie remained standing.

'If the Lund Corporation uses death squads, Banza, then I am not aware of them. I do not involve myself in such activities. Your problem, Banza, is that you believe your own propaganda.'

Banza looked up at Pixie. His face now fell, turning deadly serious. He turned to Sammy.

'Are you her prisoner?'

'No.'

Sammy poured herself another rum and sipped at it. It was warm and sugary. High quality.

Banza opened his arms to her, 'then why are you here?'

'I've come for John Barton.'

'Your lover?'

'My boyfriend.'

'And what has John Barton come for?'

She took a sip. 'Answers, I suppose.'

'Answers to what?'

'Well I don't fucking know, do I?'

She drank the rest of the rum and slammed the glass down.

'You're the one he spoke to last! You're the one sending him off to die in some fucking hole in the ground! Why don't you tell me?'

Banza looked her in the eye. He could sense her seriousness, her honesty. She could see something click inside him. He knew he could trust her.

'Many people die in these holes, Samra. If he did die in there, then your John Barton would hardly be the first. As it is, he is not heading to the mines.'

'He's not?'

'No.' Banza turned to Pixie with a knowing look. 'He is heading to the microcity.'

'The microcity?' Sammy asked.

Pixie's face was fixed, unmoving. She gave nothing away.

'You know, Sammy, Karl Marx was a very clever man.'

Banza leaned back, expansive, staring all the while at Pixie.

'He recognised capitalism as a great liberating force. It freed the serfs from the land. It freed merchants to trade freely. Yet, from all this freedom, came new slaveries. Slaveries made all the worse because they were freely chosen by free men...

'For many in the West, the size tool has become just another type of freedom. Another freedom in a vast sea of freedoms. We too, here in the Congo, have shared in this freedom. We are free now to fight, and my god do we fight. The killing, it is endless. And we are free from laws, the kind of laws that stifle your... glorious enterprise,' he gestured to Pixie, she looked back with contempt. 'We are so free, Samra Habib, so very free, that we are even now free to become free of our freedom.'

'What do you mean by that?' Sammy asked.

She had turned on her recorder.

'I mean that the Lund Corporation,' he pointed to Pixie. 'The company that she works for, is offering ten thousand pounds a person to sign into indentured servitude. SLAVERY!' He shouted. 'By any other name: SLAVERY!'

'I do not know of this, Sammy,' Pixie said, her eyes still fixed on Banza. 'I know nothing of this.'

'I have seen it with my own eyes!' Banza continued. 'We have photocopies of the contracts here in this office, just back there. I can show you. In fact, here!'

He threw a pile of folders into Sammy's lap.

'Here are fifty such contracts. Every one of them would be illegal, were there such things left as laws. Of these fifty enslaved people, only eight remain. The rest – poof!'

He made a poof of smoke gesture with his hands.

'Up in smoke! Another sacrifice for progress!'

'What is this?'

Sammy was rifling through the papers. They looked genuine. Prominent among them were photos of a tiny black box, the size of a matchbox.

'That, my sharp-eyed friend, is where you house your slaves in the twenty first century.'

Pixie leaned over, eyeing the black box with disapproval.

'How many people are in there?' Sammy asked.

'Over a hundred thousand,' Banza replied. 'That's why we call it the microcity. Those bastards at Lund call it HR. Human Resources. How about that, eh?'

'I have never heard of this.'

Sammy looked at Pixie and saw worry in her eyes. It was a deep and terrible worry, like something she had always suspected was finally revealed to be true.

Sammy turned back to Banza.

'How do we get in?'

'You know,' Banza chuckled, 'That was your lover's first question too! I'll tell you what I told him. The microcity is connected to every mine in the region through microfiber lines, a millionth of the thickness of Amazon Rail. The only people who come in and out are the miners, the guardians and certain allotted traders who provide their food and clothing. You happen to be in the one settlement through which all of these traders pass. Every day people come in and out of this town on their way to the microcity. The size tool depot is five miles out to the north.'

'You need to get us in there,' Pixie said.

Banza looked up at her, his lip curling.

'Why don't you just fly there yourself? You are with Lund, are you not?'

Sammy turned to Pixie. Was it the heat, or was she breathing a bit too heavily? Sammy poured herself another rum and downed it. This was all getting a bit much.

'Don't mind about her,' Sammy said, 'she's with me, and I want in to this microcity. What options have we got?'

Banza poured himself the last of the rum and smiled.

'You are a woman of business, Samra Habib. I like that. Now, let me see. First, we will have to get you out of those Flash Gordon costumes. Then, provided a significant donation is made to the cause of Congolese people's liberty, I should say that we can get you inside on the evening shipment.'

'What about the wings?' Pixie asked.

Banza looked up at her and shrugged.

'I don't know. Do traders have wings? I do not personally think so but perhaps I do not know the right traders, eh?'

Pixie grunted, her feathers rustling slightly.

'Don't worry about us,' Sammy said. 'You just have that shipment ready and waiting.'

She stood up and walked to the door.

'Captain, give the man his money.'

6

They crouched in the back of a truck full of fruit. Six oranges the size of space hoppers were piled up beside them, forming a leathery orange barrier. Behind that was a bunch of grapes that filled up the rest of the lorry, and a couple of small boxes containing sixty thousand bananas. They strapped themselves down with rope and waited to enter the microcity.

They were dressed in the garb of Arabic traders. Beneath loose robes they wore bundles of rags to masculinise their body shapes. They pulled scarves up, covering their faces. In a city full of men with nothing to live for, it was safer to travel male. Beneath Pixie's feet was a swollen kitbag. It ostensibly held rubber components for plumbing (a commodity much called for in the microcity) but a check would reveal it to also contain two loaded pistols, a carbine, and a set of folded, golden wings.

Outside the cabin they heard a whoosh. They were in.

*

After a series of bumpy roads, traffic jams and customs officials in need of bribing, they felt the lorry pull to a halt. It idled for a second. A door slammed up ahead. They heard shutters closing behind them.

It was the union lock-up. A nervous minute passed before they heard a friendly hand hammering on the side of the container. The rear doors slid open.

'How are you doing in there?' came the voice of their guide.

'Enjoying the heat?'

'It's like a sauna,' Sammy gasped. 'Move the fruit. Quick!'

The guide laughed and gestured to the nearby stevedores. They responded with clench-fisted salutes and began unloading. The union ran lorries into the microcity on a regular basis. They brought the kinds of items that traders wouldn't bring. Fruit, for example, may be high in vitamins but didn't return much profit. When everyone was penniless and starving, they were mostly happy with gruel and krokodil. The union weren't too happy with this arrangement, so sent in relief wagons. They barely covered their costs, but at least the workers got their vitamins. Their guide, Awax Saint-Just Ngalamulume, gave off the beatific glow of someone who thinks they're helping.

'We will be unloaded in a matter of moments, ladies. Or should I say, gentlemen?'

'You can call us whatever you like, mate,' Sammy gasped. 'Just have some water ready when you've shifted those grapes.'

'It would be easier,' Pixie announced with more authority, 'if you did not refer to us by name. We are nomads. Traders. To give you our names would be – according to the trader's lore – to give you a power over us. This would, in itself, be suspect. You will refer to us merely as traders, or as gentlemen, if you so wish.'

'Aye aye, ma'am!'

Awax laughed, giving a cartoon salute. He slapped a passing comrade on the back and yelled.

'You heard the gentlemen, boys! Get this fruit out of here, and bring some fresh spring water! With ice!'

The workers around him didn't respond. Sammy put this down to Awax being a one of those easy going bosses she'd heard about. Pixie put it down to communist insubordination.

*

Ten minutes later they sat in the microcity branch of the Congolese Miner's Union. The posters in this office were identical to the ones at the trading post, including the one reading "Solidarity with the Microcity". Charity begins at home, Sammy thought. Having supplied them with their ice water, Awax now brought out an ornate wooden jug and proceeded to pour coffees. The jug was Ethiopian, he explained, and they have elaborate coffee rituals there, just like the Japanese do for tea. Although, he admitted, he had only visited once and didn't know much about them.

'We are looking for a man called John Barton,' Pixie interrupted.

'Then it's good that I forgot the coffee ceremony,' Awax said, 'because there is a lot of small talk involved, and it is clear that you don't have time for such things.'

'No,' Pixie confirmed, 'we don't.'

'We reckon he's come to collect evidence of the microcity,' Sammy explained. 'I mean, he's kind of a journalist, I suppose? He's doing an impression of one anyway. Your boss – Banza was it? – he told us you guys smuggled him in here. Can you tell us where he went?'

'Pierre!' Awax shouted. A skinny man with a goatee poked his head in through the door. 'Pierre, did we bring a man through here by the name of John Barton?'

'I don't know, sir.'

He was a young man and didn't seem too bright.

'You want me to check the registers, sir?'

'If you would, Pierre.'

Pierre's head disappeared and they heard filing cabinets being searched. Awax sipped at his coffee.

'He is a good boy, Pierre, but he should take it easy with the Mary Jane perhaps.'

'Are there any areas that he's likely to go?' Sammy asked, recorder in hand. 'Any areas where he might get interviews or guides or… newsworthy things?'

'Well,' Awax leaned back and scratched at his chin. 'Provided he is not already dead, then he is likely to have been kidnapped by someone or other by now.'

'What?'

'It depends how long he has been here, of course.'

Pierre's disembodied head then returned to the room.

'I found him, sir. We brought him in yesterday.'

'And he has not come out again?'

'Not that I can see, sir!' Pierre smiled, pleased at his own initiative. 'Is that all, sir?'

'Yes, Pierre, you have been most helpful. Thank you!'

Awax smiled and waved away his subordinate. Turning back to the two cotton-wrapped figures in front of him he sighed.

'Yes, I'm afraid that he's definitely been taken by somebody at this point.'

'Shit…'

Sammy felt her stomach turning over inside her. She swallowed, tensed herself, pushed back the bad thoughts.

'If this is so,' Pixie straightened up, 'we must act fast.'

'I suspect the time for acting fast has gone,' Awax chuckled, 'but I commend your spirit! Everything is possible with hope, my friends. Yes! Let us find your friend.'

With that, he rubbed his hands together and pulled a dog-eared notebook out of his grease-slicked shorts. He began flicking through it, humming to himself and occasionally pausing to tap at a page.

'You have some ideas where he might be?' Pixie asked.

'A few.'

Awax furrowed his brow and closed the notebook.

'Now that I think about it, I know some people who are better qualified than I to answer you.'

'And these are?' Pixie asked, impatient.

'Come!' Awax finished his coffee and stood. 'You will find out when we get there. I will introduce you directly.'

Pixie stood and followed Awax out of the room, the kitbag slung over her shoulder. Sammy, who was only halfway through her coffee, stumbled out after them.

*

They pushed through the jostling crowds of the microcity. Sammy was growing more and more dejected. She thought of John Barton wandering these streets, lost and alone, and kind of stupid, in a charming way. She didn't think she could bear it if anything happened to him. Maybe age was getting the better of her? She felt young elbows jamming into her sides as gangs of gaunt and shirtless youths barged past her. She felt the occasional young foot stamping on her toes. The streets of the microcity were in perpetual gloom, locked as they were inside a matchbox. Streetlights and the occasional naked bulb were all that lit the city. It was a city of shadows. Masses of movement soaked up the rare light.

They kept themselves wrapped tight, but still Sammy and Pixie attracted attention. There were other traders around but none of their size and shape. Pixie stood a foot taller than even the lankiest of the starving miners, while Sammy-plus-padding was visibly better fed than anyone else in the city. If it wasn't for the waving, hollering presence of Awax as their guide, Sammy felt it likely that they too would have been picked up. As it was, everyone seemed to know Awax. He yelled private jokes to barbers, shook an elderly man's hand and shared a conversation without even slowing his pace. In another situation, Sammy thought, Awax might be a millionaire, or a laughing Buddha. He was a man of the people.

Which is why it was so troubling when they began to descend a series of stairwells and Awax dropped his banter and became visibly cautious. The darkness loomed in as they entered the microcity's underworld. They moved through storm drains and service hatches, all carved into polystyrene. It was the base of the city that they were moving through now. No soil. Not like Lund Acres, or even the most basic of private size tool created homes. This was as cheap as it got. It gave Sammy a terrible sense of impermanence, like being in a cave that might collapse, only here there was the uncanny feeling that someone would scrunch up the whole city and throw it in the bin.

Finally, they reached a cave. It had been dug out of the polystyrene. Inside, it was pitch black.

Awax turned back to them.

'We are here. Do you have torches?'

'I have one on my phone.'

Sammy offered it to him, selecting the app.

Awax looked despairingly at Pixie, who shrugged.

'Okay then, it will have to do.'

With a tinny start-up noise, Sammy's torch app flickered into life. She adjusted the settings in an attempt to keep the power low. They had no more than twenty minutes.

'That will be enough,' Awax nodded, 'I hope.'

They moved through the dark passageway. The raw polystyrene squeaked underfoot and occasionally they'd stumble over a loose sphere of it. The tunnel was wide. It was like a cavern in places. Many hands had been involved in digging it out.

Soon they saw a light ahead of them. It glowed a sickly neon blue. Sammy turned her phone off and they moved closer.

Ahead of them they saw a door carved into the plastic. Beside it was a single brazier holding not fire but a lump of raw uridium. Sammy had never seen it in its raw state before. She could see why miners had considered it cursed for so long. The centre of the gem seemed to pulse with a radioactive light while around it a sort of shredded-wheat structure of crystals grew out in a casing. This silvery, webbed outer casing looked like it was blowing in a breeze but the air in the cave was still. Instead, Sammy realised, it was the power of the core that blew through it. There was no denying it. The rock seemed alive.

Taking a deep breath, Awax stepped around the uridium. He went to knock on the door. Before he could even lift his hand, a hatch slid open and a pair of eyes peered out.

'Who is it?' the figure behind the door asked. 'What do you want?'

'You know me, comrade.'

Awax smiled while his hand shook.

'It's Awax. From the union. I am here with these travellers. They are looking for someone. For a journalist.'

'Who are they?'

The man was suspicious, as befitted a man peeping through an iron door.

Awax looked to them, shrugged and turned back to the guard.

'They are disguised as Arabic traders.'

'Yes, I can see that,' the guard rolled his eyes, 'I want to know who they really are. We can't just let anybody in here, Awax, just because you asked nicely.'

'I know, I know.'

Awax pushed his hands together and rocked back and forth in a parody of begging.

'But they've lost their friend and we really need your help. Pretty please! Pretty please with sugar on top!'

The guard rolled his eyes again, clearly a common gesture of his, and then turned his gaze on Sammy and Pixie. In a tougher voice he asked them directly.

'Who are you?'

Pixie moved forward as if to speak, but Sammy held her back.

Instead she announced, 'I am Sammy Habib, freelance journalist. I'm here to find John Barton, and to break any news that I come across along the way.'

'Sammy Habib?'

A voice echoed from behind the suspicious guard. Sammy watched as the eyes at the peephole retracted and others, less suspicious, took their place.

'You are Sammy Habib the journalist? The one who writes for the Bantz Testament?'

Sammy stepped forward.

'That's me.'

'I heard that you were the one who first discovered the size tool? The one who first broke the news of the Lund Corporation's malicious schemes to the whole world?'

'Where did you hear that?' Sammy asked.

'In the comments section,' the man grinned. 'People kept posting it and moderators kept taking it down, so it's got to be true, right?'

'Well, it is true,' Sammy beamed.

'Can we come in now?' Awax asked.

'Oh, yes, of course!'

The figure moved and they heard the slamming back of bolts. The door creaked open and inside they saw a fully furnished operations room complete with a world map and several blinking monitors hanging from the ceiling.

As they walked in, the man who had known Sammy opened his arms wide.

'Welcome, friends! Welcome, to the Frequency Underground!'

*

They sat on sofas around a coffee table. They were being served more coffee, Arabic this time. As the man began to explain the operation, Sammy wondered where the toilets were. They had drunk a lot of coffee. In keeping with the secrecy of this operation, the man explained, he could not give his name, but he did understand their plight.

'The Frequency Underground is a revolutionary organisation committed to the transformation of the world. As your journey here testifies, the size tool has brought only renewed misery to the toiling masses of the third world. I am reliably informed that the working class of your own country is suffering too, Sammy?'

'I suppose,' she sipped at the thick coffee, 'in a way.'

'We are committed to a wholesale reorganisation of the current economic hierarchies dominating the globe. The size tool has made it possible, although as you also know, that was possible long before the size tool came into existence. Without a fundamental shift in consciousness, the world of plenty will be forever withheld from the world's suffering masses.'

Sammy could feel Pixie shifting in her chair. She was glad that the guards hadn't thought to check their kitbag.

'We demand size tools for all,' the man continued, 'and a return to unrestricted size allocations.'

'Who exactly are you demanding this of?' Pixie spat, clearly enraged by the man's condescending tone.

The revolutionary narrowed his eyes.

'Do I know you?'

'Please,' Sammy leaned in, 'continue. Size tools for all. No more regulation sizes.'

'Yes,' the man lifted his coffee and sniffed at it. 'Yes, we demand the freedom of frequencies. It is a human right.'

'Who says so?' Pixie cut in.

Sammy was beginning to regret bringing her. She had behaved herself with the unions, but communist guerrillas were clearly a step too far for Captain Adisa.

'We say so,' the man continued, his eyes once again narrowing on Pixie, 'and to prove it, we have already found a number of unused sizes at which not even the world's militaries, or the Lund Corporation, or the secret state operate…'

'Secret state?' Pixie spat. 'Sammy, come on. This man is clearly a fantasist. There is no secret state.'

'If there is no secret state,' the man replied, sipping his coffee. 'Then how do you explain them taking your precious John Barton?'

'John!' Sammy leapt up.

'No, Sammy,' Pixie held her back. 'They are lying to you. There is no secret state. It is foolishness.'

'Watch for yourself,' the man said, his face a mask of total seriousness.

As he clicked his fingers, a hanging TV pivoted to face them. On it, a video played on a loop. It showed John Barton entering a shop. He was dressed in the stereotypical outfit of an adventurer, complete with leather jacket, fedora and a camera slung over his shoulder. He spoke to the man in the shop for a few seconds and then poof! A huge flash filled the screen and nothing was left but an empty till and a hat floating to the floor.

'Oh my God!' Sammy screamed, 'he's dead!'

'No, Ms Habib,' the man replied. 'He has been disappeared. It has happened to many of our best agents, and to almost all of our worst. We suspect they have been interned within a secret prison system. One that is much like this secret city, but on an international scale…'

'How do you get that from this video?' Pixie demanded. 'It could have been anything! A flashbang. A regulation size tool pro being operated by someone outside the shop. It could even be a clever edit. We do not know, Sammy!'

She set her hand on Sammy's shoulder.

'We cannot trust him! You know we cannot trust him!'

'B-but… where has he gone then? If not there, then where?'

The man clicked his fingers and a new overlay came over the camera.

'If you still doubt me then you should look at this.'

A red ring appeared on the screen. It circled a tiny patch of red static on the shop counter.

'These are heat signatures,' the man confirmed. 'We measured them. If they are from humans, which we suspect that they are, then they are operating at far below regulation size. There are fifteen of them. The exact size-'

'-of a squadron of Lund Corporation guardians,' Pixie finished.

'Yes,' the man stared at Pixie. His eyes were slowly piecing together her face behind the scarves. 'And why would that be?'

'Because it is the optimal size for stable size tool travel while accompanying-'

'-one other person,' the man finished her sentence for her. 'And, of course, you only need to worry about stability if you are operating at non-regulation sizes.'

'So you conclude that this is the work of a secret state?' Pixie snorted.

'That,' the revolutionary grinned, 'or we are wrong, and your John Barton was simply shrunk out of existence by a rogue maniac with access to a size tool.'

He noticed Sammy's eyes watering. He turned to her, speaking softly; 'there are many maniacs here in the microcity, Sammy Habib, but none who can afford a size tool. If they had such money, would they be here?'

'You are here.' Pixie said.

'We are everywhere,' the man replied, 'we are the Frequency Underground.'

He stepped forward, reached out, and pulled the scarves from Pixie's face.

'And you, spy, are Captain Adisa!'

Just then an explosion rocked the polystyrene cavern. Gunshots echoed through the tunnels. Some were booming, heavy, as if from oversized weapons. Some, screeching in the ducts above them, sounded microscopic.

The man turned and, just as he looked away, Pixie grabbed his arm and twisted it behind his back. He screamed.

'You evil bitch! I'll kill you!' he spat and wriggled. 'You planned this!'

'It wasn't us,' Sammy cried, gathering their kitbag from the floor and throwing it to Awax. 'I promise it wasn't. We just want to find John Barton!'

'Where is John Barton?' Pixie screamed at the man, wrenching his arm up behind his back. It threatened to snap clean off.

'Jesus! I don't know! I don't know!' he cried. 'The secret state has him! It's them you need to torture, you crazy bitch, not me!'

She slammed the palm of her hand flat into the back of his neck. It made a hollow thudding noise and the revolutionary's body went limp.

'Have you killed him?!' Sammy whispered, 'Fuck!'

'He's only stunned.' Pixie turned to Awax, 'Now, give me my wings. We must go!'

'We have no time!' Awax responded, turning suddenly and running for the door.

He had a point. As Pixie and Sammy ran after him they felt gunfire whistling past their ears. Sammy turned to see soldiers dressed in black moving into the cavern behind them. Sammy didn't know what soldiers of a secret state looked like, but these certainly looked like soldiers of a secret state. The three of them sprinted for the door, bullets slamming into the polystyrene around them.

As they reached the door they found the suspicious guard waving them through. He fired over their heads at the approaching troops. Awax and Sammy rushed through with the kitbag. Pixie slammed the door shut behind them.

It wasn't lockable from the outside. She looked around for a blockade.

'Step back!' Sammy shouted. She booted the brazier of uridium as hard as she could. She felt her foot swelling painfully, bursting out of her shoe. The uridium fell and smashed, scattering behind. The floor covered with impassable shards.

'Come on Sammy!' Pixie yelled, grabbing her under the arm. 'Run!'

The two of them rushed on. Sammy limped on a foot that was now three feet tall from ankle to heel. Awax went ahead of them with the bag. They would keep running until they ran out of breath.

The uridium had stopped the soldiers for now, but surely

there were more closing in.

Awax dropped the bag and turned to them.

'I don't know if I can come with you on this one, guys. This is all a bit too crazy for me. I don't like getting shot at. I'm an easy going guy. This is not for me.'

'You've done all you can,' Pixie clasped her hand to his shoulder, 'we just have one more favour.'

'Do you really work for the Lund Corporation?' Awax asked.

'I… don't really know anymore,' Pixie answered.

'What is it that you want?'

Pixie unzipped the bag. Sammy collapsed on the floor rubbing her big foot. Pixie pulled out two pistols. She threw one to Sammy and strapped one into her own concealed holster. She threw the carbine and its ammo belt to Sammy and then, from the bottom of the bag, she lifted out her wings. She turned to Awax, a gleam in her eye.

'Just help me get these on, won't you?'

7

As the last electrode was attached to the back of Pixie's head, her wings stretched out over her, wide and golden. The device plugged directly into her cerebral cortex. Her brain had adapted to it. The wings were part of her body now.

Pixie shook them out with a couple of practice flaps and ruffled her feathers. She turned around and preened them a little. Yes, she nodded to herself, she was ready to fly.

'Sammy, come!' Pixie called, opening her arms. 'We must leave. I shall carry you.'

'Wait!' said Awax, turning. He had already started walking away, his job of tying on Pixie's wings being done. 'Those things actually work?'

'What did you think they were?' Sammy asked.

'I don't know,' Awax put his hands on his hips. 'Some kind of battle dress? I'm no warrior. I don't know how to fight.'

'Well, they do work.' Sammy smiled, wrapping hers arms around Pixie's neck. 'Let's go, Pixie!'

'Absolutely,' Pixie smiled, her wings opening wide for launching.

'Wait wait wait!' Awax ran to them. 'I know I said I was done, but... you can't just leave me here, can you? Those soldiers in the black, they weren't asking questions!'

He flashed his winning smile, bowing humbly.

'I am just a lowly union representative.'

'Of an illegal union,' Pixie added.

'Yes, you are right,' Awax lifted a finger, 'but that does not mean that I am therefore skilled at combat. The CMU does not provide weapons training, my friends. Trust me, our instructions -as far as the police are concerned- are to run away or, ideally, to get killed so we can become another martyr to the cause.'

'Bullshit,' Sammy laughed.

'Okay, so that second part is merely implied,' Awax shrugged, 'but it does not mean that it will not come true as soon as those soldiers catch up with me.'

'You wanted to leave,' Pixie said, her voice hardening, 'you can leave.'

'Come on, Pixie!'

Sammy looked up at her, her arms draped around the tall woman's neck.

'He's helped us this far. He helped you get your wings on, for God's sake. Let's take him along with us.'

She smiled as Pixie met her eye. 'Pweeeze! Pwetty pweeeeze!' Pixie sighed.

'It's okay for you to say this, Sammy. You don't need to carry him.'

Still, she gestured for him to approach. He padded around them for a moment with his arms open, trying to find a way in to the huddle. Tiring of him, Pixie pushed his shoulder, spinning him right around. One hand cradling Sammy, she reached out with the other and bunched up a tight knot at the back of Awax's t-shirt. Before he could complain, she swooped her giant wings and they were airborne.

They soared through the widening polystyrene cave. Sammy was wrapped around Pixie with her giant foot swinging free below. She kicked Awax in his side as he swivelled around below them, yelling. Pixie held him aloft in one arm, accounting for his extra weight as she soared, occasionally bumping him off polystyrene stalactites as they went.

Suddenly the cave opened into microcity proper. Pixie pulled them up ever higher into the dark sky. The city spread out below them. Its mass of people writhed like water. Meagre lights were like reflections, glinting in the night.

What felt like hundreds of feet up, but must only have been a centimetre, Pixie hovered in place.

'Alright, Awax,' she said through heavy breathing. 'Where is the gateway back to the river?'

Swinging around below them, Awax shouted.

'It is hard to tell when I am upside down!'

He had indeed rolled over somehow. He now hung from his shirt with his head below him and two pathetic legs kicking out above. Sammy booted at him with her swollen foot to try and right him.

'I can't feel anything in this giant foot, you know? It's like it's just a big soft shoe.'

'I have seen the effects of raw uridium contact before,' counselled Pixie, 'and you are very lucky, Sammy. Raw uridium does not affect all parts equally. You may have a two-foot square foot made of flesh but only a regular sized set of nerve endings in it. You could have had it the other way around. Or worse.'

'I'll count my blessings,' Sammy said, finally kicking Awax the right way up. 'Now point us to the exit, comrade, or we'll all end up hanging upside down; in a secret state prison.'

As she spoke, sounds of gunfire began echoing around the matchbox. Beneath them, muzzle flashes and shrinking buildings showed that the conflict had tipped out into the merchant district. Secret state troops still had the upper hand but clearly the Frequency Underground weren't mere harmless idealists either. Far below the hovering trio, revolutionaries moved through the streets, crouching. They stood at a height of twenty storeys, using the cardboard tower blocks as cover. As they watched, one collapsed; a tank shell smashing into his forehead and blowing his brains out across four blocks. There were disadvantages to being big.

'Okay, I see it now,' Awax pointed. 'There! Beside the big cranes! There are a series of hangers there. The one with the size tool gateway is the second from the left.'

'Our left,' Sammy asked, 'or their left?'

'How can they have a left?!' Awax yelled. 'They are buildings! Now can we please get down there. This is not a dignified way to travel. I feel like a baby being brought by the stork.'

'Awwww,' Sammy laughed.

And with that, they plunged out of the sky. Sammy and Awax screamed. Pixie twisted at the last second, skimming the floor. They tore down the streets of the microcity, dodging power cables and pot-shots. They banked hard right at a junction. Pixie flipped them over and brought them in on a low, hard trajectory, down towards the hangers.

'Okay,' Pixie bellowed, her voice clear and martial.

'Ready weapons. We're coming in hot.'

Sammy lifted a hand from Pixie's shoulder and grabbed for the carbine but thought better of it. Awax simply dangled. The suppressing fire was left to Pixie, who released her hold on Sammy and unholstered her pistol.

At the last second they hung a sharp 90-degree turn and blasted straight in through the hangar doors. Inside was a single truck, part of the latest shipment moving through the gateway. Around it were a number of workers who ran for cover as Pixie started blasting. High above were armed guards who returned fire.

Pixie swung to a halt beside the truck, rolling Awax away like a bowling ball and sending Sammy skidding across the floor. Dropping to a knee and pulling a second pistol, Pixie leapt back into the sky. Bullets danced out of her weapons as she turned in the air. Sammy scrabbled for her carbine and pulled it close. She fired up into the walkways above. Gunfire seemed to come back at her, but she couldn't tell from where. It was impossible to see.

Perhaps she was killing people? She didn't know. She really couldn't tell. Is this what war is like?

Awax, rubbing his head where it had bounced off the floor a few times, looked about him and saw a group of workers cowering behind crates to his left. He waved over to them, donning his warmest and most contagious smile. Bullets whizzed past them.

'Comrades! We are with the union! Can you help us to get through the gateway?'

The workers looked at him like he was mad.

'Which union?' A small, hard-faced woman yelled back at him.

'CMU,' he grinned, lifting his t-shirt to reveal a tattoo of their logo. 'Up the miners!'

'We're with the stevedores!' The woman yelled back. 'You didn't vote with us on the proposal to suspend block voting and replace it with proportional regional polling at the last General Union Conference!'

'My sincerest apologies, comrade, but that was what our membership wanted.'

Awax's smile looked painted on.

'If you help us to get through the gateway-' a bullet ricocheted an inch from his foot, 'then I promise I shall canvass them again and try to convince them of the benefits of a proportional syst- AAAH!'

A grenade had rolled up between him and the stevedores. They all watched, eyes wide, breath still. One. Two. Three...

The grenade fizzed. The fuse was faulty.

'Okay, comrade,' the woman yelled, 'we will help you out, if only to stop those Lund Corporation bastards throwing bombs around! Get your comrades into the truck and we'll send it through.'

The plan made, the stevedores scattered. Awax yelled to Pixie and Sammy. He indicated with a series of windmilling arm gestures that they were to get in the truck.

Sammy stood, laying down covering fire as she walked backwards to the truck. Pixie flipped around in the air and landed on its canvas roof. She drew a knife, cut a hole and disappeared inside. Awax jumped into the cabin and threw the truck into reverse.

As the huge engine roared to life the firing outside seemed to intensify. It hammered off the metal around them like a downpour. Awax jammed the throttle and the truck seemed to fly backwards; first across the hangar and then, with a great wooshing sound, through a maelstrom of space and scale as well. Sammy clutched her rifle and felt sick.

When she opened her eyes they were hurtling backwards through the mud of a riverside loading bay. Blue sky was above them and soil below. Sammy gasped for breath, only to find the air thick with burning gasoline. Was it their truck?

Looking out she saw they were surrounded by figures in white robes. The loading area into which they'd reversed was scattered with burning wreckage and the bodies of guardian and secret state soldier alike. Sammy gulped when she realised the soldiers in white had their weapons trained on her. She lifted her hands.

From behind her, Pixie strode out of the hold.

'Stand down, men. It is us. We have returned.'

It was then that Sammy realised these troops were in fact the crew of their boat. They had been following the transmissions of the Frequency Underground (being secret members themselves) and, after realising the Captain had moved over to their side, they had decided to rescue her from the trap that waited on the other side of the portal.

As Pixie stepped on board, the white robed crewmembers cheered. She saluted them. Sammy turned back to Awax who followed nervously behind.

'Thanks for saving us in there, mate,' she nodded. 'You might be fake as fuck and a filthy commie to boot, but you're good to have around when it hits the fan.'

'It was nothing,' he bragged. 'I was simply trying not to die.'

'So you'll join us on the cruise?'

Sammy mounted the gangway.

'Just get me back to the trading post and we'll call it even.'

*

The boat turned slowly on the brown river. The crew moved fast. As they started to putter away down the river, a tank, black and without markings, rolled out of the jungle and lowered its cannon at them. They turned the corner just as a shot rang out. Sammy felt the shell soar through the air above them, just missing. It exploded against a tree on the far bank. Pixie stepped up to the forecastle, her wings opening wide.

'Everyone to a gun. I doubt that our return journey is to be as peaceful as our journey in.'

Then, turning to Sammy specifically, she furrowed her brow.

'You will not be using a gun, Sammy.'

Sammy smiled. At the front of the boat the crates had been dismantled and, waiting for Sammy, was the size tool. The one that looked like a cannon but wasn't. Resting her swollen foot behind her, she lifted the viewfinder. She felt it suck on to her face. Gears swirled around inside it. Then, clearer than day, the jungle blinked to life all around her, translucent and massive; filled with the infrared heat of soldiers.

'What do you see, Sammy?'

'There are soldiers!' Sammy yelled back. 'A lot of soldiers!'

A squad of five giants was moving towards them through the jungle. Four or five storeys tall each, they moved tactically but, Sammy realised, not carefully. They had made themselves too tall to find any effective cover. Instead, they simply had to wade through the undergrowth; their torsos clearly visible. Small arms fire wouldn't hurt them, Sammy thought, but she knew what would.

Sammy lowered the cannon.

'Bigger is not always better.'

She thought of John Barton's hot embrace as she squeezed the trigger and felt the cannon pulse. It had a hell of a kick. Through the scope the effect was even more impressive. Where there was once a soldier, there was now nothing. Just a hole in the air. The cannon shrank people so quickly and so dramatically that it left a vacuum. The giant soldier appeared to pop into a sphere of pure blackness. The sphere hung there for a second before sucking shut, like water pouring down a drain.

She lowered the cannon and fired off more shots. She could see the panic in the giant soldiers' body language. Finally, Sammy smiled, they're the ones that are out of their depth! She felt the cannon's kickback thumping pleasantly into her body as she counted down the troops. Two left. One left. None left.

She reached up to the handle above the barrel and re-cocked the cannon. No one had shown her this, she just somehow knew how to do it. A steaming hot canister of uridium cycled out and a fresh one was loaded in. Sammy enjoyed the metallic sound of it all clicking into place. The fuzzy hum of it powering back up. Yes, she could get used to this fighting life.

She felt a hand on her shoulder.

'Sammy.' It was Pixie. 'I know you're having fun but you must come out of the cannon now.'

'No thanks. I wanna stay in here.'

'Awax is taking over the cannon, Sammy. You have more important things to be doing.'

'Awax?'

Sammy disengaged the cannon's viewfinder.

'What the hell's he supposed to do with it?'

Awax shrugged, his t-shirt now hanging limply off him, a wide rip added to the damage done by Pixie's airlift.

'I don't know either, Sammy, but I would like to be useful.'

Pixie pushed Awax towards the cannon and told him to figure it out. She wrapped her arm around Sammy and marched her back to the Captain's table. Charts lay out there and now, alongside them all, Sammy's electronics.

'My spy kit!' Sammy rubbed her hands together. 'You had it all along!'

'I thought it might come in handy,' Pixie nodded, 'and I was right. Sammy, we must use your skills. All those years ago, you were the only one to locate the size tool. You used only this equipment and your insatiable curiosity. Now, that same attitude has led us here.'

As she spoke gunfire sounded off the port bow. The crew huddled down and returned fire. Awax swung the cannon around and fired pulses into the canopy.

'We have heard a lot about the secret state, and about the Frequency Underground. I cannot say that I entirely trust our information. All I know is that something more is going on. The Lund Corporation is involved. It is something I was not privy to, even as one of Zane Lund's top commanders. I cannot say that I will not return to them, but first I need answers. You, Sammy, need to find out just who these people are that are called the secret state. Who are they working for?'

'-and where have they taken John Barton?' Sammy nodded. 'Yeah, I'm a bit baffled myself, to tell the truth. I don't know if I'll be able to find much online. I mean, secret is right there in the name.'

'Secrets are not secret because nobody knows them, Sammy.'

Pixie looked to the horizon.

'I have learned this now. Secrets are things that we refuse to hear. Things that do not fit our narrative. They are truths that are the wrong size, or the wrong shape, and so they do not fit alongside our other truths. I was blind for too long, Sammy. Not because Zane Lund's secrets were not visible, but because I refused to see them.'

A bullet slammed into the table in front of them. A tiny poof of map paper sprung into the air. Sammy nodded.

'That's some deep shit right there, Pixie. Now what do you say we split up? You kill the bad guys and I do some Googling?'

'It would be my pleasure!'

Pixie opened her wings and launched herself skywards, an assault rifle clung in her arms.

*

As Sammy opened up her browser she had no idea where to start. Perhaps she had grown rusty in the long years of drifting, or perhaps it was a side effect of the gunfight going on around her. Either way, Sammy started in the most obvious way. She opened Google and typed in: Secret State.

Okay, as predicted there was nothing there but conspiracy drivel. She scrolled down the results. Bilderberg. NWO. Alex Jones. Some videos that seemed to mention the Frequency Underground.

She clicked on one of these but, without audio, all it seemed to be showing was Prime Minister Mosley's ridiculous Hitler moustache. Sammy sighed and rolled her eyes.

She scrolled down. Past the duplicated results, more moustaches, and then wilder and more elaborate titles including words like [TRUTH!] and SHOCKING REVELATION. There was nothing here. She checked social media feeds: same thing. She checked online videos: double the garbage.

Sammy put her head in her hands. She had no idea where to start. She folded her arms and lay back in the chair, trying to think. Across the deck, Awax was going wild with the cannon. She heard the electric fizzle of things getting shrunk and wondered why she was the one cursed with the boring job. She would definitely rather be shooting a cannon. Maybe that could be her new career? Instead of being the woman who discovered the size tool, she could be the woman who was the best at blowing shit up with it.

She sighed and returned to her phone screen. She needed to get back to the earlier internet to have any hope of finding anything. Back before routine censorship. She needed to go back to the back-ups. She needed to call Bantz.

*

On a leather-topped desk in the City of London, an ivory-handled phone rang. A man, forty but grey, his handlebar moustache curled with a hint of irony, reached out and lifted the receiver.

'Marley unt Moi, financial investors. How can I invest you, yeah?'

'Marley! It's me!'

'Bloody hell!' His laugh rolled down the phone, slow and languid. 'Is that bloody blackballed Sam-Sam? How's it hanging Sam-site? Mumznet keeping you in chocolate milk, yeah?'

'I'm off the bottle, mate,' Sammy tried the old banter, 'but you know I still like a bedtime story from Daddy every once in a while. You still got access to the Bantz back-ups?'

'I haven't worked at Bantz for six years, Samwise.'

Even with all the gunfire she could hear him rolling a diamond ring around on his finger. What a twat.

'So yeah, of course I bloody do! Got a backdoor in there. Loose as a hooker's chuff.'

'Jesus Christ, Marley. I didn't think it was possible for you to be any more of a prick.'

'Can't hear you, darling. There's some kind of gunfire your end. Saying that, could be all the money just faaaaalling into my account now that I'm a bloody millionaire banking bastard, right?'

'It could be that, yeah, Marley.'

She ducked as a jet zoomed overhead, its minigun strafing a line just off starboard. Water sprayed across the boat. Awax span the canon around and shot up after it.

'Now, can you give me the decryption keys or what? I'm in a bit of a rush here.'

'Sure thing, babes.'

She could hear him tapping at his phone screen with long fingernails.

'Just sent them over to you on Tinder, lols. Remember when we matched on there? What would those babies look like, eh? Anyways, consider this one a freebie, Alexander Sammleton. I guess I owe you since I was the one who took your name off the size tool story back in the day, right? Anyway, money to make, hearts to break. Ciao ciao!'

'WANKER!'

Sammy yelled down the phone, but he'd already hung up. Begrudgingly, she logged onto Tinder and scrolled past his nudes to the bottom of the messages. There, as promised, was a set of keys that would get her into the Bantz backups.

She didn't know what she was looking for, so she'd start at the start. She ran searches: 'secret state' in 2020 – nothing but conspiracies – 2021 – same, nothing – 2022 – nothing – 2023 – nothing.

She began to wonder if she'd find anything at all. She went all the way through. Nothing. Pictures of illuminati symbols, sometimes Zane Lund, and then the ever-recurrent Hitler moustache of Prime Minister Mosley. Sammy groaned. A missile seemed to shoot overhead but she ignored it. She decided to search the databases again, this time going by month.

The monthly searches worked, or worked better at least. It was May 2034, when the governments of the world started debating 2035's universal size tool regulation, when Prime Minister Mosley had made a (soon-to-be-infamous) speech. In it, he decried surreptitious and bad faith actions made by governments utilising size tool technology. She opened a video and put on her headphones. As a crewman fell screaming to the deck, blood pouring from his middle, Sammy switched on the sound-cancelling function.

'My fellow Englishmen, I regret to inform you, that there now exists every possibility of a secret state.'

He said the words slowly and carefully, tapping each one with a wag of his finger.

'A state operating at the widest extremities permitted by our new proportional technologies. In good faith, we reach out to the nations of the world. We must, I emphasise, must regulate this size tool before it becomes a scourge. Great upset has already arisen from its implementation. It falls to us now to relieve the unhappy burden of our providence. Let us bring an end to this question of a secret state, or else, threatened by the malignity of our enemies, we shall soon be lowered to undertaking dastardly practices ourselves.'

That, Sammy blinked, could mean only one thing. She looked around vaguely, her hand pointing at the screen.

'Secret state!' She mumbled. 'Secret state!'

There was definitely a secret state, she knew it now, and Mosley was right in the middle of it. By worrying publicly about his enemies doing it, he was signalling that he, himself, was doing it. He was setting it all up as he spoke. That Hitler-stached bastard!

*

The boat rocked. Horns blew, filling the air with sound. Ahead of them, horns blew back. Sammy fell to the ground. Up above her, she saw Pixie dancing and dodging between other flyers. They wore black. They flapped around on dark wings, but they had none of Pixie's ability. The secret state flyers only hovered. Their bodies were vertical, lifted up by their wings like slack packages beneath Amazon drones. Pixie cut through them like an angel, weightlessly flipping and flying, cutting them out of the air with perfectly-placed pistol blasts.

Sammy sat up. She noticed the crew all running to the front of the boat. They were running and firing. A couple fell dead under a hail of fire.

Their enemy was dead ahead, Sammy realised. They had run straight into them.

She still wasn't really sure who this enemy was. All she knew was that the government were in on it, Lund was in on it and, somehow or other, John Barton had got himself mixed up in it. He'd brought them all here, in fact. He, she realised, had got them to his point. The secret state had followed him, not them.

She raised herself up on unevenly-sized feet and picked up the nearest weapon. A grenade launcher. She cocked it, her heart swelling, and began climbing up to the driver's cabin.

Up there, she crawled past the drying driver and peeked out of the smashed windows.

They had hit a hovercraft. A large one. Both ships took the blind corner at speed and collided. Now they were wrapped up in each other; the hovercraft's cushion punctured and draped over the smashed front of their boat. They were both heavy in the nose, presumably taking on water. The only thing keeping the two vessels afloat was their collective engine power, driving into each other in high gear. The two motors kept their noses up and out of the water for now, but their slow descent was inevitable.

The hovercraft was swarming with black-suited soldiers. Many had already fallen to the fire from Pixie's crew but the weight of numbers was on their side. Sammy swallowed and lifted her grenade launcher. She pointed it down at the huddled black-clad masses.

This time, when they died, she'd be certain that she'd killed them.

Frozen for a moment, hesitant to take a life, something of her old freelance anger started to boiled up into her brain. It was them or us! Winners and losers! No room for lazy bastards in the gig economy! She pulled the trigger and watched as bodies burst into pieces across the deck in front of her.

It only took one barrage and the secret state forces were broken. The crew charged and drove them back. Pixie, above, chased down the retreating flyers. Sammy slid down the ladder to join them, picking up a lost-looking Awax on the way and running with him over the deck, into the enemy hovercraft.

By the time she got there the place was empty. Her white robed comrades were now splashed with the red and black stains of combat.

Pixie called out to them. She had flown through a window. She was already below deck. Sammy and Awax descended a ladder and joined her. In the hold was a large, neon-blue room.

'It's…' Sammy's mouth fell open.

'An exact replica of the size tool at Lund Acres,' Pixie said, finishing her thought. 'A reinforced-uridium size tool portal. Perfectly designed to operate at any scale desired. I would like to say that it is a relic of the early days – a mk.1 - but, looking at its controls, this technology is brand new. It has been developed alongside commercial size tools. A distinctly military enterprise.'

'Or, an enterprise of the secret state.' Sammy added.

'So, it is real. You found evidence?'

Sammy nodded.

Pixie tilted her head back. She did not question it. If Sammy had found evidence of the secret state then Pixie would believe her.

'Look!'

It was Awax. He had climbed on to a raised platform surrounded by thick, radiation-proof glass.

'These must be the controls. They are… destinations, I think.'

'Then this is the secret state transport network that the communists were talking about,' Pixie nodded. 'Bring all the men in here, and bring weapons. All of the weapons.'

The crew gathered round in a defensive formation. As they reloaded their guns and patched up minor wounds, Sammy climbed up to the control panel. There were over a hundred destinations listed there on the glowing buttons. All were listed as single words.

'Is it a code, do you think?' Awax asked.

'If it is, it doesn't matter,' Sammy smiled. 'I know exactly where we're headed.'

In the middle of the panel was the button she was destined to press. She held her finger over it and praised God for internet conspiracy theorists. How else would she have worked it out?

The label next to the button read: MOSLEY.

8

If Pixie still had doubts, they were now settled. They had come through the portal into a hangar. After a brief firefight, they secured the room. They now looked out over Black Site MOSLEY.

The landscape was otherworldly. The cracked red ground was soft underfoot, jellyish. They were surrounded on all sides, and overhead, by an opaque blackness.

'Are we on Mars?' Awax asked.

'We're still breathing.' Sammy shrugged.

'They could have terraformed it,' Pixie replied. 'I heard Zane talk of such things, but I didn't believe him. Now, I don't know what to believe.'

In the valley ahead of them a military compound stretched out, barracks and mess halls interspersed between prison blocks and tents. Prisoners in orange jumpsuits could be seen limping through the streets or conducting mandatory exercises in the parade ground. All of it was overseen by troops in black.

Overhead, Pixie could make out two flyers. Their movements were clumsy, like the flyers she'd just killed. What she had put down to a lack of practice, she now realised was due to the poor quality of their government-issue wings. Their flaps lacked manoeuvrability. Their ST-units were underpowered. The final effect was unimpressive.

Pixie narrowed her eyes and looked again at the black-clad soldiers.

'Sammy, take a look at those men,' she pointed. 'Do these seem like elite warriors to you?'

Sammy peered at them. Still not seeing well enough, she took out her phone and opened the Zoomr app. Looking through her digital binoculars, Sammy confirmed Pixie's suspicions. Most of the guards were fat. Some had limps. Those posted at the front gate appeared to be sitting on a sofa that they'd dragged out from the staff room.

'Yeah,' Sammy blinked. 'They're hardly supersoldiers.'

'Government cut-backs,' Awax nodded. Pixie and Sammy traded glances. Awax continued. 'You see how even the top soldiers of the secret state are suffering in this economy. Austerity has gone too far!'

'I agree,' Pixie nodded. 'It calls for revolutionary action, doesn't it? You will clear the gate for us?'

'So be it,' Awax nodded grimly. 'You have both proved your value, so now I must prove mine. I think it will be best to go in disguise.'

As they spoke, three of the ship's crew stepped forward with suits of black armour. They had stripped them from the guards they'd just killed. Awax rubbed his hands as he took one and ran off to change into it. Pixie turned to her troops.

'It is lucky that these uniforms come in a size suitable for Mr Ngalamulume. Did you find any among the dead with the measurements of an actual soldier?'

'No, ma'am.' A sailor snapped to attention. 'The few we found were covered in blood or torn up from explosives.'

'Fine,' Pixie folded her arms. 'Who among the crew will fit into an extra-large?'

One particularly burly sailor stepped forward and, after some prodding, so did the cook.

'Good.'

Pixie sent the two of them to change into disguises.

'Now don't let that communist do anything moronic.'

Sammy crouched behind a fold in the red, spongy ground, her

carbine held close to her chest. Beside her, stretched out in a line, fourteen crew members readied their weapons and waited. They all wore white Lund Corporation robes, now spattered with blood, dust and gunsmoke. On their heads, each now wore a black secret state helmet. Sammy, still dressed as an Arab trader, was glad of the extra protection. Lund guardians weren't issued helmets. It was a pride thing, she suspected. Or perhaps it was because helmets did nothing to protect from instant shrinking.

Peering out from cover, Sammy could see Awax and his two accomplices in conversation with the guards. Two sat on a sofa by the front gate. The other had come down from the guard tower to join them. Awax looked raggedy and unprofessional in his uniform, but then so did the guards. Sammy watched as he gestured widely, spoke with his usual enthusiasm and peppered his conversation with closed-fisted salutes. Surprised at first, the guards were now nodding along.

'Of course they're in a fucking union,' Sammy grumbled silently to herself. 'Of course. Typical public sector. Even here...'

Above them, blood burst from the neck of a secret state flyer. Pixie had pounced on her from above. The other flyer's body was already smeared across a high rooftop. She had attacked at an angle where no patrols could see them.

A few tense minutes passed and, finally, Awax came through. Scratching as they heaved themselves out of their sofa, the guards moved inside. The three replacements took their positions. Once the coast was clear, Awax gave the signal. The crew jumped up from their cover and ran to storm the gateway. Sammy was the first one up, sprinting as fast as she could, but she was soon left behind. As the white-robed crew took the gatehouse, she ran up after them, coughing and spluttering. Her too-large helmet bounced about on her head. Her too-large foot dragged behind her. Behind them, the corpse of the last flyer lay on the ground. Ahead, Pixie landed.

'I am familiar with the design of these buildings. This is

a British secret prison. I have infiltrated them before in Zimbabwe. The large concrete tower: this is where they hold captives for permanent interrogation.'

'Interrogation?'

Beneath the adrenaline, something twinged in Sammy's guts. They were so close, but now the danger was greatest. What would they find when they found John Barton? If they found him?

Pixie led the crew off down a side street. They were headed for the concrete tower. Sammy followed and, behind her, Awax shuffled along with the other two disguised crew members. Sammy turned.

'Awax, you've done enough. You don't need to come. It's fine.'

'Are you sure, Sammy?'

He was nervous, caught between intentions. 'I'm very happy to join you. I just fear that I am not very good at these military things.'

'Don't worry, comrade. The world needs lovers more than fighters. Why don't you take these two back to the gateway and make sure everything's secure? We're going to want a rapid escape, after all.'

Awax seemed quite relieved at his new mission, as did the cook. The buff crewmember, however, was not so pleased.

'Come on! We finally get a bit of action and you're sending me back? I'm the strongest bastard in the whole damn crew!'

'Yeah,' Sammy nodded facetiously, 'and you're wearing an enemy uniform. How do you think that's going to play out in a firefight? Go back, guard our escape route, and maybe change into something a bit lighter while you're at it.'

The crewman nodded.

As the three of them retreated to the front gate. Sammy turned to catch up with the rest of the assault team.

*

280

Sammy could have sworn that they'd taken a left. She had run blindly forwards and now, caught in a warren of little passages between huts, she realised she had lost them.

'Fuck.'

She tried to remain calm. She held her carbine close and leaned against a wall.

She knew they were heading for the concrete tower. She would just have to meet them there.

The huts here were so close together, though. She couldn't see. Damn her height! She felt herself breathing heavy. She was lost, alone, surrounded on all sides, and too damn small to do anything about it.

Still, she had to move on. Lowering her rifle, she edged to the side of the nearest hut. She peered around the corner. No visible troops. She fell to her knee, controlled her breathing, and listened.

No, she couldn't hear any either. She edged on. She jogged the length of a hut and leaned around another corner. Empty. She moved on. It was slow going.

She berated herself. The slower she moved, the further ahead they got. She was being left behind.

She began to rush. But another voice in her head said you don't even know which way you're going.

'Damnit!' she cursed.

Feeling powerless, she dragged her phone out and launched Googlemaps. She doubted she would find anything. Just by putting these coordinates into Google she'd probably set off an alarm at GCHQ. But she had to try.

The screen took a moment to buffer. It was struggling. Then, with a high swooping zoom, it dropped her down slap-bang in the middle of the House of Commons.

'Shit!'

She shook her phone.

'Why did you do that? Some redirect or something? Damnit!'

She groaned, 'and what kind of soldiers don't carry walkie-talkies, eh? What the hell is going on…'

Hearing footsteps, she dropped to the ground and rolled beneath the hut to her left. She crouched there a while as two black-clad soldiers ran past. When she was sure they were gone, she rolled out. As much as it pained her to do it, she realised she'd have to follow them.

She followed, her foot dragging loudly behind her. She tried a sort of hopping run, but without any feeling in her flesh it was hard to gauge exactly when her foot would hit the ground. The thumping boomed loud in her head as she stumbled through the sheds. Surely someone would hear her?

Then, being heard was the least of her worries.

Far ahead of her, the sound of gunfire filled the air. Above, sirens whirred into life. She swallowed down her panic and sprinted in the direction of the noise.

She passed one hut, two, then hung a left. She pulled around a corner at a full sprint, realising too late that it opened on to a courtyard where secret state troops were gathering. 'Shit!' Sammy screamed inwardly and kept running. Her heart raced as she rounded another corner. No-one saw her. The sirens kept blaring.

As she ran, the gunfire grew louder. Two soldiers rounded the corner, she lowered her weapon and fired a burst into them. They fell immediately, bullets tearing easily through their armour.

'Now it's serious.' Sammy whispered.

She found herself at another corner. This time, her heart pumping with adrenaline, she rolled around it with her weapon raised. She was ready.

Before her was a scene of carnage. White-robed crew lay dying on the steps of the prison tower. Above them the surviving crew fired down from hastily constructed barricades. They faced dozens of secret state soldiers. The black shirts had the whole building surrounded. Shots echoed inside the building itself. There was a fire in the rear. Smoke gushed from the windows. Glass smashed, and objects were launched out at the black masses advancing below.

A line of six guardsmen lay between Sammy and the rest of her forces. Three crouched behind a watertank, firing off potshots, while the other three were sprawled on the ground.

'Right, Sammy,' she told herself, lifting a grenade from her pocket. 'Make this count.'

She pulled the pin, and it rolled.

'Sammy!'

She looked up. At the top of the stairs, waving. It was him! John Barton!

He was waving right at her. The six troops all turned their heads toward her. She swallowed.

Just then the grenade detonated. The three guards around the watertank were flung into the air. Shrapnel shot through the neck of a prone guard. Without blinking, Sammy lowered her rifle and pumped the remaining guards with two short bursts of lead. They collapsed motionless on the ground.

Turning back to John Barton and waving, Sammy clutched her helmet tight to her head and began sprinting toward the besieged doorway. Seeing what she was doing, Pixie flung open her golden wings and launched herself from the door. As if in slow motion, Sammy's small and imbalanced figure bounced over the courtyard, bullets ricocheting through the dust around her, as the fire of the guards was drawn by Captain Adisa. From Pixie's outstretched wings rolled four grenades. Each flew through the air towards a different group of advancing guards. Completing her arc, pulling a tight loop over the battlefield, Pixie watched as blooms of fire burst among her enemies, black cloth and body parts flying everywhere, lacerated.

Sammy sprinted up the stairs. She threw her rifle down and dived into John Barton's arms. She kissed him, deeply.

'Bloody hell, John Barton,' she smiled, tears in her eyes. 'I've heard about playing hard to get, but this is ridiculous!'

'You've used that one before,' he smiled back. 'I can tell!'

Pixie came out of her loop and flipped herself around, landing behind the pair.

'Inside!' she yelled. 'Now!'

She dragged them through the doorway. The air inside was cool and, more importantly, far less riddled with bullets.

'As wonderful as it is to see two lovers reunited.' Pixie's deep voice rose clear over the sounds of battle. 'We must get you out of here, now. This is not a place for those who can't fight.'

'Get us out of here?' Sammy yelled back. 'Why? Are you planning on fighting here without us?'

'You have served your purpose, Sammy,' Pixie replied. 'You have discovered the secret state. You showed us it was a real thing. You led us here to one of its most secret black sites. Now you must step aside and let us finish the job.'

'What are you going to do?'

'I cannot leave until I know the reasons for this prison's existence. I must know what this secret state is. I must work out what part the Lund Corporation plays in it... what part I played in it!'

'But Pixie...' Sammy shook her head. 'You aren't responsible for this! You knew as little about it as the rest of us. You can't take all of this on yourself. I'm not going to let you! It's my business as much as yours. It's the world's business!'

'The Lund Corporation offices are on the fifth floor at the back of the prison tower,' John Barton offered. 'I saw them going in there from my cell. They have a rolling presence here. Some days they're in, some day's they're not.'

'...are they in now?' Sammy asked him.

John looked her in the eye.

'Yes. At least, I think so.'

Sammy turned back to Pixie.

'I'm not leaving. You can fly, Pixie. Take John back to the gateway. I sent Awax and the other two there to guard it. It should be safe. Take John and come back. We'll solve this mystery together!'

'You what?' John balked. 'But you've only just got here! Now you're sending me home and running off again?'

Pixie, ignoring him, lifted John Barton up by his belt and spread her wings.

'Okay, Sammy. I will humour you this time. I will fly your lover out to where he is safe. Just promise me that you will not take on Lund without me!'

'Sure thing!'

Pixie lifted into the air. Sammy pulled her hand from her pocket, revealing crossed fingers.

'Sorry, Captain, but I've learned by now when somebody's trying to fuck me over and take my story. Get me to safety? Psht!'

She turned and scanned the gangways, working out which ones would take her up to the fifth floor. There were running battles going on within the building but these were mostly prisoners settling scores. The guards were all dead. She spotted a fire escape that would take her straight up to a fifth floor entryway.

'Finally,' she said, preparing her phone's video function. 'A story from the legendary Sammy-fucking-Habib that will actually have her name on it.'

She ran to the ladder and began to climb.

*

It was a long climb, but worth it. She moved low through the Lund offices, grabbing any paperwork she could find and passing it in front of her phone. No time to read now, but she would go back frame by frame and take it all in. Perhaps she and John could read it together? She rifled through filing cabinets, unrolled plans and schematics, before finally entering a sheltered office. Everything passed before the camera's electronic eye.

The office was quiet. Too quiet. It must have noise cancelling, Sammy realised. Some kind of hermetic sealant. It was cool too, and smelt vaguely of ozone. The office was styled in white wood, ornately carved and run through with neon blue lighting. Hanging from the walls were heads of dead animals and, as she approached the desk, Sammy realised that the chair behind it was furnished with lion skin. Slowly, cautiously, she sat herself in the chair, placing her weapon on the floor beside her. Lifting her phone, she panned it along the desk and tilted it down to an open drawer. Inside, as she had suspected, was a cigarette holder marked with the name she had expected.

'Don't move!'

Sammy froze. She knew the voice. She had almost expected it. She swallowed and spoke.

'Zane Lund? Imagine seeing you here.'

'Shut up, Sammy.'

He kicked her gun away from the table, out of reach. He grabbed her phone and held it for a moment before launching it out of the window.

'You know this weapon, Sammy?'

She turned. He was pointing a shotgun at her. It was snub-nosed. Black. Very carefully crafted.

'It's a reminder of the first time we met.'

He spoke quietly, his voice sinister.

'It was the first time I used a weapon in anger, Sammy. You surprised us, you see, after we had already had too many surprises. There's only so much a man can take, you know?'

He seemed to smile, but Sammy's eyes were still on the shotgun.

'We are only human. We all make mistakes, eh? And this was a mistake. An honest one.

'You realise, Sammy, that if it were not for this shotgun then none of this would have happened? You were the first person outside of my company to see the size tool in operation. It's what saved your life. If I had fired at full size - as I am now, for instance - then there would have been nothing of you left to patch back together. As it was, I was already a third of my previous size when you burst in.'

'Like a baby,' Sammy finished.

'A baby wearing a suit, I guess… but I see what you mean.'

'So you shot me?' Sammy said, her eyes still fixed on the weapon. 'I mean yourself? Personally? And I came back to find you? I still don't see how that results in us being here now.'

Zane Lund's malicious smile opened wider. He leaned out with the shotgun and rubbed it up against Sammy's arm.

'Of course you do, Sammy, you don't have to pretend. You knew that it was my plan to keep the size tool a secret forever. You knew that it was only by threatening to make it public that you would force me to change the world… and change the world I did.'

'Not necessarily for the better,' Sammy added.

'If there is blame, Sammy, then we share it equally. I brought the size tool into the world, but you were the one who told the world about it. Once that happened, there was no going back.'

'Then how do we get to secret prisons, Zane? How does that follow logically?'

She was still frozen stiff. The barrel now held inches from her face. Nevertheless, Sammy was growing angry.

'How are you going to blame this whole evil corporation, big government, corrupt conspiracy on me then? Please explain.'

'Come, Sammy, you saw Lund Acres. A secret state was part of the plan from the moment of its first inception. You saw the guardians. You knew that they weren't just masseurs and waiters. A utopia must be ruled by wise warriors. Like you and me, perhaps?'

He stroked her chin with the gun.

'But until the world can face reality, these enlightened governors must remain secret. Those that are secretly ruling must appear to be servants. This prison is simply an extension of that.'

'Then where are the guardians now, Zane?' Sammy pulled her face away from his prodding. 'If this prison is part of your glorious utopian plan then why is it staffed with fatsos?'

Lund inhaled deeply through his nose and frowned.

'Guardians are expensive, Sammy. Compromises had to be

made. The government, they…'

'Sammy!'

BANG!

It was Pixie. She had entered the office through its front door. Her weapons weren't drawn. She expected only to find Sammy. Hearing her cry, Zane span his shotgun around and blasted her out of the door. Flying backwards with the force, her wings caught on the doorframe and snapped inwards. Pixie slammed to the ground in a mess of blood, feathers and splintered wood.

'Pixie, no!'

'I see you know my lieutenant.'

Zane turned the gun back on Sammy. There was a new fury in his eyes.

'At one time I thought she was the one who would take over when I was gone. But now I know her to be just another one of your puppets.'

'Puppets?! Jesus, Lund, you're messed up, man.'

Sammy was shaking her head.

'She just wanted to know what was going on. She was just trying to help me find John Barton.'

'John Barton?' Zane Lund froze. 'The spy?'

'He's not a bloody spy, you paranoid idiot! Don't you trust anyone? Can't you take it that some people are just good? That they're not out for anything! John's not a bloody spy, mate, he's just a boy who was trying to impress me. He's just a harmless idiot.'

'If you are talking about the John Barton who until very recently was a guest in this facility, then you are very wrong Sammy!'

Was it her, or was Lund uncomfortable?

'No no no, Sammy, he was not an idiot. We picked him up from deep inside a revolutionary stronghold. He was connected. He was deep into the underground.'

'I saw the footage!' Sammy cried out. 'He was going to the shops! He was going to the shops and you kidnapped him and dragged him off to prison!'

'That was not a shop, Sammy,' Zane Lund's eyes were wide with panic now. 'That was an armoury. An armoury that we have been searching for for way too long! These degenerates, Sammy, they don't understand the careful balance of forces, the play of cause and effect. They don't understand us, Sammy. The way we do things, right? Cat and mouse, right? They don't see the big picture!'

Suddenly the windows behind Zane Lund blew out, one by one. From outside a noise of strange engines roared. He dropped to the ground as Sammy fell off her chair. The last thing she saw was Zane pulling a string from a hidden socket in the wall. He took it firm in his hand.

'You've not won, Sammy Habib! Be assured, you have not won!'

'Yet!' Sammy smiled, 'I've not won yet!'

She watched him shrink away. For a fraction of a second he was there again, a little suit-wearing Pakistani baby. Then he fizzed away, beamed down the fibre optic wire to some distant location.

Whatever was hovering outside touched down in the courtyard. Two sets of boots slammed on to the metal and ran towards them. In the doorway, Sammy spotted the red crosses of a medic running up the stairs toward them. The figure leaned over Pixie and began clearing her airways. Sammy, thankfully, heard the Captain breathing. Her breaths were heavy and agonised, but she would survive.

Then came John Barton. He still wore the orange jumpsuit of a secret state prisoner, but over it was a leather bomber jacket, around his neck were dust goggles, and on his head he wore a beret. Sammy had seen the outfit before.

'John! You're…'

'I brought help.' He charged in and lifted up Sammy in his arms. 'What happened to your foot?'

'Long story,' she kissed him. 'What's with the hat?'

'I joined the Frequency Underground!' He smiled. 'I found them at that trading post in the Congo. I told them I was after evidence of bad conditions in the mines. They said I should join up.'

'Oh, John Barton,' she wrapped her arms around him and kissed him again, 'is that who you've brought to rescue us? They were trying to kill us just a few hours ago!'

'I explained all that,' John smiled.

'How?'

'I said you were the legendary Sammy Habib and that you were a bit of a stuck up cow sometimes but ultimately your heart's in the right place.'

'...and you let them all in through the gateway?'

'Yeah, there was a guy there. Awax, is it? Good guy. Knows his way around a ship radio.' John blinked. 'You know that gateway leads out to a couple of crashed ships, right?'

'I do,' Sammy smiled. 'I crashed em!'

'Bloody hell,' John rolled his eyes. 'Well, that Awax guy told me he's found another setting on the size tool at the gateway. He was having a look at it, right, and it turns out that we're a hundred times smaller than a speck of dust here. This whole secret prison is like a millionth of a millimetre or something. So no wonder it's secret. What he's suggested, is that we use the size tool and turn the whole thing back to a normal size.'

'John! You beautiful boy!'

She wrapped her arms around him as they walked out of the office. Together they hopped onto his Frequency Underground hover-bike. As she turned around in the saddle she saw Pixie on another bike behind her, tightly secured and breathing steadily. Their eyes met. Maybe it was just the morphine, but the unsmiling Captain Adisa seemed to manage a smile and, more than that, a wink.

'Right!' Sammy slapped John's helmet. 'Take us home John! I want you to get big for me!'

*

In the Commons, a hush came over the house. Prime Minister

Mosley stepped forward to speak. The debate was once more about the size tool, and how politicians could keep their citizens from using it in ways they thought irresponsible. Mosley, whose decade-long stint as PM was largely due to his experience on size tool matters, cleared his throat. Before him, in note form, was the outline of the speech he would give. He would implore the house to vote on his proposed bill prohibiting the use of the size tool for secret meetings. All Family Size meetings of any more than five unrelated individuals, he was to argue, was tantamount to a conspiracy.

He needed to get the speech over with. He was due at his club in an hour.

He was planning to meet with the young Zane Lund. They would discuss the future of extrajudicial authority and the possibility of perfecting a new state of public order.

As he opened his mouth to speak the cameras in the house were all, as usual, centred on his moustache. After ten years the novelty of the Hitler toothbrush had never really worn off. This was important, as it was this footage that the news would replay frame-by-frame, analysing what exactly happened.

As the PM opened his mouth, you could see on the tape a single frame where something appeared in his moustache; a little piece of dirt or grit, no bigger than a bit of dandruff. In the next frame this was a grey sphere of around six inches in diameter. It was pushing hard against the PM's face, and had ripped out some of his moustache hairs, which were visible on its surface. The next frame was too bloody for the news, so they cut to a longshot.

Where the PM's head had been a moment before there was now a bloody explosion and a ten-foot-cubed miniature prison hovering in the air. By the next frame even the longshot was too close.

The secret prison at the heart of the secret state was, it turned out, located deep within the moustache of Prime Minister Mosley. By bringing it back to normal size, Sammy Habib, John Barton, Captain Pixie Adisa and Comrade Awax Saint-Just Ngalamulume, had assassinated the Prime Minister, wiped out the rest of the government, and destroyed the Houses of Parliament.

The news showed a group of hover bikes rising from the rubble. In particular, they focused on the face of a woman some journalists recognised as a writer for Bantz Testament. She hung on to a rider in bright orange trousers. The cameras clearly picked up the shock on her face.

Across every news station and YouTube channel in the world the face of Sammy Habib was seen to mouth, 'Fucksake!' before the whole gang of hover-bikes roared their engines. Hanging out of a sidecar, Awax opened a window on a holographic UI.

He opened the size tool, dragged and clicked, and the column of bikes fizzed out of sight in a neon-blue haze.

Acknowledgements

My deepest thanks to the team at Northodox for all their hard work bringing this book to life. Writing is a team sport and there's nobody more dedicated out there.

FIND US ON SOCIAL MEDIA

@northodoxpress

@northodoxpressofficial

@northodoxpress

@northodoxpress

www.northodox.co.uk

SUBMISSIONS

CONTEMPORARY
CRIME & THRILLER
FANTASY
LGBTQ+
ROMANCE
YOUNG ADULT
SCI-FI & HORROR
HISTORICAL
LITERARY

SUBMISSIONS@NORTHODOX.CO.UK

Printed in Great Britain
by Amazon